Don't Ask

Brie Kraus

For everyone who have only wanted to find love.

Don't Ask

Brie Kraus

Chapter 1

The sound of my alarm clock pierced the quiet stillness in my room. Groggy from sleep, I reached for the source of the annoying ring and turned it off. I got up and stretched a bit before putting on black shorts and a white tank top. While I tied my brown hair with a rubber band, I went down the stairs to go jogging in the morning. In fact, I've never really been a morning person. I'm used to it though, after a lot of early morning shifts at the bakery my mother owned.

I inhaled the crisp, autumn air and ran as I took a step outside. Running was something I always did to take my mind off of things. It is like I forget everything as I spring forward, whenever my feet hit the pavement. As I finished my second lap around the park, I couldn't help but feel like I was being watched. I looked around and my eyes landed on a car that was parked conveniently behind some bushes, but it wasn't just any car; it was one of those nice, fancy, black cars with tinted windows. I looked closer and saw that there were flags, red with a gold colored crest on them, on both sides of the car. Shrugging my shoulders, I decided to let it go and keep on running.

After several more laps around the park, I made my way back to my house and took a fast, cold shower. It was always refreshing after a long run. I toweled myself dry and put on some dark wash jeans and a purple satin blouse. After I finished putting on some light makeup, I made my way downstairs and smelled something cooking in the oven, and followed the delicious scent.

"Hey mom!" I greeted my mother as she leaned over the oven.

"Good morning, Melanie!! Guess what? I'm trying out a recipe for a new kind of bread. Do you want to try some?" She gushed, as energetic as always. She is like a stereotypical baker…you know the ones you see in clip art? She has rosy cheeks and a slightly rotund belly. Her favorite hat is one of those floppy chef hats, and her apron is always smeared with flour. After my father died of a heart attack, my mother became even more interested in baking—her way of coping with my father's death—and took over the shop.

"Sure, why not?" I shrugged. I loved my mother to death. Although she could really get on my nerves for being so cheerful and talkative all of the time; she was a caring person. I knew she did everything out of love. After spreading a little butter on the warm slice of bread, I took a big bite of her creation. She looked at me expectantly.

"So…what do you think?" She giggled; I noticed the nervousness in her voice.

"I dunno mom," I faked a grimace. "It seems a little too dry for me. And did you put in too much salt again?" As she began to panic, I decided to save her nerves. "I'm just kidding!! It's delicious…as usual." I stood up to leave and gave her a quick peck on her cheek. "I'm off to work! I'll see you in a few hours."

"Okay honey, drive safe!! Have fun at work!" She yelled from the kitchen.

I used to work with her in the bakery, but we realized that it would be better if I worked at a higher paying job. Our shop had a few loyal customers, but it was never enough to pay all of our bills. So now, I worked at an insurance office. Yes, it was boring, but it provided us with a sufficient amount of money.

I parked in front of my office building twenty minutes later. Locking my car, I made my way to my work space.

"Hey girlie. How is your day so far?" Jessica, my co-worker, and best friend, asked. I started working here about a year and half ago, and she was the first person I met and soon became good friends after we discovered that we had a lot in common.

Although we have similar interests, we look nothing alike. She has deep red, structured, wavy hair and her eyes are a sparkling emerald green. The two colors accented one another and as a result, she looked amazing. On the other hand, there's me, boring brown hair that's unmanageably wavy and dull blue eyes.

"It was fine. I went running, as usual. Nothing special." I sighed. Sometimes, I wished something exciting would happen to me. Don't get me wrong, this town is great, but it is sort of like a bubble. It feels secluded from the outside world.

Suddenly, she gasped and whispered in a rush, "Well, don't worry. Your day is going to get infinitely better. Don't turn around, but Karter is walking our way. Act normal." I laughed in response. "Me? Act normal? I should be saying that to you!! Calm down and take a deep…"

"Hi, Karter!" Jessie nearly screamed while I rolled my eyes.

"Hello Jessica. Hey Melanie. " A deep voice greeted us.

"So how's work treating you? Are you getting the hang of it after being here for a month? Oh by the way, I totally love your tie!" Jessica rambled.

"Yeah thanks. Everyone here is so nice and welcoming." He winked at her. I swear she swooned in response. He then turned to look at me. "Anyway, Mel, when is your birthday? You're gonna turn twenty one, right?" His deep hazel eyes met mine.

"Uhmm…yeah. December 14. Why?"

He grinned and replied, "I was just wondering cuz I heard it was coming up soon."

"Oh. Well, I have to get back to work. We don't want the boss to come around and yell at us do we?" I attempted to wink at him, but I'm sure it came off as a random twitch in my eye.

"Good point. I will see you guys later." He flashed one last smile at us and walked away.

"Oh my gosh. Did you just flirt with Karter Johnson? Since he flirted back, that means he is totally into you. And what's with that birthday question? I bet he wants to get you a romantic present!!!"

Jessie overanalyzed everything. I just laughed at her. Sometimes, I wondered why I was friends with such a spaz.

I realized something. His tie. After Jessica complimented it, I looked at it. It was a plain red tie, but there was something else on it. If I hadn't paid more attention to it, I probably would've missed the tiny golden crest at the collar. That gold emblem reminded me of something, but I really couldn't place my finger on what it was. I knew it had to be important because I had that nagging feeling inside of me.

"How are you not even reacting to what I'm saying? HELLO?! Earth to Melanie!" Two fingers snapped in front of my eyes.

"Oh right. Sorry. I just remembered something." I apologized. After that, the conversation died, and we returned to our own cubicles.

An hour later, I jumped out of my seat as I remembered what had bothered me about Karter's tie. "The fancy black car," I gasped.

Why is Karter wearing the same crest on his tie? Does he own that car? That means he is rich!! Then why is he even working here? My brain was working a hundred miles per hour, but I couldn't seem to put the pieces together. It just didn't make any sense at all.

I squirmed in my seat for the next three hours, willing the clock to move faster. I needed to tell Jessie what happened and see if she could figure anything out. Finally, it was 11:30 and we had a one hour lunch break. Jessica came by my desk a few minutes later, and we walked to a nearby café together.

"Guess what?" She asked as we entered the café. "Karter is here too! Maybe we can sit with him today."

I rolled my eyes. I couldn't tell her the story, now, but I could ask Karter a few questions about himself. I smiled to myself as we ordered our food and slid into the booth across from my suspect.

"Hello ladies. How was your morning?" he asked.

"It was boorringg!" Jessica whined.

Karter turned to me and waited for an answer. Instead, I asked him a question. "So, pardon my asking, but where did you move from?"

"Uhmm. I…uhh…lived in…Chicago before I moved here." He ran his hand through his glorious, thick, brown hair.

"And why did you move in the first place?"

"I got…laid off from my old job. Anyway, it's a good thing that I switched jobs. This one is a lot better paying than my previous one

"Oh okay, I'm sorry for being so nosy." I was still a little suspicious, and I knew I wouldn't get a satisfying answer from him anytime soon. "Oh and by the way, I really do love your tie. The color really suits you. What does that little gold crest represent?"

His eyes shifted as he responded, "It's probably just the company's logo. Like you know, Polo Ralph Lauren has that little man on the horse, Tommy Hilfiger has the flag, and Lacoste has the green …"

"Yeah we get it!" Jessica cut him off and laughed. I caught her questioning glance. I was acting a little weird by playing twenty questions with our newest coworker.

I stayed silent for the rest of the meal and thought about

how I must've made a fool out of myself and took the time to think about the situation. Why was Karter lying to me? Or was I just making a big deal out of nothing? By the end of lunch, I decided that the latter thought was correct.

"Hey Karter, do you wanna walk back with us?" I offered, trying to be friendlier.

"Nah thanks, I need to make a phone call. I'll catch up to you guys later." He answered while waving his cell phone at us.

"Okay, suit yourself."

Jessie and I took our time walking back to the office. On the way back, I told her all the things that I noticed today, from the fancy car to Karter's tie so that she understood why I acted the way I did at lunch.

"I'm sure it's just some big old coincidence! It's not like a super-rich guy is going undercover for no reason." Jessie laughed at her own joke. "C'mon seriously. Nothing happens here, and you know it."

I nodded in response and convinced myself to believe her. By the time we made it back to the office, our lunch break was over. Once again, we split up and headed to our respective desks. The rest of the workday went by without any incident.

As I grabbed my car keys, I yelled bye to Jessie. The drive home was uneventful, until I pulled up to my house. Parked in front of it was the same black car that I saw in the morning. Okay. This could not be a coincidence. I thought to myself as I cautiously walked up to the house. When I opened the door, I heard an unfamiliar voice talking with my mom.

"That's not possible!" my mom cried, almost in hysterics. "Why didn't you find her sooner? Why now? Is this some kind of joke?"

"No ma'am. We are serious when we say that she is the granddaughter of Ralph McKinley." I gasped when I heard what they were talking about. Ralph McKinley is basically the Bill Gates of the music industry, possibly even more successful.

This time, a familiar voice reassured my mother. "Yes. We have been keeping a close eye on her for the past month, and we have just confirmed that it is true." I turned the corner and came face to face with none other than Karter Johnson.

"What the hell is this about?" I screeched, "And I thought that you moved here from Chicago! You are such liar. I thought I could trust you! But no, you happen to work for the richest man in the nation."

"Actually, that's not entirely correct. I don't work for your grandfather. I live in the mansion with him because I'm training to take over the company." He amended.

I just stared at him in disbelief. He is the heir to the biggest music company ever.

A man stood in the corner next to my mom and cleared his throat to break the silence, "Sorry to interrupt, but we have to get on with this."

I nodded and questioned, "Excuse me, but you are…"

"My name is Evander Montgomery, and I am Ralph McKinley's personal butler. I am also a good friend of your grandfather, and he asked me to do this favor for him. On behalf of Mr. McKinley, I would like to invite you to stay at the mansion with us."

Chapter 2

"WHAT?!" I yelled without thinking. To me, it was a knee jerk reaction. "I'm sorry, but I can't! Does he really want to see me? If so, why did he put me up for adoption in the first place? He obviously didn't care about me for the past twenty years!"

With an expressionless face, Evander explained the situation to me, "Of course he wanted to find you! In fact, I don't think he even took a break from looking for you for the past twenty years. It's just that it has been very…difficult to locate you. Everything will become clearer when you come to the mansion. There are some issues that your grandfather wants to personally talk to you about."

My mother and I exchanged wary glances. Right now, we didn't know what to believe. During this whole time, my mom remained silent. Finally, she spoke up and asked a single question, "So he wants Melissa to permanently move in with him?"

"Yes."

She nodded in response. Suddenly, a wave of remorse washed over me. I couldn't just leave my mother here and let her face the world all by herself. Reality hit me and I realized that life wasn't a fairytale. It's not practical to leave everything behind just to live in a luxurious, high class world.

I took a deep breath, "Once again, I'm sorry I have to decline the offer. I can't just leave and forget everything that happened here. I have to be here to help support this family."

"If money is an issue for you, don't worry about it." Karter stated, "Because if you come back with us, your mother will get compensated. In other words, we will financially support her. Think about it. She will have more money if you came with us than if you stayed here."

I laughed dryly and gave him a cold look, "If you think that we want your money, then get lost. We were doing perfectly fine before you guys came, and I'm sure we will be fine after you leave. You just don't get it. Family and friends are more important to me than money is." Karter looked stunned by my tirade.

Sensing the tension between the two of us, Evander took hold of the situation. "Okay. I know this is a big surprise to you, and it will take time to sink in. We are going to leave you alone right now so you can think about your decision. I suggest that you take everything into consideration. Let's not forget that your grandfather is family too."

Without another word, the two of them left, leaving my mom and me in silent shock.

"Mom…" I whispered, completely unsure of what to say or do.

She walked over to me and pulled me into a tight embrace. "Don't worry about me honey. I will be fine wherever you are. This is entirely your choice, and I don't want to influence your decision."

We stayed where we were for a couple of minutes before I went to my room. In the safety of my room and the comfort of my bed, I was able to digest the news I was given. Pressured by the decision, a few tears escaped from my eyes. I usually don't cry, but when I do, it was for silly things. I didn't think that I needed to cry over this stupid situation.

A few minutes later, I reached for my cell phone and pressed the number two speed dial. Jessie picked up on the third ring. "Hey Mel! What's up?"

I sighed, preparing myself to tell her the news. "Well, something big happened and I really need to talk to you about it."

"Oh gosh. That doesn't sound too pleasant. Don't worry, I'm here to listen. Tell me what's wrong." I loved Jessica for this reason too. Although she is a spastic person most of the time, she can be really serious. And when she is, she is probably the best person to talk to and get advice from. She is not only fun to be around, but also loyal and trustworthy.

"So it turns out that Karter really is a super-rich guy going undercover. But that's not even the big news." I took a deep breath and continued. "He came to my house with this other man, and they told me that I was the granddaughter of Ralph McKinley." Saying that out loud made this situation sound even more ridiculous.

Under any other circumstances, she would have probably made a joke or teased me about it. But now, she didn't even question me about it, even though it sounded absolutely absurd.

"Okay. Is there anything else? Why did they find you just now?" she asked.

"Apparently, he was looking for me ever since I was adopted. But I don't know what to believe. And he wants me to move to his mansion so I can live with him." I answered her questions and added, "But I'm not sure what to do because I don't want to leave my mom and make her fend for herself."

"You know what? This is a once in a lifetime opportunity. Do you realize that your dream is finally coming true? You've always wanted something big and exciting to happen to you, and here is the chance. But you chose not to take it. Although I think you are just a little insane, I totally understand your reasoning. Is there any possible way you could reach a compromise with your grandfather?" Jessica spoke in a passionate tone.

I was confused, "Compromise?"

"Yeah, like maybe you could stay with him for half a year and then come back. I'm sure your grandpa will understand. I mean, that's better than not seeing you at all." she explained.

"You do have a point. But these people are multimillionaires." I stressed the last word. "They seem so proper, and I think that they are used to having things their way."

"Melanie," she stated. I could tell she was getting a

little annoyed. "If a person is rich, it doesn't mean they don't have a heart. Your grandpa will be able to empathize. I promise you that."

"Okay. I'll talk to Evander about it and see what he can do." A knock on my door interrupted the conversation. "Shoot. My mom's at the door. I have to go, but I promise I will call you back. Thanks so much for talking to me." I hung up the phone after we exchanged our goodbyes.

"Come in," I yelled in the general direction my door. My mother was probably brining up some food. Whenever I'm sad, she would always do that. The door opened slowly, and I smelled some delicious cookies that were fresh from the oven.

I immediately sat up on my bed when I saw who it was. "What are you doing here?!?"

"I'm sorry. I had to come back here and apologize for my behavior." Karter's low voice carried through the room. "You're mom let me in."

Quietly, he made his way over to where I was sitting and gently placed the cookies on my nightstand. With his eyes, he asked permission to sit down, and I gave a small nod in return. I felt the springs underneath the mattress shift as he sat down next to me.

"I'm sorry I lied to you. I didn't know what to do or say when we were at the café, and I sort of freaked out. Since your grandfather and Evander were in charge of this whole thing, I wasn't sure if it was in my place to tell you." He explained to me. "The phone call I had to make afterwards was to your grandfather. I told him that you noticed some things and pieced together a lot of information. That's when we decided that we should tell you the truth when you came home from work."

"I guess I understand why you lied to me. I appreciate that you just told me what happened, but what happened, happened. You lost my trust about two hours ago. I don't know if and when I will forgive you." I didn't realize how much he hurt me until I said that.

I looked up into his deep hazel eyes and to my surprise, I saw pain. "Melanie, I really got to know you over the past month, and I don't want to lose what we had…or could have." He muttered the last part so softly that I wasn't sure if I was supposed to be able to hear it. "I would do anything to gain your trust back."

I thought about what he said and realized that he wasn't lying when he said that we bonded during the past month. I didn't notice how close we got because it was so gradual and smooth. But the problem is, I still didn't know where we were in our relationship. Acquaintances? Friends? Maybe something more?

"I don't know. Maybe after some time, I will be able to trust you again. The main problem is just that you are so secretive. I barely know anything about you, and I'm not sure if what I know is true or not." I admitted.

"I was only secretive because I couldn't let you find out about Ralph McKinley until Evander said it was okay. Now I can be myself around you instead of the guarded person you think of me as." He sighed in exasperation.

I really did start to feel bad for him. Now that I think about it, it really wasn't entirely his fault. If I were in his position, I probably would've done the same thing he did.

Therefore, I decided to cut him some slack. "So…you will do anything to gain my trust back right?"

He nodded warily. I continued with my plan, "Well, tell my grandpa that I need to talk to him about some living terms because I don't think I am ready to permanently move in with him. Ask him if I could stay for a year and then come back. As a matter of fact, I want you to call him up right now."

"I can NOT believe I am doing this for you, but I really want our relationship to go back to normal." He whipped out his cell phone as I stared at him with wide eyes. I really didn't think he would go through with it. He dialed a number and patiently waited for someone to pick up.

"Hi Mr. McKinley, this is Karter." Pause. "Yeah. She's fine, but she didn't make up her mind yet." I could faintly make out some sounds coming from the cell phone. "She wants to tell you that she's not ready to permanently move into the mansion. She needs a year of living with you before she can make up her mind. After the year is up, she will make her decision on whether she wants to stay at the mansion or not." The pause after this was heart-wrenchingly long. I could tell that my grandpa was thinking about it really hard. Finally, the silence was broken. "Okay, I see. Thank you. I will see you soon."

"Well…" I looked at him expectantly.

He had a grim expression on his face. Then, I noticed the corners of his mouth turning up, fighting against a smile. "He said that was a fantastic idea!"

Without thinking, I launched myself at him. I hugged his broad chest and laughed with joy. "So I take it you forgive me now?" He asked me with one of his trademark grins.

"Yeah…I guess so." I felt his arms slowly wrapping around my waist. My laughter died as the atmosphere became more serious. I became acutely aware my racing heart and how his body was wrapped around mine.

Never being in a situation like this before, I awkwardly coughed and pulled out of his embrace. "Sooo…when are we going to leave to go to the mansion?" I quickly found something to talk about.

He laughed nonchalantly and dismissed my awkwardness. "Believe it or not, we are going to leave in three days. It should give you enough time to pack and say goodbye to everyone here. I hope that's okay with you." I looked at me worriedly.

I nodded and remembered that I could always come back after a year. It's not going to be that bad. I kept on telling myself.

Karter left a few minutes later, and everything that happened finally caught up to me. I'm going to live in a giant house with the richest man in the whole country. And that man happens to be my grandfather! Also, I will get to see Karter every day. I smiled at the last thought. Suddenly, exhaustion hit me like I ran into a brick wall, and I fell into a dreamless sleep.

Chapter 3

Saying bye to everyone wasn't as bad as I thought it would be. Since I didn't have a lot of close friends in the first place, I didn't have to deal with a lot of tears. But when it came to my mother and Jessica, it was a whole different story.

The two of them accompanied me, Karter, and Evander to the airport. Sunny California was going to be a very long commute from the ever so bustling New York. I didn't live in NYC, but it wasn't a very long ride from my house to the city.

"I'm going to miss you so much! Make sure you call or email me EVERY day, so I don't get Melanie withdrawal." Jessica teased and then lowered her voice, "If anything happens between you and Karter, I expect to be the first to know. Or any guy for that matter."

I laughed. I could always count on her to lighten up the situation. "Of course! Who else could I tell? My imaginary friend? You know you are my best friend, and I am glad that you are always there for me." I really meant that.

"Aww…" She cooed, tears forming in her eyes. "You are my best friend too!! I can't wait to see you again, and maybe I can visit you sometime!"

"You will always be welcome…as long as the other people are okay with it," I added. I gave her a big hug and she returned it as enthusiastically.

When we broke apart, I turned to my mom. "I'll miss you a lot mom."

"And I will miss you too. Make sure you have fun there…and don't ignore my calls!! Or else I will be very mad!" she warned, "I can take care of myself, I promise you that. So don't worry about me too much when you are enjoying your time at the mansion."

"Why would you think I would ignore you?" I asked my mom with a smile. "And I'll try not to worry too much. If you ever need anything, call me!"

My mom smiled at me and pulled me into a bear hug. "Shouldn't I be the one saying that to you? Sometimes I think you baby me too much." She joked. I just hugged her tighter in response.

Finally, all of our goodbyes were said and I boarded the plane with Karter and Evander. When I stepped on the plane, I looked at my plane ticket for my seat number. I really hope I don't have a middle seat!! I thought to myself. Usually, I saw a number like 38F, but this time I saw 04A. I did a double take a realized that there was a huge FIRST taking up most of the ticket.

"Hey! Where are you going?" Karter curiously asked me.

I looked up and realized that I was already at row 6. "Oh. My bad. I'm not used to sitting up in first class." I apologized. "I usually make my way to the middle of the plane before paying attention to what row I am at."

I turned around so I could walk back a few feet to my row and sit down in my seat. As I stared out the window, Karter slid in next to me. Although the seats were very spacious, I was aware of how close he was to me. I took in a deep breath to clear my mind, but that was not a good idea. Instead of fresh air, I breathed in his cologne.

Did Axe always smell this good? Maybe it's just because he's the one wearing it. I grinned stupidly to myself.

"I see you are in a good mood," Karter said, looking amused.

I immediately scowled and turned away from him as a blush slowly made its way up from my neck to my cheek. Oh boy…this is going to be a long plane ride.

What seemed like a few minutes later, someone was shaking me gently. "Hey, wake up sleepyhead. We're landing soon." A deep voice woke me up.

"Mmmmmm…" I moaned in protest. I hated waking up because it was so comfortable. Never in a million years would I have imagined calling a plane comfortable. Suddenly, hands were attacking my stomach.

"Stop!" I laughed. "I…am super…ticklish! Don't! Oh…you are going to…get it!" I gasped for breath between my sentences. I grabbed his hand and tickled his stomach. No response. I moved my hand to his side and poked him there. Still no response.

Frustrated, I looked up and saw that he was laughing at

me. "That's not fair." I pouted and crossed my hands over my chest.

"Poor Melanie! I'm sowwy for making you cwy. I pwomise I won't do it again." He said in a baby voice and pulled me into a reassuring hug. I laughed and batted him away with my hands. At the same time, the plane bumped against the gravel of the runway, signaling the flight was over. It wasn't as bad as I thought it would be.

After we gathered all our luggage and belongings, we headed out to the pickup part of the airport. Right as we stepped outside, I saw I giant, black stretch limo waiting for us.

"Is that ours?" I asked in disbelief. I have never been so close to a limo before, let alone been in one. I noticed that this limo also had the little red flags and gold crest on it.

"Of course! It's actually your grandfather's personal limo." Evander answered as if I just asked a stupid question.

"Oh…" I didn't have anything to say in response. I slid into the car and was dumbfounded yet again. It had lights circling the floor and roof, and there was a mini bar with crystal glasses on the left hand side. The privacy divider that was separating the front and back of the limo had the crest on it also. This thing was going to haunt me in my dreams.

As I looked around even more, I realized what I got myself into. I came from a lower middle class and now, I have to get used to a first class, luxurious lifestyle. Feeling totally out of place, I looked at Karter for support. As expected, he just looked at me weirdly with a hint of worry.

He doesn't get how I feel like right now. I let out a mental sigh. How would he be able to know how I'm feeling?

He is used to all this lavishness. I'm sure he grew up in a world like this.

I stared out the window and looked at the scenery that we were speeding by. There were a million palm trees and miles of sandy beaches. I was anxious to get out there and enjoy the sun. Although it was mid-August, the weather was still great here. The landscape changed, and we were driving past houses now. As we drove further, the houses just got larger and larger. The spacing between the houses grew too, and by the time we finally stopped, we were in front of a palace. I now understood why they always called it "the mansion" instead of "house" or something like that.

I gasped at the house in front of me. This is like the one you see in movies, and I'm not even exaggerating. In order to get in, you had to go through a wired gate that was probably guarded 24/7. The driveway was a perfect rectangle with a patch of lush green grass in the middle. Then the road split to reveal even more green lawns with fountains in the middle. After driving three minutes up the driveway, we were finally at the front door.

The front door alone was probably the most elaborate thing I have ever seen. I could only imagine what the inside of this house looked like. After dropping the three of us off, the driver drove away with our luggage. He said that it would be waiting for me in my room.

"So…" I said when I was able to take in my surroundings. "How long have you lived here for?" I asked Karter as we walked up the marble stairs that led up to the door.

"About 4 years," he answered as we stepped under the arch that hung over the door. He pressed the doorbell, and someone answered it almost immediately.

"Hello Mr. Johnson. It's nice to have you back. I hope your trip was enjoyable." A man greeted Karter. "And it's nice to see you again Ms. Cartwright. It's been very a long time." I gave him a confused look, but decided to ignore it. I'm pretty sure I've never met him before.

"Thank you." I replied, not knowing what else to say. He closed the door behind us, and Evander led the way through the massive house.

"I have been instructed to bring you straight to Mr. McKinley." Evander directed to me. I started to freak out because I was going to meet the richest man in the country. I probably looked really bad, especially after the 6 hour long plane ride here. My hands shot up to my hair, and I attempted to make it look somewhat presentable. Then I moved to my clothes and tried to smooth the wrinkles out. I was wearing sweatpants and a comfortable cotton tee shirt, which was not as fancy as they should be.

"Don't worry," Karter whispered in my ear, as if he sensed my distress. "You look beautiful." I whipped my head around to see if he was telling the truth. When my eyes met his, I could see that they were full of sincerity. I gave him a small smile in return.

"Here we are." Evander announced as we arrived outside a giant wooden door. "Wait out here while I tell Mr. McKinley that you are ready to see him." He pulled open the door disappeared into the room.

"Your grandfather is a really nice man. You shouldn't feel intimidated or nervous. I'm sure he is really excited to see you, no matter what you look like. Also, you have no idea how much he has talked about you ever since I got here." Karter smiled at me, and immediately, I felt slightly better.

"Mr. McKinley will see you now." Evander told me as he stepped out from the room and held the door open for me. I took a gulp and walked into the room.

Sitting on the couch in front of me was an old man who looked like he was in his seventies. His hair was all white, but he had an air of friendliness around him. I walked closer and saw his mouth form a big grin. Afraid to step any closer, I hesitated.

"Now what are you waiting for?" His hearty voice boomed. "Give your grandpa a hug! It's been almost 20 years since I've last had you in my arms!" He stood up and started walking towards me with his arms spread out.

Awkwardly, I walked forward too and gave him a hug. When he finally let me go, he held me at arm's length and studied me.

"I see you have your mother's eyes. They were the brightest blue I have ever seen." He said with a hint of nostalgia. I smiled slightly. "And your father's smile. His smile could always light up the darkest days."

I nodded and looked around the room. There were bookshelves covering the wall from the floor to the ceiling, and one of those rolling ladders you could push around. I could tell that he really enjoyed reading, just like me.

"Sit down. We have a lot to talk about." He motioned towards a chair that was next to the one he got up from. We both moved to sit down. "I know you have a lot of questions right now, but hear me out first."

He took a deep breath and started his story. "You were born in this exact house 20 years ago. Your mother and father both lived here with me, and it was just the four of us for almost a year. Those times were filled with happiness and joy. One night, your parents decided to take you out to the park. I waited all night for the three of you to come back, but you never did. It tore me apart when I learned that your parents got into a fatal car accident. But when I heard that your body was missing from the scene of the crash, I had some hope. It may sound stupid, but I was determined to find you. I believed that you weren't dead like your parents. For 20 years, I have been following hints, but they all led me to a dead end...until now. I was almost about to give up hope, but I am so glad that I didn't."

As I listened to him talk, tears started to form in my eyes. I looked up and saw that he was beginning to tear up too. Silently, I got up and gave him a sincere hug. It wasn't awkward at all this time around. In fact, it felt natural and loving.

"I guess that's enough of that sad talk for today." He smiled. I nodded in return. Then, I realized that I haven't said anything to him this whole time.

"Yeah. I agree." I said in a small voice. "So, do you live alone now? Or did you find someone else?" I attempted to make small talk.

"I did not find 'someone else'," raised his hands and made air quotations. "But I do not live alone either. You already met Karter right?"

"Yes. I did. He seems really nice." I answered. "So it's just you two?"

"I glad you like him. But it's not just us. There are two more people living here. Their names are Pierce Young and Blake Miller. The three men are all training to take over the company. I have not decided who will become the next president though." Mr. McKinley explained to me.

"Wait. All three of them are training to be the president?" I asked incredulously, "I thought it was just Karter! How can they live with each other? Do they even get along because of this competition?"

"They are actually quite close…almost like brothers. And yes, all three of them are in training. In fact, I called them down for a meeting that should start in a few minutes. You are also invited to attend." As if on cue, someone knocked on the door. "Come in." My grandpa yelled.

And in walked Karter, along with the two hottest guys I have ever seen. They looked like they were all around the same age, about 23 or 24. The three of them lined up in front of us while I sat there drooling.

"Melanie, meet Pierce and Blake. Of course you already know Karter." Grandfather introduced us. Karter threw me a lopsided grin, and I smiled back in response. They took turns shaking my hands, starting with Karter and ending with Pierce. Blake was gorgeous with his sharp features and dirty blond hair. I smiled when I felt that he had really soft hands. For some odd reason, I really liked it when guys had hands like that. After the handshake, he took step back while Pierce stepped forward.

When he stood in front of me, my eyes locked onto his. They were an amazing shade of silver, a color that I have never seen before. His hair was tousled and I had to refrain myself from running my hands through it. As I shook his hand, I noticed he had a firm grip. I also noticed that my heart was racing and trying to escape from my ribcage.

As I sat back down, I tried to calm my beating heart.

Why am I acting this way? I asked myself, confused. I never react this way with a guy…let alone three! Am I now a slut or something?

I forced myself to stop thinking those thoughts and focus on the scene in front of me. They were talking about some business plan and how grandpa was going to choose the new successor. My head snapped up as I heard my name being said.

"…and whoever is the successor to the company will have the honor of marrying my beautiful Melanie."

Chapter 4

"WHAT?!" I had a sense of déjà vu. Why do I always have to react this way? Or more like…why are people always deciding my life for me? "Since when was this decided?" I demanded as I shot up out of my chair.

The three guys looked just as stunned as I was, but definitely more calm and collected. I'm sure that they were trained on how to react to big news like this.

"I have actually been thinking about it for a couple of years now." My grandpa admitted. "My dream is to make you happy, and I wanted to leave in you in good hands when I pass away. I know this is a big shock for you, especially because you just met me for the first time in twenty years. But for me, it feels like I have known you my whole life."

I looked at him with mixed feelings. I knew he meant well by it, but I really thought he was crazy for believing that I needed money and a husband to 'be in good hands.'

"I'm okay, even without the whole arranged marriage thing." I felt a little silly saying the last part. It sounded so…old fashioned. "I am actually really happy, and I probably wouldn't have ever thought in my wildest of dreams that I would be here right now. I am sure that my life will never be the same." I reassured him, not knowing if it was a good or bad thing.

"I know that you think I may be controlling, but if you do marry one of these wonderful lads, my mind would be at peace. Will you please do this for me?"

I looked at him incredulously and finally understood how he was so successful in business. I bet he made everyone feel so guilty that they had to agree with him. "I'm not so sure…"

"Oh come on Mel, is it that bad for you to marry one of us? Are we that awful to be around?" Karter cut in and asked me jokingly. I was slightly surprised that he was supporting my grandfather's decision, but I decided to let it slide.

I looked from him to Blake to Pierce. Of course they were all heart throbs, and good looking in their own ways, but I had no idea of what their personalities are like. I knew a little about Karter, but not enough so I would want to marry him. My biggest nightmare is to be stuck with an arrogant, cocky, albeit good looking guy who treats me like trash. Although none of the guys seem to be like that type, I still wanted to take caution.

"I don't know, Karter. You seem to be a pain in the ass sometimes." I teased back, forgetting about the other people in the room. When I finally remembered that we were in a fancy mansion, I apologized. "Sorry for my language, Mr. McKinley."

My grandfather only laughed. "Don't worry! We aren't that uptight around here. I want you to be yourself because I need to get to know you better. And don't call me Mr. McKinley. Call me Chief."

"Why Chief? It doesn't have anything to do with Ralph or McKinley." I asked curiously.

"Well, I called him that when I got really frustrated with him one day." Pierce finally spoke up for the first time that night. "He was telling us all what to do and stuff and we all got really tired of his bossiness. So I said to him, 'Why can't you do this yourself, Chief?' And I guess it sort of stuck from then on." The other three guys laughed at that memory.

I smiled at how close the four men were. Even though I could tell they all had different personalities, I knew that they mixed together really well. But I could also tell that they were trying to change the subject away from the arranged marriage thing. Truthfully, I didn't really mind because I was in no mood to talk about it right then.

After a few more minutes of small talk, I started to feel exhausted. California time was three hours behind New York time. Although I know it's not that big of a time difference, I still felt really tired. Maybe it was because of my new surroundings and all the big news.

"Hey, Chief. I'm really tired, so is it okay if I go to bed right now?" I waited for a reply.

"Of course." He smiled warmly at me. Then he turned to the guys, "Karter, will you show Melanie up to her room? It's the guest room that's on your guy's floor."

Karter grinned at me, and we left the room silently. When we closed the door behind us, we began to talk. "So, how do you like the other guys and the mansion?"

"I think the mansion is giant and super extravagant. I might need a map in order to get around this place!" I exclaimed. "And the guys seemed nice. I just need to get to know them better." I was actually thinking about Pierce when I said that. You know how there are some people that you just want to get to know better, not necessarily in a romantic way? Well, he was number one on my list. He seemed like a very mysterious and intriguing person.

"Yeah. It took me about a week to get the hang of this place and be able to locate everything. " Karter laughed. "All three us moved in at the same time. Since everyone was new and had no idea what to do, we all bonded and got to know each other."

I nodded as we climbed up the remaining few steps of the grand wooden staircase. Taking a right at the top, I noticed that we had reached a wide hallway. The floor was super shiny and tiled with black and white patterns. On one side of the hallway, there were windows that reached from the ceiling to the floor with red velvet curtains that framed it. Since it was dark outside, I couldn't really see anything, but I'm sure that the view would be amazing during the daytime because we were on the third floor of the mansion. Opposite of the windows was like a lounge area with couches, a huge flat-screen TV, and a foosball table. I assumed that's where the guys hung out during their free time.

Continuing down the hall, I was able to count out three doorways. I turned around to look behind me and saw two more doors to the left of the staircase. Karter finally came to a stop in front of the last door on the right.

"Here is your room." He gestured towards the door in a lavish hand movement. I laughed and braced myself when I opened the door.

It was breath-taking. I sort of expected it to be like one of those bedrooms where you see in a castle...like lavish canopies, chandeliers, red and gold themed, something fit for a king. But this was a really modern bedroom. The walls were all different colors/styles. On the far side of the room, the wall was painted red, and the adjacent one was made out of wood with my bed leaning against it. Across the wood wall was a wall of giant windows like the ones close to the lounge. And the wall with the door was all white. Although it seemed a little weird, it actually looked really nice.

"Oh. My. God. This room is all mine?" I asked Karter in disbelief.

He just chuckled in response, "Of course, you silly girl. My room is right next to yours." He pointed his thumb in the direction of the wood wall. "And Pierce's is just right across from ours. Blake is a loner and sleeps by himself down at the other end of the hall."

I laughed. "Okay. Well, I'm really tired, so I'm going to go to bed right now. Thanks for showing me to my room. I'll see you tomorrow." I smiled and gave him a hug.

He squeezed me against his body. "Sweet dreams. Don't let the bed bugs bite." Then, he was gone.

I collapsed on my new bed and immediately fell asleep, not even bothering to change into my pajamas.

The natural alarm clock in my body woke me up at six

in the morning. It wasn't that bad, since I actually got eight hours of sleep last night. I groaned as I sat up and remembered where I was. As I stretched, I decided to go out for a run because it would really help me clear up my head.

I made my way to a two door mirror that I assumed was my closet. I guess I was right because I found my suitcase lying in there. I closed the door behind me, and started to change. When I turned around to open the door again, I gasped.

I could see my whole room from inside this closet. I brought my face just inches away from the door and inspected it. It looked like a normal glass door. I quickly opened the door and looked at it from the outside. It was a mirror. I laughed as I ran from the inside of the closet to the outside several times. Amused, I realized it was a one way mirror. Of course there would be one of those in this house. I smiled to myself.

I carefully opened and closed my door behind me as I stepped out into the hallway. There was a peaceful silence, and I bathed myself in the sunshine that poured through the windows across the lounge. I looked at the gorgeous scenery below me. I looked closer and saw that there was a little trail that made its way around the mansion. It was perfect for running.

Fifteen minutes later, I was finally able to find a door that led to outside. I immediately took off running, enjoying the rhythmic crunching sound of the gravel beneath my feet. When I finished my first lap around the mansion, I was suddenly aware of a second pair of feet behind me. I turned around and saw a glistening Blake running behind me. After a few more feet, he was running next to me.

"Good morning," I greeted. "You're a runner too?"

He turned his head to look at me, and turned it back to face forward again. "Yes."

Guess he is a man with few words. I sighed. It was always challenging to keep a conversation with those kinds of people. I wanted to know him better, though, so I decided to make an effort. "So…it's a nice day. Is it always this sunny? I really hope so. Do you like living here? Is this whole competition this stressful?"

He looked at me strangely for a second, as if not knowing what to say. Finally, after a few seconds, he cracked a grin. "You talk a lot."

"I know." I blushed, feeling a little embarrassed. "Are you going to answer my questions?" I attempted to put the attention on him again.

He paused, deciding whether or not he wanted to. "The weather is really nice, and it is usually like this. It is also a really great time to go to the beach right now." He answered the first part. I waited for him to continue. "And I do enjoy living here, although some people can be really annoying at times. I feel that the other two don't take the competition seriously enough."

"Mmhmm." I mumbled in response. I could tell he was really serious too. Blake probably wanted to win this whole competition from the start…even before I was dragged into the whole thing. "But you still like Karter and Pierce." I stated. It wasn't a question.

"Yes. They are really awesome to hang out with and talk to." He stated in agreement. We talked about those two for a little bit and some more things about the mansion. After running three laps together, we decided to go back inside.

He walked with me to the top of the stairs, and said a quick goodbye as we parted ways.

I took a quick shower in the super cool bathroom that looked like it came straight out of a bathroom design book. The shower was really nice because it was like a waterfall style showerhead. There was also a bathtub that sat under a panoramic window. To the side of tub, there was a door that led to my closet, which was actually very convenient.

I put on a dressier outfit than I wore yesterday, and made my way downstairs. My stomach was grumbling and begging for food. It was easier to find the dining room because all I had to do was follow the scent of warm breakfast. When I turned into the room, I saw that everyone was already sitting down and eating.

"Good morning, Melanie. How was your sleep? Do you like your room?" Chief asked me.

"Good morning! I had a nice sleep, and the room is amazing!! I noticed the one-way mirror. That was very interesting." I responded as I sat down between Pierce and Chief.

Everyone just grinned and laughed in response. Right then, a waiter came up to me and sat down a silver dish filled with food in front of me. I eyed it hungrily and dug into the scrambled eggs and sausages.

After we all finished our breakfast, Chief spoke up. "Pierce, will you show Melanie around this mansion? I know it is a bit overwhelming and it is easy to get lost if you are new."

He simply nodded, stood up, and waited for me at the doorway. I would be lying if I said that I wasn't the slightest bit excited. Slipping next to him, we made the way around the house. The tour wasn't awkward at all. We did talk the whole time, but it was only about the mansion. Halfway through the tour, I still didn't know a single thing about him.

"Do you like living here?" I asked him, trying to make a conversation.

"Yeah. I don't really have a family other than the guys and Chief, so it feels like I belong here." Pierce told me. I wanted to ask him more about it, but it felt like I should wait until I got to know him better.

"So, do you want to win this whole competition?" I wanted to find out if everyone was as serious about it as Blake.

He hesitated before he answered. "Uhm. I don't know." I didn't push him farther, but I knew there was something more to him that I had yet to find out. He was so guarded around people, and for some reason, I wanted to be the one who broke down that wall.

We walked around for a little more before the tour was over. He was walking me to my room, but we were interrupted by a parade of workers who were pushing silver carts full of food past us. The hallway was narrow, so I was pushed against Pierce for the time being.

When we touched this time, it was like the first time we shook hands. I felt a zap of some kind of sensation flowing through me. My heart raced and I was sure that he felt it because it was pounding so hard. I looked up at him, and he gave me a smoldering grin back. The parade of carts was over too soon, and we separated. The atmosphere felt different to me, and it was probably because of my stupid hormones. Trying to distract myself, I started up a conversation again.

"What was all that food for? Are we feeding a mob?" I joked.

He looked amused. "Actually, sort of. There is going to be a mob of people at the house tonight. We are hosting our semi-annual company ball tonight. Chief has always been a fan of those old-fashioned balls. I think that he made it tonight because he wanted to introduce you too."

"Oh. A ball. This is going to be interesting." I gulped nervously. I was never good with crowds and being at the center of attention. When are the surprises going to end?

Chapter 5

After lunch, I went straight for my bed so I could sit down and relax. After a few minutes of my needed silence and peace, I decided to call my mom and Jessica. I called my mother first.

"Hi, mom! I've missed you here!" I greeted her after she picked up the phone.

"Oh! You finally decide to call. I've been worrying nonstop about you!" She rambled, "So, how's living in first class?"

"It's actually really overwhelming. The mansion is giant and so elegant that I'm afraid I might break something whenever I move," I explained, "And I never do anything by myself here, unless I'm in my room. There are workers everywhere, and I just feel so spoiled sometimes."

"What else do you expect, Melanie? Ralph McKinley is the richest man in the country. How is Mr. Multi-Mil-

lionaire-Rich-Guy treating you? Does he talk to you at all?"
She asked.

"Of course he does…he's actually really nice and definitely not as arrogant as you expect. We already did a considerable about of talking. I found out that his nickname is Chief. It's sort of weird, but I'm sure I will get used to it," I explained to her.

We continued to talk about how extravagant the mansion was, and of course the one-way mirror closet. Finally, we said our goodbyes, and I called Jessica.

"MELANIE CARTWRIGHT!! You didn't call me right when your flight landed!! I am so mad at you!!" She seethed as she picked up the phone, skipping all salutations.

"Jeez, Jessica. I'm sorry! But I have news that will make you a lot happier." I tried to appease her.

"Fine. I will give you three seconds to tell me before I start to yell at you again. One…" She warned.

"Okay so it turns out that Karter isn't the only guy here. There are also two other really, super, amazingly gorgeous guys here." I spewed out really quickly. Jessica seemed interested since she didn't say anything, so I elaborated. "Karter is only training to be the next owner of the company, but there are two other guys that are training with him."

"Ooohh. That sounds like drama." Jessica commented.

"Sort of, but not really. I don't quite know all of them that well, but I do know that all three of them get along really well. Apparently, they are like brothers." I explained.

"So, what are the other two hotties' names? And what do they look like?" Jessica questioned.

"The first one is Blake Miller. He has dirty blond hair and looks really clean…not scruffy at all. He also has hazel eyes with flecks of gold." I guess I paid more attention to him than I realized. "And the other one is Pierce Young. He has chestnut brown hair and silver eyes. It's amazing. I didn't believe silver eyes existed until I saw his."

"Oh my gosh. I would die to be you right now. So which one do you like the best? I think either Karter or Blake is the best looking…from what you described. " She analyzed for a second. "Of course Karter's on my list because I actually know him."

"Blake is definitely good looking, but he doesn't talk much. He also runs, so I spent this morning with him. I was only able to get a few words out of him. He's not the type of guy who would initiate a conversation." I told her, "Personality is a big part of a guy's attractiveness."

"You sound like a psychologist right now. But who says you can't get him to open up more? It's so romantic. You can be the girl who gets the quiet guy to open up! I can totally see it." Jessica cooed, caught up in her own imagination.

"Yeah, right." I laughed at her, "We'll see. I really don't know who I like the best…Oh shoot. I forgot to tell you something." I paused, suddenly remembering the whole arranged marriage thing. "Uhm…I'm sort of engaged."

She laughed at me, "Funny joke." Pause. "No, seriously? You've got to be kidding me. TO WHO?!?!"

"I'm not kidding you. My grandfather offered my hand in marriage to whoever ends up taking over the company…so I really don't know who I am engaged to right now. It's definitely one of the three guys though." I explained.

"Wow…" She was at loss of what to say, "At least you

know all of your potential husbands are very attractive?"
She stated that like a question.

"Whatever. I'm going to have to talk to my grandfather about that sometime later…it's actually not quite clear
right now. I'm just really confused about the whole thing."
I dismissed the topic. Thinking about it just made me angry, confused, and sad at the same time.

Sensing that I didn't want to talk about it, Jessica tried
to change the topic. "Soo…Did anything exciting happen,
other than moving into a giant-ass mansion?"

"Well, not yet. But it will. Chief, I mean Mr. McKinley,
is hosting a ball tonight for his company. He's also going to
introduce me to all his corporate friends and colleagues."

"You are a lucky duck." Jessica sighed. "First, the mansion. Second, three hot guys. Third, an elegant ball. What
next? A million dollars falling out of the sky?"

A knock at the door interrupted our conversation.
"Sorry, Jessie. I have to go…someone is at my door." I
quickly hung up and walked to the door to open it.

Evander stood there, carrying hanger that was attached
to a bag. "Good afternoon, Miss Cartwright. I hope you
have had a good day so far."

"I have. Thank you. What's in the bag?" I eyed it suspiciously. I had a feeling I knew what it was, but I didn't
really want it to be that.

"It's a dress for you to wear to the ball tonight. Mr.
McKinley is having his semi-annual company ball tonight,
and he wishes that you attend it." He answered formally.

"Okay." I sighed and reached out to take the hanger.
Don't ask me why, but I never liked wearing dresses. I do
love the idea of them because they are so pretty, but I don't

enjoy wearing them. I guess I don't like all the attention, and I really didn't have the opportunity to wear one…until now. "Thank you, Evander."

"You're welcome." He nodded his head and started to walk away. "Oh yes, one more thing. Lukas will be coming to do your hair and makeup for tonight. He will be at your room approximately an hour before the event."

Not surprised that I have my own makeup artist, I closed the door as I stepped back inside my room. I placed the dress flat on my bed, and unzipped the bag to reveal the dress.

It would be insulting the gown if I said it was beautiful. It was beyond words to describe. Gingerly, I touched it, afraid that I would taint its beauty. I was grateful that the tag wasn't on it anymore because it probably cost more than I made in a year.

I looked at the clock, and it said two thirty-eight. Great. I have two and a half hours to kill before I can start getting ready for the ball. Deciding to get out of my room, I stood up and walked out the hallway. As I walked down the hall, I heard some clicking, like someone typing on a keyboard or something.

Rounding the corner and stepping into the lounge, I was greeted by Karter. He was playing some sort of video game and hitting the buttons on the controller forcefully.

"Hey, Karter. Long time no see." I joked. The last time I saw him was two hours ago at lunch.

"Hey, Mel." He finally looked up at me as he put down his controller when he lost. "What's up?" He asked me while I walked across the room and plopped on the couch next to him. He casually slung his arm around my shoulder.

"I'm bored. What's there to do here?" I complained into his chest. He smelled so good. I could stay in this position and that would cure my boredom.

"There's a lot of stuff to do! Were you even paying attention during your tour?" Karter joked. I looked down guiltily. I paid more attention to Pierce than what he was saying during the tour. "For example, we can always go walk around outside; go to the pool; watch a movie; drive around."

I considered what he said. Since I didn't really want to do anything energy consuming (I was saving all of it for the ball that night), I chose to take a stroll around outside. We slowly stood up and made our way to the outdoors.

"Want to see my favorite place to go?" he asked me as we walked further into the gardens, "It's a nice peaceful place. Pierce, Blake, and I found it when we first moved in. They stopped coming here, but I didn't."

I nodded while he lifted up a heavy looking tree branch. It revealed a small pond with a small bench made out of stones. It looked like the guys placed the stones there so they could sit without getting too dirty. Karter and I sat down and we resumed the position we were in when we were at the lounge.

I leaned on his shoulder and he asked, "What do you think of the people here?"

"Well, I don't know them that well yet. So you have to help me get to know them better." I stated. "But this is what I could gather from our conversations so far. Blake is the quiet and serious one, who puts a lot of effort in whatever he does. He definitely cares the most about the company...no offense." I looked at him and he shrugged his shoulders dismissively. I continued, "Pierce is more of a mystery. He seems more detached and guarded. He talks about everything but his personal life. And you. You are the laid back one, and you just go with the flow. Truthfully, I'm the most comfortable around you." I admitted.

"I'm glad to hear that," He smiled down at me, "And you have the most general aspects of their personalities down. Blake is definitely the most competitive out of the three of us, but strangely enough, Chief likes Pierce the best. I think we all know that Pierce will end up taking over the company." He explained to me. "I don't have a problem with that, but Blake sure does. It doesn't get in the way of our friendship though."

I tried to process that information. If Pierce was Chief's favorite, then it means that he was the most likely to be my fiancée. Oh god. I don't know whether to cry or be happy.

"But who knows?" Karter seemed to realize what I was thinking about. "Maybe something will change Chief's mind."

We avoided that tender topic of mine for the rest of the time. Eventually, we walked to dinner together. After dinner was over, we all went to our separate rooms to get ready for the ball. I made my way to my bed and picked up the dress again.

I slipped it on over my body. Amazingly, it fit perfectly. The dark silver colored satin hugged my curves perfectly and accented some of my best features while hiding the bad ones. It had a V-neck that was pleated and embellished with some beads. It also had a cowl drape back, exposing some of my back, but not too much.

I stared at my reflection in the mirror. I was so entranced at the dress that I almost missed the knock at the door. I quickly turned around and opened it.

"Hello, dah-ling." A blond haired man with nerd glasses stepped in my room. He had to be Lukas. "Let's see what I am working with." Circling me, he began to take mental notes.

"Uhm. Okay. You're Lukas right?" I asked.

"Of course," He drew out the last word, "The one and only. Okay, missy. Sit down right here, and I'm going to do your hair right now. Ahh!! What do you to do your hair? It's as dry as straw!!"

I could tell he was a diva and most likely gay. What I love most about gay people is their straightforwardness. They are really blunt about things, and for some bizarre reason, I like it. I sat there in silence as he worked wonders to my hair.

"That's so much better! Now for your makeup. You have such pretty eyes…we just have to make them pop." He made some wild hand gestures. When he finally finished beautifying me, he jumped and clapped his hands. "I am proud of my creation. Now, you can see the new you."

I spun around in my chair so I faced the mirror. A girl that I didn't know looked back at me. She had bright blue eyes that sparkled in the light. Her lips were delicate and her cheeks rosy. I smiled at Lukas and gave him a bear hug. "Lukas, you are amazing."

"Okay, honey. Thank you, but you have to get off me. You are ruining your hair!!" He said sternly as I giggled. My usually unmanageable brown hair was now in structured curls that fell across my shoulders and back gracefully.

He looked at his watch and looked back at me. "Darling, you have five minutes before the party starts. Chief wants me to bring you to his office when you are ready. Are you ready now?"

"Yes, I think so." I nodded. We made our way out of my room and walked to the library where I first met Chief.

"Here you go. Be my little butterfly at the party." He air kissed my cheeks, "Muah. Muah. Bye bye. Don't forget to have fun."

I opened the giant oak door and saw Chief all dressed up. He smiled at me and held his arms wide open, "Melanie! You look gorgeous. Do you like the dress?"

I hugged him and answered, "Thank you so much! You look quite good yourself. And I absolutely adore the dress." I did a quick twirl in front of him.

"Good. Karter picked it out for you." I was surprised. Who knew Karter had such a good taste in clothing? I remembered to thank him later. "Are you ready to go now?" Chief asked me.

"As ready as I will ever be." I answered as I took a deep breath to calm the butterflies forming in my stomach.

"Come on." Chief ushered me out of the room. We walked down an empty hallway. I could faintly hear talking and wine glasses clinking. As we neared the ballroom, the talking got louder. We finally reached the doorway, and an usher nodded at us.

The man took in a deep breath and called out, "Now presenting Ralph McKinley and his granddaughter, Melanie Cartwright."

As we walked into the room and down the stairs, we were greeted by awed silence. I could feel everyone's eyes on me, especially three specific sets of eyes. The three hot successors stood at the bottom of the stairs waiting for me and Chief.

Oh, boy. This is going to be interesting.

Chapter 6

The three guys seemed to be in shock as they stood there speechless. Pierce was the first one to recover and greeted us, "Hello, Chief. Melanie. You two look very nice." He nodded at each of us.

He seemed more gorgeous than ever tonight. His black tuxedo fitted him perfectly, and his silver eyes held a little more excitement than usual. Karter looked very cleaned up, too. And Blake seemed very natural in a suit. Maybe his personality was best fit for formal environments, like tonight.

"Thank you, Pierce. All three of you look quite handsome and perfect, too." I blurted without thinking. I felt my cheeks heat up, and I knew I looked like a tomato. Karter grinned and gave me a wink. It did not make me feel better. In fact, I'm pretty sure my face turned a deeper shade of red.

The five of us walked closer to the dance floor in order

to mingle with the other guests. The first few hours were pretty agonizing because we had to go through all the formal introductions and stuff. By the end of the formalities, I felt worn out. Just thinking that there was still three more hours left of the ball made me want to cry. I closed my eyes and took a deep breath.

Suddenly, someone came behind me and tapped me on the shoulder, "Ms. Cartwright, will you please honor me with your first dance?"

I spun around and grinned, "Of course. It would be my pleasure." I mimicked Karter's old fashioned way of speaking and placed my hands in his waiting, extended hand.

He led me to the center of the dance floor, and we faced each other. I stared into his eyes as we took a step closer to one another. Gently, he snaked his arm around my waist and took a hold of my right hand. I placed my left hand on his shoulder.

The music started, and I could tell it was a waltz. I freaked out a little because I had no idea how to waltz. When it came to dancing, I only knew how to jump up and down and step side to side. I was the type of person who preferred to stand at the wall during dances.

Karter seemed to notice the panic in my eyes. He leaned his head closer to mine and brushed his lips against my ear. I couldn't help but shiver a little at his touch, "Don't worry, I'm a good leader. Just go along with what I do." I could almost hear the grin in his voice.

"I'm not sure…" I began to say, but we already began to move. I counted the beats in my head as we started. One, two, three…one, two three…

It turned out that he was actually a great teacher and

dancer. We started off with a simple move…I think he called it a box step. And then, he started to do something more difficult.

"What are we doing?" I asked as I accidentally stepped on his foot. "Oh, sorry! I can't do this!"

"Yes, you can. I am a guy, and I can do it. It just takes some getting used to." He winced as I stepped on his foot again. "Come on, concentrate!"

I looked down at our feet and noticed a pattern. Back, right, step, turn, forward, left, step, turn, together. Hoping to hammer it in my memory, I chanted that in my head over and over.

"Hey! I'm starting to get the hang of…oomph." I grunted softly as I crashed into his chest when I took a wrong step. Bodies still molded together, I slowly looked up at him. He didn't seem to want to move back either. Instead, he shifted his head closer to mine ever so cautiously.

I stared at his lips as they came closer. When they were only an inch away from mine, my eyelids fluttered closed. I anticipated his soft lips crashing down onto mine, and my stomach filled with butterflies.

"Ahem," someone cleared his throat, interrupting our soon-to-be kiss. "Karter, do you mind if I dance with Melanie?" My eyes flew open in surprise. A wave of heat went to my cheeks for the second time tonight.

Karter didn't move his head back from mine, so we were still only a few inches apart. I stared into his eyes and saw him roll his around. A little pissed, he replied sarcastically, "Of course not. She's all yours."

Slowly, he stood up and straightened his jacket. While

giving me a meaningful look, he walked away into the crowd.

I was disappointed when we were interrupted, but I almost completely forgot about it as another person stepped in right where Karter was going to kiss me moments before. My heart seemed to quicken its pace even when I tried to seem calm and indifferent.

"Hello, Pierce. Forgive me, but I suck at waltzing. I'm sure you know that from watching me and Karter dance." I greeted.

He looked back at me with expressionless eyes, "That's fine. I'm used to it."

What was that supposed to mean? I screamed in my head. He's supposed to say, "You're not that bad!" Does he really think I suck?

I gave up thinking about it too much in my head and concentrated on dancing. Surprisingly, dancing with Pierce was a lot more successful. With the exception of two slips, I was able to dance gracefully. We twirled and made our way around the whole ballroom.

I was acutely aware of where his hand was placed on my waist. Underneath his hand and the material of my dress, my skin burned. Although we weren't standing as close as I was to Karter, it seemed a lot more…intimate.

Looking up into his eyes was a mistake. Once I did, I couldn't pay attention to anything else. Not even the dance. I took a wrong step and broke the spell of whatever was going on between us. In the few seconds that our eyes met, there was definitely something there. And I'm sure we were both very aware of it.

The rest of the dance was slightly awkward, and he

walked away quickly after it was done. I couldn't help but feel a little hurt. Finding somewhere I could stand where there wasn't much attention, I walked towards the food.

I grabbed a crystal goblet and filled it up with the red fruit punch sitting on the table. As I stared absent mindedly ahead of me, I brought the cup up to my lips and drank a little. My head was on overload right now, filled with conflicting thoughts and emotions. I'm sure you could guess what I was thinking about.

Karter. Pierce. Karter. Pierce. Karter. Pierce. Karter. Blake? The great debate in my head was interrupted as I saw Blake sitting alone at one of the tables. I decided to make my way over and join him. He might be able to distract me from my thoughts.

"Hey," I said as I pulled a chair out from under the table.

"Hi," he looked at me kind of strangely. I guess he wasn't used to having company.

"How do you like this party so far?" I asked him.

"Truthfully, I hate parties." Blake admitted. "They are so…overwhelming at times. There's too much drama for my taste. And I hate dancing."

I hadn't been to a party in a long time, and I thought that this one was fun so far…sort of. I could understand what he meant when he said that there was too much drama. "You can say that again. They are a lot to handle, and I suck at dancing too."

He grinned at me and joked, "I didn't say I suck at dancing…I said I hate dancing. There's a difference." I slapped him playfully on the arm. "Anyway, look. There's some fresh drama unfolding over there." He pointed to the large crowd on the dance floor.

It took me a while to see who he was pointing at, but when I did, I felt my heartbeat quicken. "Who is that girl all over Pierce?" I asked.

"I can't really see from here," Blake replied. "But I feel sorry for him. He obviously finds her annoying. See? He just pushed her away."

I felt a little better now that I knew he wasn't interested, but I still felt a little stab of jealousy. "Are you sure? Wait, do any of you guys have girlfriends?" I asked when I thought about that topic. It was silly not to think about it before.

"Yeah, I'm sure. Now he's walking away from her. And no, we're technically not allowed to have girlfriends. But that doesn't stop some people…" Blake stressed the last two words with conviction. I knew he had someone in mind.

"And…who might that someone be?" I asked curiously.

"Who else? Karter The-Womanizer Johnson." Blake said it as if it was his middle name. "He always has a girl hanging off each arm at any given time…like right now."

I scanned the crowd for Karter. Blake was right, he did have several girls drooling after him. But I wasn't sure Karter realized that he had that effect over girls…at least I didn't think he knew. Another wave of jealousy and hurt hit me.

And to think he almost kissed me an hour ago…I thought silently to myself. I could've been one of the girls who he plays with and tosses aside a moment later.

"C'mon…let's dance," I almost begged Blake because

I wanted to get my mind off those two guys. It took a few minutes, but I eventually got him to cave in.

For the third time that night, I was led around the dance floor. With Blake, it felt natural. There was no drama, no mixed emotions, no confusion. Because of the smoothness, we were able to be ourselves around each other. I don't think I'd laughed as much as I did then with Blake. He was a truly funny guy once you got to know him.

"I actually had fun tonight," Blake laughed in a carefree manner. His eyes were shining with water from all the laughing and his hair was slightly messy because he ran his hand through it so many times. I think it's one of his main habits, and I found it absolutely adorable.

"Same here," I grinned, "At first it was really boring and confusing, but then it got a lot better. All thanks to you."

"Don't flatter me," He smiled back.

"I'm serious! Good thing I persuaded you to dance with me. And I guess you were right about the whole suck at dancing thing. You were only okay." I poked him in the chest.

"Ouch. At least I was better than you were," he retorted.

"Oh, shut up. Don't rub it in." I pouted.

"Hey, the party is almost over." Blake looked at the clock. It was ten till midnight, "Only forty minutes left. Time passed by pretty quickly."

"That's because you were hanging out with me," I couldn't help myself. It was too fun to tease him, "Time flies when you are having fun."

"If I agree with you, will that make you stop talking?" He asked. I nodded in return. "Okay. Tonight was really fun and awesome because I got to spend my time with the beautiful and stunning Melanie Cartwright."

His blue eyes bore into mine as he said it, and all trace of playfulness was gone. I was a little stunned by what he said. It wouldn't have bothered me as much if he was joking when he said it, but he said it with a very serious tone.

I half-laughed nervously and tried to make the conversation light again, "Thanks for finally admitting it. I guess I will have to stop talking now." I pretended to zip my mouth shut, lock it, and throw the key away.

Blake just smiled and looked away for a moment. Right then, the old clock began to chime. I counted the number of chimes. One, two, three, four…

Five. I looked around and saw Karter holding on to a girl and nipping playfully at her neck. My stomach twisted in revulsion. Six, Seven, Eight…

The annoying girl that kept bothering Pierce was back. But this time, something changed in Pierce's attitude towards her. She was on her tiptoes and whispering something into his ear. She laughed and pulled back a few inches. Then, I saw Pierce lean his head towards hers. I quickly turned my head so I wouldn't have to see what happened next, although I already knew. Nine, ten.

Eleven. All I knew was that my heart was almost ripped out of my chest. Sure, I didn't know them that well, but I couldn't help how I felt when I was with those two.

Twelve. A tear slipped out of my eye without my permission. I sort of felt like Cinderella right now because her dreams were crushed at midnight. But the only difference is that she had Prince Charming running after her, and I didn't.

A thumb wiped away my tear, and I looked up to see a worried Blake. He pulled me into a hug and didn't ask me any questions. Maybe I did have a Prince Charming after all…

Chapter 7

The morning after the dance was brutal. My eyes were practically glued shut from the dried tears from the night before. I knew it was irrational to cry so much over the guys, but I guess cared more than I wanted to. I couldn't help how my heart felt.

Taking a deep breath and rubbing my eyes, I decided that running would be a good way to clear my mind for an hour or so. I quickly slipped into my workout clothes and made my way outside. While stretching outside on the patio, I heard someone running towards my direction. I smiled as I saw Blake's figure in the distance.

"Hey, Mel. How was your sleep?" Blake stopped when he finally reached me.

I gave him a big smile back. This was the first time he initiated a conversation between the two of us. "It was nice. When did you wake up? You seem to always be out here."

"I got up at around 6:30, which means I got about five

of sleep last night. I don't know why, but my body doesn't need a lot of sleep in order to function." He grinned at me.

"Wow. I need sleep or else I might die in the middle of the day," I said in awe. When I finished stretching, we started to run together. Our footsteps fell into sync and we made our way around the house.

"So, what did you think of the dance last night?" I realized that Blake was discreetly trying to ask me why I started to cry.

"It was really fun up until the end," I answered, struggling to think of an excuse to why I was crying. "I don't know what came over me, but I suddenly started to think about home. I missed my mom and my best friend. It just seems so foreign over here. I have yet to get used to everything."

He nodded and accepted my response, "I know exactly how it feels to be thrown into a world that is so different from your old one. It definitely is a bit overwhelming at first, but you get used to it eventually, especially if other people are there for you. I had Karter and Pierce with me, and you know that I will be there for you." I looked into my eyes.

I smiled warmly at him. I felt a little uncomfortable with the intensity in his eyes, so I shifted my focus on the road in front of me, "Thank you so much. That means a lot to me, and I'm glad I can count on you." Unlike the other guys in this house, I added in my head.

The conversation flowed into a topic that was much less serious, and Blake went back to being his humorous self that I discovered last night. Before I would have never thought I could carry a conversation with him with no awkward pauses but he obviously proved me wrong. He was actually really fun and nice to talk to.

"You know, you are actually an okay runner. I would never have guessed that," Blake commented as we made our way back to the mansion, walking past the pool. The sun just rose, and the rays of light hit the water. The reflections of light created a playful, dancing light show.

"And why is that?" I asked skeptically.

"I don't really know. You just don't seem like the type of girl who runs. You're more like a girl who stays at home and bakes or something." He joked.

I faked a gasp and gave him a little shove in the shoulder. I guess I shoved him harder than I meant to, and he managed to fall over into the pool. My eyes flew open in shock and guilt as I made my way to the side of the pool to check if he was okay.

He made his way to the surface of the water and spluttered. With a mischievous glint in his eye, he warned, "Oh, you are so going to get it."

Quick as lightning, his hand reached out and knocked my legs out from underneath me by pulling on my ankles. I screamed as I fell forward and hit the water with a graceful belly flop.

I pushed off the bottom of the pool and spit out the water that got in my mouth. While treading water, I looked around to try and find Blake. He was nowhere to be found. Suddenly, something was pulling me underwater by my legs.

"BLAK..." was all I managed to get out of my mouth before I was submerged underwater yet again. I forced myself to open my eyes underwater. After the initial sting of the chlorine, I was able to make out the blurry outline of Blake's body.

In a flurry of bubbles and splashes of water, we fought against each other to see who could reach the surface of the water first. With one final push off his muscled chest, my head popped up out of the water. While gasping for breath, I waited patiently for Blake to surface.

"That was brutal," Blake exhaled as his head finally broke the surface of the water. "Remind me to never fight with you again….and never to get on your bad side." Blake joked.

I splashed him in return. Since he made no attempt to fight back, I knew he was tired. I walked closer to him and held out my pinkie, "Truce?"

He looked up into my eyes and gave me a suspicious grin, "In your dreams."

He grabbed me by my waist, and I wrapped my legs around his in an attempt to bring him underwater. I realized a little too late that it was impossible because he could easily stand in this shallow of water.

When I stopped moving, I realized that my eyes were finally level to his. His hold tightened around my waist as I looked into his eyes. I was hyperaware of how close we were and how good his hands felt on my body. Slowly, he slid one hand up to my face to cup my check. Unconsciously, I brought my face an inch closer to his. I looked at his eyes, and I noticed they were dark and filled with determination. He stared at my lips, and I brought my head even closer to his. My eyes fluttered closed as I felt his breath fanning over my face. It felt like an eternity of just staying like that, and my stomach almost exploded with the feeling of anticipation.

Slowly, he brought his head closer to mine and ever so softly brushed his lips against mine, as if he was testing how I would react. The butterflies exploded inside of me, and I couldn't help but tighten my grip around his neck and press my body closer to his in order to properly kiss him.

Our lips moved against each other's while our bodies molded together. Blake's hand moved from my cheek to my hair and twined his finger through it so he could deepen the kiss. I felt his tongue slide across my bottom lip, asking for entrance. I smiled and parted my mouth a little to grant him access. As his tongue met mine, I let out a soft groan into his mouth.

Finally, we broke apart after a few moments. He pressed his forehead against mine, and we both waited until we caught out breaths. We smiled goofily and just looked at each other. After a few minutes, we broke apart, and I felt cold on the parts of my body he was holding on to.

"Come on, we should probably go back inside. Chief and the others are probably wondering why we aren't at breakfast." Blake held his hand out to me, and we got out of the pool.

We walked the rest of the way into the house dripping wet, hand in hand. I'm sure we were an interesting sight to behold. Thankfully, we didn't run into anyone on our way to our rooms. On the top of the stairs, we parted ways. Blake bent down and gave me a quick peck on the cheek.

Twenty minutes later, we met up and went down to breakfast together. When we walked into the room, everyone gave us suspicious looks. I blushed and walked quickly to my seat.

"So, Melanie. What did you think of the dance? Did you like it?" Chief asked me.

"It was fine. I actually had a lot of fun at times," I answered truthfully.

"That's good," he smiled, "And where were you two this morning? Why are you so late?"

"We went out for a run and lost track of time," Blake answered for me. His answer was a lot better than the one I came up with. He looked up at me and his eyes were full of humor.

"Right, I didn't know you ran too, Melanie," Chief directed his attention on me again.

"Yeah, I have been ever since my freshman year in high school," I told him while spearing a few eggs onto my fork. "I did track and cross country as a sport, and I never gave up running since."

"I see," he looked between Blake and I one more time before giving up and returning his attention back to his food.

After everyone finished breakfast and was about to leave, we all heard someone knocking on the door. The sound echoed through the house. Evander excused himself and went to go answer the door.

From where we sat, we all heard, "Siri! What a nice surprise. Did you tell your mom that I won't be able to go home this weekend?"

Everyone else at the table seemed to know who the visitor was. I gave Chief a questioning look, and he whispered, "Siri is Evander's daughter and she comes and visits very often. She happens to be friends with the guys…maybe you can talk to her too."

A few seconds later, a gorgeous girl with blond curly hair walked into the room. She had full lips, so it looked like she was eternally pouting, which I am sure all guys liked. Her eyes were made up beautifully, and I could tell she was the type of girl who cared about money…a lot. Evander followed her in the doorway a few moments later.

"Pierce!" she ran up to him and gave him a kiss on his cheek. The position they were in gave me a flashback of the night before. Gasping, I realized that she was the girl that was all over Pierce at the dance.

I turned away and looked at Blake, hoping that he could give me some reassurance. I laughed when I saw the look of disgust on his face. Obviously, some people didn't like that girl. I looked over at Karter to see his reaction. I could tell his eyes were filled with amusement.

Taking a deep breath, I mustered up the courage to look at Pierce once again. Was it just me? Or does it seem like he is a little annoyed? I noticed his irises roll ever so slightly around his eyes as he talked to Siri.

"Oh! Where are my manners?" Siri suddenly exclaimed, "I forgot to introduce myself! I'm Siri Montgomery. And you are?" She turned to look at me.

I wanted to rip of the fakest smile on her face, "I am Melanie Cartwright, Chief's granddaughter?" I stated in almost a question to see if she knew what I was talking about.

"Of course," she waved her hands dismissively and turned back to Pierce, "Last night was amazing! I wished the night would never end, but you know how things are… the best things never last." She babbled on at him.

I felt a knot forming in my stomach, and I couldn't stand listening to her high-pitched voice any longer, "Chief, can I be excused?" I asked.

"Me too?" Karter chirped beside me.

"Of course," Chief nodded in approval.

Karter and I made our way out of the dining room. He turned to me and started to talk, "It feels like I haven't seen you in such a long time! I think we should change that." He winked.

I'm surprised that I didn't notice his confident and cocky personality before. Even though he is sort of pompous, I didn't hate him. I couldn't, "I know. We didn't see each other after we danced."

"Yeah! Oh, by the way, did you like that dress?" he asked.

I remembered that he was the one to pick it out. Of course he would have a nice taste in women's clothing. It wasn't because he was gay; it was because he had so much experience. "I really like it, thank you. You have a very good taste in clothes."

"I know…what can I say?" Karter joked and I laughed in response. It was impossible to hold a grudge against him. He was the first person I knew here, so it felt like we had a connection. "What are you doing today?" He asked me.

"Uhm. I don't really know. Do you have an idea?" I asked.

"Let's go to the beach. The weather is perfect, and it's not going to last for long." Karter suggested, "Pierce, Blake, and Siri can come along too."

Suddenly, we heard I high pitched giggle coming from behind us. Great, I thought to myself, perfect timing. The other three came around the corner and made a little circle.

"You guys want to go to the beach with me and Mel today? The weather is great, and I'm sure Mel wants to get out of this mansion for the first time in three days." Karter invited the bunch. I didn't even realize I was inside the grounds of the mansion for the past few days. Thinking about it, I really did want to get outside and away from the house.

"Sounds good. We're in," Siri accepted for both her and Pierce. Pierce just gave a curt nod in response.

"Blake?" I looked at him expectantly.

"I wouldn't miss it," He flashed me one of his brightest smiles. I nearly swooned.

Then, I thought of the whole situation. Three guys. In the sun. Wet with water. All shirtless. I couldn't help but smile to myself and get a little pumped.

Chapter 8

We all quickly got changed and packed for the beach. I wore a white sundress with floral patterns on top of my bandeau bikini. I haven't worn my suit for so long that I was sort of surprised there were no cobwebs on it. At least it will be able to see the sun today. Anyways, I was super excited to be able to finally get out of the house. It has been full of drama that it would be nice to have a break from that place.

The three guys drove their separate cars there and Evander almost made me take my own limo, but I refused. I couldn't show up at the beach in a limo because that would be way too flashy for me...although Blake's silver Mazda RX8 isn't much better. In fact, all the guys had their own sports cars. Karter had a red Porsche while Pierce had a black Maserati. I have to say that I'm not totally surprised.

Siri rode with Pierce, and Karter drove alone. The

whole way there, Blake and I talked about California and interesting things to do here.

The conversation flowed nonstop as we whizzed by the Californian palm trees. I admired them silently while I stared out the window. The silence in the car wasn't an awkward one that needed to be filled in with talk. We were both the kind of people who didn't really mind the quiet.

Blake's hand eventually found mine after a few minutes. We entwined our fingers together, and he drew circles on my hand with his thumb. He spared me a quick glance with a small smile and continued driving forward. When he smiled at me, I felt at ease. It was comfortable being around him, and I felt like I could always trust him.

We reached the beach after Karter but before Pierce. Karter was a maniac fast driver, and I could tell he loves to push the limits of his car to the max. Typical trait of a womanizer, I thought ruefully in my head.

After Blake parked his car, I climbed out of it slowly. I stared at the beach, excited to just jump in and feel the cool water around me.

"C'mon Blake!!" I pulled on his arm, willing him to go in the water with me.

"Hold your horses, Mel," Karter looked at me with amusement dancing in his eyes. "We have to wait for Siri and Pierce. They seem to be taking their time." He nodded his head in their general direction.

I rolled my eyes as I took in the sight. Leaning against the car was Pierce, being the "hot guy" he was, while Siri played the role of the desperate girlfriend who was all over her man. She literally squirmed her way between his legs and leaned her face in towards his.

"Do we have to wait for the two lovebirds over there?" I asked sarcastically. Apparently I said to too loud because Pierce shot me a death glare. I just stuck my tongue out in response. Childish, I know, but it made me feel better. It looked like Pierce rolled his eyes, and he lightly pushed Siri off of him.

"Well, someone here is very impatient," Pierce accused me as he casually made his way towards the three of us. Siri followed behind like a dog.

"You were taking your time. The whole world doesn't have to wait for you," I retorted.

He scoffed in disbelief at me, "Are you kidding me? Now you think you are the whole world? Well you aren't as high and mighty as you think you are."

"Me? You think I am self-absorbed?" I was almost screaming at him. We were literally nose to nose at this point. "Of all people, I think that you are the least qualified to accuse me of being high and mighty. Seriously, what is your problem with me?" I jabbed my finger into his chest.

"Guys! Break it up! Both of you as stubborn as hell and acting like children," Blake stepped in between us and pushed Pierce a little further away from me. I stared at Pierce from behind Blake's massive frame. He just glared back at me.

"So…who wants to get in the water?" Karter laughed nervously. I guess he didn't feel comfortable at all…which I don't blame him one bit.

I just sighed and turned away from Pierce. Thanks to him, my good mood was completely ruined.

"Melanie, don't be a party pooper!" Karter shared a devious glance with Blake and gave a slight nod. Suddenly, I felt a strong arm wrap around my waist, and in a matter of seconds, I was thrown over Blake's shoulder. Behind him, I could see Karter running just behind him towards the ocean. Karter and Blake ran until they were knee deep in water, and then Blake half threw me into Karter's arms.

While my shoulders were supported by Karter and my legs by Blake, they swung me from side to side. Finally, they counted down from three and dropped me into the salty water. I let out a squeal as my body hit the water.

"You jerks!" I screamed playfully as I surfaced from the water, "You made me get my dress soaking wet! Couldn't you have waited and let me take it off before I was thrown in?"

The two guys looked at each other and suddenly burst out into a fit of laugher. "No way, your reaction was too priceless." Karter managed to say in between his laughs.

"Fine. Then it's your turn to get wet," I ran at them and tackled both of them into the water at the same time. Usually I could tell it would've been an impossible feat to bring them both down, but I was able to catch them off guard.

They both spluttered as they stood up in the water. I smirked, "Payback is a bitch."

"Hell yeah," Karter grinned, "You are one strong woman."

"Uhm, thank you?" I replied uncertainly as I waded out of the water with the two guys following close behind.

We made our way to where Pierce and Siri laid all our towels out, "Thanks" I muttered to Siri as I walked past her to reach my towel. I took off my dripping wet dress and used the towel to dry myself off.

"No problem!" Siri chirped in her girly, high pitched

voice. "How was the water? Warm? I usually never go in the water. I prefer to lay here and bask in the sunshine."

I could tell she was attempting to make conversation, but truthfully, she wasn't the kind of girl that I usually hang out with. But still, she was probably the only girl I would be talking to when I was here, "Yeah, the water was warm. You should try and go in sometime today. But lying in the sun can be relaxing."

"I know! Omigosh. We have so much in common!" Siri exclaimed. I mentally laughed at her. We have nothing in common. I laid my towel out on the sand a plopped down on it next to the blond haired girl.

"I guess we do…" I trailed off as I looked at the three guys. They were all playing Frisbee, and all shirtless.

'Great,' I thought to myself. 'This is just wonderful. Now I am drooling after three guys. But only one of them is the good one. The other one is a mean, cold hearted jerk. And the last one is a man who takes advantage of women.' Even as I thought that to myself, I couldn't help but lust after the three guys. 'Now what? Am I a whore?' I shook that though from my mind and tried to think about something else.

"Don't the guys look so adorable to you?" Siri sighed in admiration.

"Sure. They are all really good looking." I agreed with her, trying to act like it didn't affect me that much.

"Especially Pierce. He is such a nice guy. I love him so much," she looked at me when I scoffed at what she said. "What? Pierce is such a sweetie…I just don't know why he is so mean to you."

"Yeah, I wish I knew too." I told her truthfully.

"Well, he did mention one thing," Siri tried to lure me in. It worked.

"What did he say?"

"Something about how you were stuck up and he didn't want to marry you," she sighed. "I heard about the whole arranged marriage thing, and it's too bad that he is Chief's favorite. I really thought that Pierce and I would get married in the future. We've been friends for so long, and we did have a conversation about it before. I guess he hates you because he thinks you are getting in the way between me and him."

I looked at her in disbelief. I had no idea that she was so deeply involved with Pierce. "Wow…" I didn't know what to say or how to feel.

Siri suddenly clasped her hand over her mouth, "Oh my, I wasn't supposed to tell you that! Pierce and I wanted it to be a secret. We didn't want Chief to know about how serious our relationship is. And I am so sorry that I was brutally blunt to you. I should have known better."

"It's okay. I understand if you are mad at me too," I replied honestly.

"No! I don't hate you! This whole thing isn't your fault. Your grandpa made the decision, and I know you can't go against him. But maybe you should talk to him about this whole arranged marriage thing. It may not be the best idea." Siri held onto my hand and whispered in my ear as if it was some kind of big secret.

"That's good advice. I think I might do that later this week," I gave her a smile. Although something was very fishy about this girl, she gave me no reason to hate her. We could possibly be friends in the future.

"And I'll try to talk to Pierce and tell him to lighten up on you. Nothing is your fault," she nodded in Pierce's general direction.

"Thanks, Siri. It's nice to finally talk to a girl again. I was worried that I would be surrounded by guys this whole time," we both laughed together.

At sunset and we all walked along the boardwalk together. I held hands with Blake as we hung towards the back of the group.

"Thanks for making today such a great day," I thought back on all we did. We made a giant sandcastle, climbed on the rocks that led out into the ocean, and buried Karter in the sand. Even though the start of the day was a little rough, it was one of the best days of my life.

We stopped walking and Blake took both of my hands into his, "No. Thank you for making it so enjoyable. You are definitely a great person to have around, and I'm glad Chief found you."

I was touched by his speech and freed one of my hands from his. I slowly caressed his face in my palm, and he moved his head closer to mine.

Our second kiss was as good as our first one. We both still hesitated at first, but it was more natural this time. His arm slinked around my waist in order to pull me in closer, and his other hand made his way to my face. I could feel the line his fingers drew as they travelled up my arm, leaving a trail of fire. In response, I wrapped both my arms around his neck and tilted my head so we could deepen the kiss.

A wolf whistle interrupted us, "Hey, lovebirds! Hurry up or else we're going to start the party without you guys!" Karter joked.

I blushed a deep red and Blake just grinned at my sudden shyness, "He's right. We don't want to keep them waiting." Blake grabbed my hand and led me to the rest of the group.

By then, they had started a bonfire. I smiled as Blake and I found a suitable log that we could sit on. We dragged it over to the fire and plopped down next to each other. Blake slung his arm around my shoulder.

"Woohoo Blake. Nice catch," Karter winked at me and Blake. I turned crimson again as Karter continued to torture us. "I wonder what Chief would say." He joked again.

I paled. Was I supposed to be getting close to anyone while I am here? I asked myself. What if Blake isn't the one to take over the company? What will happen then? And what am I supposed to do when they announce who will take over? Am I supposed to pretend to be a happy stay at home wife? What will happen to my mom and friends back at home?

Needless to say, I was distracted for the rest of the night as I thought about those questions over and over. The severity of this whole situation finally sunk in. I needed to get away from these people for a moment, so I excused myself from the group.

I walked several yards away and sank down into the sand right in front of the ocean. The sound of the waves crashing into land was relaxing, but it didn't really help my confused brain. Sitting there with my knees curled up, I realized that I had to go talk to Chief and get some questions answered.

Chapter 9

That week, I decided to confront Chief and get some answers. The questions that ran through my head had bugged me since the day at the beach. I could barely sleep because of them. I knew I may be overreacting, but the answers seemed very important to me at this moment.

It was right after lunch so everyone went their own ways to relax. Not knowing where Chief went, I wandered around the house and peered into each room. Opening the door to the living room, I noticed that there was someone sitting in the giant chair that faced the opposite side of the room.

"Chief?" I asked hesitantly.

I heard the slam of a book and saw a figure standing up. Guarded silver eyes met mine, and I felt my heart beat quicken. Why? I'm not entirely sure...but I didn't like the feeling. After what seemed like forever, Pierce's facial expression slightly relaxed.

Feeling slightly uncomfortable and really awkward, I spun around to get out of the room. I quickly muttered, "Sorry to bother you. I thought you were Chief."

Before I could take another step, Pierce quickly yelled out, "Wait. Melanie, stop." I froze in mid-step and took a deep breath to face him. I was in no mood to argue with anyone...especially him.

He continued to talk when I was facing him, "Look. I know I've been a jerk to you the whole time you were here, and I'm sorry." I probably looked like a fool, standing there with wide eyes and my mouth hanging open. I was in complete shock as to what he was saying. "It's just that I..."

"PIERCE!! Baby! I was looking all over for you!" An annoying screechy voice called out, interrupting his speech. Pierce's expression towards me turned distant and cold in a matter of seconds. I was stunned once again by his ever changing personality. I wished that Siri never interrupted us. Was so close to figuring out why Pierce was so mean to me.

"Hey, Siri. I was just telling Mel that Chief was in the library. She seemed to be looking for him." I found it weird that Pierce had to explain himself to Siri. I shrugged it off and walked towards the door.

"Thanks, Pierce." I mimicked his coldness. Then I turned to Siri, "Maybe when I'm done talking to Chief we can do something. I am super bored and tired of just sitting around." I tried to sound genuine and nice.

"That sounds great!" She gushed. "Just find me when you're done."

I made my way out of the room and walked down the hallway that I walked through when I first moved in. Although I have been here for almost two weeks, the grandeur of the house never lost its skill to take away my breath. I stopped outside the heavy oak door and used all my body weight to open it a crack. Sure enough, Chief's sitting silhouette was in his favorite chair.

"Good afternoon, Melanie. What's up?" Chief put down his book and set his reading glasses on top of it. He probably sensed my tense mood.

"Chief, I have some questions that we never really talked about when I first arrived," I sank into an old, antique chair.

"Okay, shoot." Chief looked completely at ease. I'm sure he had to deal with people who ask him a lot of questions.

"Well, first off, I want to know more about this arranged marriage. I don't know if it is the best decision. There are a lot of things that you have to consider before forcing me to marry anyone," I tried to sound professional.

"I hope you fully understand why you must marry the successor. It's not only because I want you to be happy, but also because I want this company be passed down to family. This company started out as a small business, and I want to know it's going to be in good hands." Chief confessed. It sort of made sense to me, so despite the fact that I slightly sad and angry, I just nodded and accepted his explanation.

But it still didn't answer my other question, "But what if I don't like the guy I'm going to marry? Or what if I'm in love with another person?" I blushed when I said the last part. Of course I wasn't in love with Blake yet, but I was definitely attracted to him.

Chief raised an eyebrow at me, but didn't comment any further on my redness, "I'm not an evil grandfather who likes to tear two people apart. I do believe in love, and I will take your relationships with each guy in consideration. You know, I am more observant than you think." He winked at me. It sounded like a lighthearted joke, but I knew what he said carried some weight. "All the guys are well equipped to take on the business, so it doesn't matter which one you like the best."

What he said slightly made me feel better, but I still wasn't satisfied. "Okay. That sounds reasonable. But what about my mom and my hometown? Where am I supposed to live after I marry?"

"I know you miss your mom and friends a lot." Chief nodded in empathy, "And I have thought a lot about it. For you to move away immediately is too much to ask of you. That's why I decided that you are going to live in the mansion for only four months. By the end of the four months, I will announce who will succeed the business. The wedding will take place one year later. During that year, you will be able to choose whether or not to stay or spend the time in New York."

I tried to digest that information as Chief continued, "That way, you will have a year to say goodbye to your friends and family before you officially move in here. But keep in mind that you will be able to visit New York very frequently, so the move won't be that bad." Chief tried to make me feel better as the reality of this whole situation sunk in. I tried to swallow the lump that was forming in my throat.

"So...there's no other option? I have to marry the successor and move in here?" I asked in order to clarify his answer.

Chief simply nodded, "I know this isn't what you expected or wanted, but I really believe that it will benefit the both of us in the long run."

Bowing my head in defeat, I stood up to leave the room. Before I could get out of the room, Chief got up and pulled me into his arms. While I was engulfed in his embrace, something snapped inside of me and tears started flowing down my cheeks.

"Shhh...Don't cry. I'm sorry, Melanie. Everything will work out in the end. I promise. Please do this for me." Chief tried to comfort me.

I know I should've been mad at him or something, but I really didn't feel any resentment. He was my only real family, and I knew everything he did was out of love. I couldn't just push him out of my life. Trying to be the bigger person, I calmed myself down and didn't argue any further.

"Thanks for explaining everything, grandpa. I'll try and do this for you," I hiccupped. It wouldn't be that bad, would it? All the guys were fairly nice, and if what Chief said was true, I could end up with Blake.

"Oh yeah," I remembered what Karter said to me before the ball, "Someone told me that Pierce is your favorite." Chief nodded in response. "Why is that?"

While sighing, Chief responded, "I think you will be able to see why he is my 'favorite'. All the guys are extraordinary, but I think that he shines the brightest because of his personality and attitude." He took in my expression, "But don't worry. That doesn't guarantee that he will be the successor. And it seems like you don't really like him...why is that?"

I gulped. An hour ago, he seemed friendly at first but something happened. It was all so confusing. "It's nothing," Chief raised an eyebrow at me. "Okay, fine. It's just that he's really cold sometimes, and I really don't know why he dislikes me so much. He doesn't even know me."

"Well, I think I will have a talk with that kid. I'm sure he has a pretty good reason though. He is usually really friendly and caring," Chief explained.

My face paled, "NO!" I said too forcefully. I changed my tone so it wasn't nearly as loud, "I don't want him to think I'm a tattletale. Maybe I can talk to him some more." I tried to persuade Chief.

Chuckling in response, he said. "Suit yourself." Chief looked down at his watch, "And now, I have to go and listen to a bunch of boring people talk about the finances of the company. If you want, I can walk you back to your room."

I shook my head and joked, "It's okay. I'm a big girl, and I don't want to keep the other people waiting. I'll just walk back myself." Chief held the door open for me and followed me out the room. From there, we split ways.

Deciding not to go back to the room, I started to wander around the house. I was getting a little sick of sitting in my room doing nothing. Exploring the massive mansion would be a good way to pass my time.

I rounded a corner and found the narrow hallway that Pierce showed me the first morning I came to the mansion. I sighed as I remembered the initial shock as our bodies met. Why is he so mean to me?

I continued to walk down the hallway. Not remembering where it led to, my curiosity sparked. I cautiously walked down the hallway and found myself standing in a giant foyer of some kind.

This was definitely not on the tour, I thought to myself. The place was extremely extravagant, but it gave off an eerie feeling. I walked closer to the giant staircase leading to the second floor. There was a thin layer of dust coating the railing, which was weird because the rest of the house was squeaky clean.

I walked up the stairs cautiously and found that it lead to a single door at the end of the hall. The window curtains in the hallway were drawn shut, so it was slightly dark. I gulped as the shadows seemed to grow and dance around me. I hesitated at the door, but decided to open it.

The room was highly anticlimactic. I almost laughed at myself for getting scared and letting my imagination run wild. It was just an old guest room.

As I wandered the room, I realized that it was occupied. But I haven't seen anyone in the house that could live here. I spotted a photo frame and walked towards it, hoping it might give me some answers.

The picture was really simple. It seemed like the photographer just snapped the picture right when a couple was laughing, so it was candid and natural. The frame was just as simple. It was plain silver with etchings into it. I looked closer and read it.

'Live, Laugh, Love' it said on the top. On the bottom, it said, 'Sarah and Rob Cartwright 1991'.

I gasped when I finally realized that I was looking at my parents for the first time. They were a beautiful couple and I could slightly see how I looked like them. Nostalgically, I smiled and picked up the photo

Not knowing how long I've been staring at it, I suddenly heard footsteps coming up the stairs. I felt like a guilty robber being caught in some sacred place and I frantically looked around for somewhere to hide. I ran into the closet right as the door opened.

My parents' closet was similar to mine, so it was like a one way mirror. I gasped when I saw Pierce and Siri walked in.

In a harsh whisper, Siri yelled at Pierce, "I thought we were in agreement."

He scoffed, "Agreement? So that's what you are calling it?"

Siri rolled her eyes in exasperation, "What? Do you prefer business agreement? Whatever. You know that isn't the issue. The issue is that you were talking to her. I said you could argue but not TALK."

"Before I knew you, I actually thought you were nice. I can't believe you are such a bitch. She never did anything to you, and you are just so fake to her. I can't be like you." Pierce retorted.

Siri slapped him. Literally slapped him on the face. I held in a gasp. I never actually saw anyone do that to a person before. Strangely, I felt bad for Pierce.

"You deserved that. You should be glad I'm not going to tell Chief your dirty little secret because I'm letting your comment slide." Siri crossed her arms over her chest in triumph.

Pierce sighed in defeat, "Fine. Whatever. I'm not going to talk to her. If that's what you want. But I'm not going to be a jerk. I think she already hates me, so you have nothing to worry about."

"Good. And please be more convincing when you are being my boyfriend. You are such a bad actor." Siri added.

"Your wish is my command, your majesty." Pierce mocked her and bowed sarcastically. He left the room without another word. Stomping her feet like a little kid, Siri followed him out.

I sat there in the closet at loss of what to do. Were they talking about me? What the hell just happened?

Chapter 10

I sat in the closet still unsure of what to make of that little exchange between Siri and Pierce. All I got from it was that Siri didn't want Pierce to talk to a girl that was possibly me. And that Pierce did something that he didn't want Chief to know about. My head hurt from just trying to figure out what it was.

Thinking about everything for a while, I realized that I might've seriously misjudged Pierce. I never thought that someone could blackmail him like that. It just seems like he is the type of guy who would always be in charge. Maybe that's why he is so mean to me.

But then again, maybe he did do something really awful. Siri could have a valid point in using it against him. Although she was the one that seemed like a total bitch, maybe her actions were nothing bad compared to Pierce's.

UGH!! I didn't know! Everything was just so confusing. This whole place messed with my mind, and I definitely needed to get out of the house sometime soon.

Finally, I forced my hands and legs to move. Slowly crawling out of the closet, I stayed close to the ground, making sure no one else was in the room or out in the hallway. It would be bad if I was caught listening to Pierce and Siri talk.

I made my way to the door of the room and looked back. I sighed and made a mental note to come back here another time and spend some alone time with my parents. It just seemed so serene and peaceful.

Standing up and wiping my hands off on my pants, I silently closed the door behind me. I crept back down the stairs and walked around the house to my room. Right as I passed the lounge area, I heard someone say my name.

"Mel! It feels like I never see you anymore!" Karter's voice called out from behind me.

I turned around and plastered a fake smile on my face. Truthfully, I wasn't in the mood to talk to anyone at the moment. "Hey, Karter! It does feel like a long time. Are you playing video games again?"

"You know me too well," he joked as he patted the empty space on the couch next to him while setting down his game controller. "Come join me. I'm lonely."

Reluctantly, I slowly walked to where he was sitting and plopped down next to him. It's not that I don't like Karter, it was far from that, it was just that my head was a mess and I have no idea what to make of this whole new life at the mansion.

"So, what's up with you today?" he asked me. I thought about telling him about the conversation I overheard, but

I had a feeling that I really shouldn't. There was something really fishy about it, and I'm sure Pierce wouldn't want Karter to know about it.

"Not much. I just wandered around the house and talked to Chief. He's a really nice person." I commented, and he nodded in response. "What about you?"

"Well, my day was very boring…up until now," he grinned and winked at me. "But in all seriousness, I have to ask you a question." His voice suddenly got a lot deeper.

I looked at him and nodded, willing him to continue. When he paused for a bit, I encouraged him even more. I was curious to find out what he was thinking. "Sure, what's up?"

"Don't take this in the wrong way, but do you like Blake? I mean, really like him?" That was not what I expected to come out of his mouth. I paled and raked my head for an answer. I really like to spend time with him, but I guess it feels like I still don't know him well enough.

"Why do you ask?" I said back, trying to buy time for an acceptable answer in my head.

"I was just wondering," He shrugged as if the question wasn't a big deal. "I mean, Blake is probably the nicest guy you will ever meet, and I want to know if you just think of him as a fling or whatever. I know he's got his heart broken by some girl before, and I don't want that to happen to him again. I'm pretty sure he likes you, so you should tell him how you really feel before he dives in too deep again."

I stared at Karter for a moment. I never saw this side of him. From this admittedly awkward conversation, I could tell he cared a lot about Blake, and he is making sure I'm not messing with him.

"Thanks for telling me that. But truthfully, right now, I don't know him well enough to make a judgment of whether or not I want to marry him or whatever. I do know that I really like to hang out with him, and he has a wonderful personality." I looked into Karter's eyes and thought I saw a flicker of disappointment. But for what? I don't know.

"Does that mean I still have a fighting chance?" Karter looked frighteningly serious. As I scrambled for a response, his gaze lightened and he chuckled. "Don't be so flustered. I was just joking. You know I care more about Blake."

Punching his arm, I let out a forced laugh. That was not funny. At all. It didn't really help that I still felt the most natural around Karter. And that he was insanely good looking.

"You are a jerk. And do you use that line with all the women you try to get? 'Do I still have a fighting chance?' Psh." I scoffed and quoted him.

This time, I caught him of guard. "I have no idea what you are talking about. What women?"

I laughed in disbelief. Does he honestly not realize that he is a womanizer? "I'm sure you noticed all the girls that were fawning over you at the ball that one night."

"Oh yeah. All the girls? More like one or two. But then again, I guess it's because they can't resist me." He joked.

I sighed in defeat. He can't take anything seriously, and I am just sitting here, inflating the giant ego of his. "Fine. Pretend you don't know what I'm talking about. That's cool."

For a second, I thought that he was going to take me seriously. But then, he shrugged nonchalantly and picked up his video game remote. "You want to play?" He asked me.

I looked at the screen and saw bright flashes of light coming from a machine gun and virtual people being killed. Looking at the game's layout, I assumed it was Halo.

"Really? Me? Play Halo?" I asked incredulously.

"Yeah, why not?" Karter asked, "Afraid you will lose to me?"

"You wish," I retorted while picking up the second game controller that was lying on the table where Karter's feet was propped up. I'd actually played this game before with some of my guy friends when I went to high school, but it had been years.

Karter paused his current game and went to the main screen. Selecting the two player mode, he grinned, "Get ready to be dominated."

"Bring it on."

I admit it. This game was slightly addicting. It took me a while to figure out the controls, but once I got used to the whole concept, I played like a pro. Okay, so I'm sort of exaggerating, but oh well. After being killed countless times by Karter, I finally killed him for the first time.

Jumping up and doing a victory dance, Karter watched me with amusement. "I BEAT YOU!!" I pointed my finger in his face and laughed. Sadly, my moment of victory was interrupted when someone started chuckling behind me.

"Oh, no. Karter, please don't tell me you got Mel hooked on video games, too! One insane person is enough."

Karter and I both looked up and saw Blake standing behind us. "Shut up, Blake. You know you play video games all the time, too."

"Not nearly as much as you do. And you know I can beat you within a second, which is really sad, considering you get a lot more practice than I do." Blake countered as he found his way to the seat next to me.

"Argh. Touché." Karter grumbled. He looked back to the screen and continued to play his game.

"Hey, Mel." Blake greeted. Glancing at Karter and making sure he wasn't looking, he gave me a quick peck on the lips.

"You guys! GET A ROOM!! I can see you!" Still staring at the screen unfazed, Karter screamed at us. Shaking our heads, Blake and I just ignored him.

"Hey. So what have you been up to today?" I asked him in a low voice, not wanting to 'disturb' Karter again.

"Nothing, really. I've just been in my room. And I went downstairs to study a bit."

"Study for what?" I asked. Then I realized what he was talking about.

"Tests and other things about the company and how we should run it." His answer confirmed what I thought.

"Oohh. That doesn't sound too fun." I commented, "How come Karter doesn't have to study?"

"Because he is a lazy ass and all he cares about is video games." Blake responded loudly enough so Karter could hear. In return, a pillow hit Blake square in the face. Tossing the pillow aside, Blake continued to talk. "But seriously, he does study. He's just so laid back that you don't even notice. And Pierce was downstairs with me. He actually knows when to study and stuff."

I nodded, and thinking about Pierce just made my mood slightly darken. Blake seemed to notice, and quickly changed the topic.

"So, what are you doing tomorrow?" he asked me.

Raising my eyebrow, I looked at him. "I dunno. Do you have anything planned?"

"As a matter of fact, I do."

I joked, "What? Like study more for the test?"

"Of course not. I already did all my studying today, just so I could go out with you tomorrow..." Blake smiled that amazing smile of his. "Only if you want to." He quickly added.

"Sure. What do you want to do?"

"It's a surprise." He winked. Yes, winked. I almost melted on the spot. But I didn't. Because the thought of surprises made me uneasy. I think I have had enough surprises in a lifetime.

I pouted at him and put on my puppy dog face, "Please? Please tell me?" Clamping my hands together, I bent down on my knees and groveled.

"Get up, Mel!" he laughed, "If you keep on doing that, I think I might give in. Don't make me ruin the most perfect date in the world."

Groaning, I got up and sat on the couch. "Fine. Be that way."

"I will." He grinned.

Karter looked at us and shook his head in amusement, "You guys are both so stubborn, it is sort of funny. And cute...in a creepy way."

Blake and I shared a look with each other and nodded in agreement. In a flash, we both picked up pillows and started pelting Karter with them.

Thinking about the date the next day, I almost forgot about the whole Siri and Pierce thing. Almost.

Chapter 11

I felt the rays of sun shining on my face, making my skin flush with warmth. Suddenly, the mattress on either side of my pillow sunk down. Refusing to open my eyes to see what was going on, I sleepily moaned in protest.

I heard a slight chuckle and gasped when someone breathed into my ear, "Good morning, sleepyhead."

I rolled onto my back and opened my eyes to see Blake's eyes boring into mine. His face hovered a feet above my own, and his arms supported his upper body from either side of my pillow.

"You didn't run this morning," he commented, obviously amused by me being in my groggy state of mind.

I looked at him more closely. It was obvious he just came back from his morning jog. His arm and face was slightly shiny from sweat, but instead of making him look gross and unclean, it made him look sexier. Of course. He was always perfect like that. "I guess I was just saving my energy for later on in this day," I responded when I remembered that we were going on a date.

My response was rewarded with a grin as Blake slowly pushed himself up and stood straight. He ran his hand through his already messy dirty blond hair, "Okay then. Let's not waste any more of this day. I'll take a shower and meet you downstairs in an hour."

"Fine," I slowly sat up in bed and raised my arms above my head and arched my back, as if I was reaching for the sky. After hearing a little pop from my back, I sighed and brought my hands down. "Is there a dress code? Formal? Casual?"

"Just wear normal clothes. Nothing too formal," He responded and gave me a mysterious smirk. And with that, he left the room, making me wonder what we were going to do on our date.

After taking a shower and putting on a pair of dark wash jeans and a simple blue and white striped t-shirt, I made my way down the stairs. I walked into the kitchen and saw Blake and Pierce sitting at the table.

"Good morning," I said chirpily, testing to see if I would get a response out of Pierce. From that conversation yesterday, I assumed that he wouldn't even acknowledge me. I was right.

"Grab something quick to eat, and we'll head off soon." Blake smiled and got up. He pulled a chair out and pushed it in as I sat down. I guess chivalry isn't dead.

I grinned to myself as Blake sat back down in his own seat. After eating breakfast, Blake and I left the room.

"Bye Pierce. Tell Chief that Mel and I aren't going to

be back until later tonight," Blake yelled over his shoulder to Pierce.

"Sure thing. Have fun, you guys." Pierce waved and grinned at Blake. Once again, he didn't look over at me at all. So he was pretending that I didn't exist at all. Fine, that's cool with me. I'll just have to do some more snooping myself...after this date, of course.

Blake opened the car door for me and closed it after I slid in. He was being such a gentleman, that sometimes it just felt a little awkward. I guess I'll just have to get used to a guy who isn't a jerk.

The scenery outside became a blur as we sped down the highway in his silver sports car. "How long are we going to have to drive for?" I asked him, after five minutes of peaceful silence.

"It's going to be almost an hour, but trust me, it's worth it." He grinned as he drove with one hand and fiddled with the radio.

Teenage Dream by Katy Perry blasted through the car, and I laughed at how fitting this was. If you had ever seen the music video, you would understand what I am talking about.

All the windows were down, and the wind rushed into the car. The feeling of it running through my hair was exhilarating, and it finally gave me the sense of freedom I was craving for. The mansion was just so overbearing that I always felt...trapped. But now, I really did feel carefree. So much so that I sang and danced along with the music like I was a twelve year old. Blake chucked at my silliness and weaved his hand into mine.

"You are so insane, you know that?" He joked.

"And you are so boring." I retorted. "Have some fun!"

"How am I supposed to have fun when I am driving?" Blake asked.

"Touché," I nodded, dumbfounded and unable to come up with a better response.

"Well, I guess there is a way…" He gave me a devious look and let his sentence trail off. Slowly taking his hand out of mine, he gripped the wheel with both hands. "Ready?"

Before I could even respond, my head jerked back and my hair became a wild mess in the wind. Pressing his foot harder into the accelerator, he laughed at me and continued to speed down the conveniently empty highway.

"BLAKE!! WE'RE GOING TO DIE!!" I screamed as I gripped the armrest.

"C'mon. Don't be so boring. Have some fun," He used the words I said to him against me. "Anyway, don't you trust me?"

I gave him a very skeptical look, but the puppy dog face he had on was too priceless. I couldn't help but laugh and feel my body relax a little.

"Fine. I trust you. But don't try anything funny." I warned, as I saw the little needle going past 100 mph.

"Just let go, and pretend you are on a roller coaster." Blake took a hold of my hand again. "And do realize that I like you too much to hurt you. So you are safe with me."

I looked at him, and found comfort in his words. So I decided to follow his advice. Looking him in the eye, I smiled and sang along to the last few lines of the song, "This is real, so take a chance and don't ever look back. Don't ever look back."

The rest of the ride felt like a blur. It was probably the most fun I have had in a very long time. Singing and talking to Blake really did make me feel so much better and happier. Finally, we pulled up to our destination.

"A farm?" I asked incredulously as I stepped out of the car. I felt a little out of place, especially arriving in a sports car.

"Yeah," Blake laughed as he walked up behind me, "I wonder when the last time you ever went to a farm was."

"Truthfully, I don't know. It definitely has been a while." I said as he guided me forward by the small of my back.

"C'mon. The main attraction is in the back." Blake grinned as we kept on walking ahead.

"No way!" I squealed when I saw the signs. "This is so awesome!!"

As we walked towards the entrance, I saw a huge crowd of people. This was one of those farms where there was tons of stuff to do in the fall, around Halloween. A giant corn maze was what the farm advertised the most, but there was also zip-lining, pumpkin carving, apple picking, pig racing, and the list goes on and on. Of course, there is a haunted house.

After Blake paid for the admittance fee, he turned around and smiled. "So, how do you like this little surprise?"

"This is so amazing. I can't wait to do all of these things!! I have never been to a place like this before. I've only heard about them." I looked around in wonder.

"Well, what do you want to start off with?" Blake asked. "Something scary?" He joked.

"No way!" I am deathly afraid of scary things. Whenever I watch a scary movie, I always hide under a pile of blankets and surround myself with pillows. It always made me feel more secure, but it also made me really hot. Basically, I am a puffy-eyed, sweaty, chicken whenever I watch horror movies. I'm sure it's a very ugly sight to see. That's why all of my friends back at home always had to fight to not sit next to me.

"How about we start with the corn maze?" I suggested. It seemed safe and horror-free.

"Good idea. But since you decided what we are going to do first, I call making some of my own rules." Blake's eyes danced with deviousness. I looked at him skeptically before waiting for him to continue. "I say we race to see who can find their way out of the maze first."

I nodded. Okay, that isn't that bad. But Blake continued to talk, "And whoever loses, has to go into the haunted house first."

"WHAT?" I screamed. I quickly cleared my throat and lowered my voice, "No way. I'm not doing that."

"Why not?" Blake asked. "If you lose, I'm still going to go into the haunted house; I'm just going to be behind you the whole time."

I thought about the situation, "If we didn't do this whole race thing, you would probably still make me go into that house anyway, right?" I asked.

"I guess you know me too well," he smiled. "Anyway, it's a life experience, and you have to do it at least once."

"Fine," I gave in, knowing that I would have to go in either way, "It's on."

He grinned and gave me a big hug. "Aww. Thanks, Mel! And by the way, you're going down." He quickly let go of me and sprinted towards the maze.

"You little cheater!!" I called out behind him and followed him into the maze.

The corn stalks were a few feet taller than me, which slightly intimidated me. The first few minutes were fun. I kept on running, believing that I would make it out of the maze before Blake. After a few minutes though, I became discouraged. I totally had been past the same stalk several times. I tried jumping and seeing if I could see anything, but the stalks were too high.

After a few more minutes, I began to completely freak out. I hated being lost and not knowing where I was. There was no one around me, so it's not like I could ask for help. Suddenly, I noticed a checkpoint. I ran towards it and looked to see if there was a map.

Luckily, there was. I found the fastest way to the exit and repeated the steps in my head. Left, right, right, left, right, turn, left. Running at full speed, I made my way to the exit. I saw the clearing ahead of me, and the corn stalks were becoming less dense. I almost cried for joy when I finally made my way out of the maze.

But Blake wasn't there. He wasn't anywhere. I turned around to look at the people around me. Just as I was about to feel lost again, I felt strong arms wrap around my waist.

"Did you have to wait for a long time?" Blake whispered in my ear.

I quickly spun around and punched him several times in the chest. "That was so scary. Don't ever leave me alone like that again." I looked down towards the ground, trying to stop the tears that were forming in my eyes. I wasn't a weak girl. I just hate the feeling of being lost.

Blake's hand tilted my chin up and he looked into

my eyes. "I'm sorry, Melanie. I didn't know it would be that frightening. We don't have to do that again." His arm wrapped tighter around my waist and he pulled me closer to him.

Not wanting to be a party pooper and hold a grudge against him, I decided to return the hug.

"And you really don't have to go into that haunted house if you don't want to." Blake said after I calmed down a little bit.

I half smirked. "If you are too scared to go in first, you can just tell me."

Blake grinned, "No way. I'm not afraid."

Spurred on by the thought of winning the maze race, my confidence soared. We walked hand in hand towards the looming dark house in the distance. As I heard some piercing screams and saw some spooked people walk by, my eagerness stalled.

"Tell me if you want to go back. I'm fine with it. And remember that I'll be there for you…since I'm going first." Blake tried to make me feel better.

"Oh, shut up. I'm fine. Let's go." I joked, trying to hide my apprehensiveness.

We reached the entrance of the haunted house and got in line. I gulped as I saw the sign. 'Dungeon of Doom: Try to Survive the Horror'. This was not going to be fun.

Chapter 12

"Blake?" My voice quivered in the darkness. Although there were people surrounding us, who were also waiting to get into the house, I felt isolated and scared.

This was the worst thing ever. The line itself to get into the haunted house took two whole hours. And it wound through a warehouse where there were people jumping out and scaring you. There were also TVs where they showed live video clips of people inside the haunted house. And trust me, it did not look fun.

"Yeah?" A voice whispered into my right ear.

"I'm just making sure you're still there…" I whimpered. I was still clinging to his arm, so I don't see how he could've wandered away. Nevertheless, I was still paranoid.

An arm started rubbing my back in soothing circles, and I felt my muscles begin to relax. He continued to soothe me, and his hand worked its way up to my shoulder.

In the middle of giving me a shoulder massage, he suddenly clamped his cold and clammy hands around my neck.

"BLAKE!!" I screamed and hugged him even tighter.

The real Blake whisked me up in a hug and started to pat my hair, "Shh…it's okay. I'm here. What's wrong?" He was oblivious of the creepy guy who was pretending to be him.

A pale figure with bloody scratch marks that ran down his cheeks started cackling. With one hand, he held out his long, sharp nails and pointed at me. His other hand was holding a knife covered in blood. "You will be buried either dead or alive. Ashanti Levi marks a doom." As he began to chant the words, his eyes turned to the back of his head and a tremor ripped through his body.

"STOP!!" Beginning to cry, I buried my face into Blake's shirt. From what I could tell, Blake was also scared out of his pants.

The man just gave one last cackle and sauntered away, looking for another group of people to scare.

"Blake…I don't think I can stand this anymore. Can we please go out?" I cried into his shirt. Somehow, his scent comforted me, and my tears began to dry out.

I could feel him nod his head. Taking my hand in his, he led me towards an exit. The people were smart enough to construct several exit places in the line, so cowards like me could exit before actually going into the haunted house.

The exit here was slightly awkward because the ceiling was low and it slanted at a 45 degree angle. Looking ahead, I could see the bright afternoon sun that looked so cheery and happy.

Completely caught off guard, I shrieked when a blood-ied and maimed person landed on the ceiling right above me. As I looked around me, I realized that the walls and ceiling were made out of Plexiglas. More people surrounded us, and they started to moan and pound on the walls. I could hear the glass shaking, and I was scared that it would break sometime soon.

Accidentally pushing Blake over in my haste of getting out of the haunted house, I literally trampled over him and ran out into the sunlight. Even after I got out of that house, I didn't stop running. My natural instinct was to get as far away as possible from the horrific house. Thank god I was a runner, or else I probably would have died from all the running.

I slowed down my pace after entering the area where there were normal activities going on – such as face painting, pumpkin carving, berry picking, etc. After a minute or so, Blake finally caught up to me.

"I guess you made up for not running this morning just now." Blake teased, although his complexion didn't look so good. I'm sure mine wasn't any better, judging from the way people were staring at us.

"Okay, so maybe this farm wasn't such a good idea to go on a date…" I started to say, but Blake held up a finger to cut me off.

"Don't say that too soon. All we've done is the corn maze and haunted house. Just be glad we got the two scariest things over with." His large hand wrapped around my tiny one, making me feel small and insignificant.

I looked at him skeptically. "I don't know."

"What's so scary about apple picking?" Blake asked me as he led me towards the rows of apple trees. "Anyway, the best apples are in season right now. The honey crisps are to die for."

And Blake was right. They were delicious. As the day went by, I started to have more fun. The scarring experiences of the morning were behind me as Blake and I sailed through the countryside on zip lines.

The feeling was exhilarating…almost as good as going 100 mph on the highway. I grinned to myself as I thought about the day. Although it was not fun at the beginning, it got exponentially better as the day went on.

We walked through the lines of fruit and vegetable stands, where local farmers sold all their homemade goods and stuff.

Meandering through the market, the vibrant colors of the fruits attracted the attention of lots of people. The smell of freshly baked bread wafted through the air, and I couldn't help but think of my mother's bakery. I remembered her rosy cheeks and her flour covered apron.

I smiled nostalgically to myself and made a mental note that I had to call her and Jessica. I missed them so much, and I felt guilty that I haven't talked to them in a while.

"Come here. Look at this!" My thoughts were interrupted as Blake tugged on my arm and pulled me to a stand where a lady was selling flowers.

"Hello, darlings!" the friendly old lady smiled at us. "What brings you here on this lovely crisp autumn day?"

"Oh, we're just here to have some fun and look around," I smiled back at her. There is something about this lady that makes you want to smile and talk.

"That's fun. Are you two a couple? Because you guys

look so cute together!" She gushed, ignoring my inflamed cheeks and downcast eyes.

"Yeah," Blake responded nonchalantly. I don't see how he could act so cool whenever someone talked about him. "Anyway, I saw those flowers, and I've never seen anything like them before. What are they called?"

The lady gave him a knowing smile, "They're known as the passion flower. It represents purity, holiness, and the truth. Of course, it may not be the most fitting to give to you girlfriend. But the flower is such a beauty."

She continued to talk. "If you are looking for a flower to give to your lovely lady, then may I suggest the white anemone with the black center? It is thought to bring luck and protect against evil." Blake and I shared a look and his lips turned upwards to form a smirk. "It also represents magic and anticipation."

Blake didn't hesitate to pull out his wallet to pay for the flower, "I'll buy one. How much does it cost?"

After the lady handed over the gorgeous flower, she called out after us, "Wait a minute! Here's a passion flower. You guys are just so cute, and I really hope you stay together. I remember what it felt like to be in love when I was so young."

Once again, I blushed at her comment. But I thanked her profusely and accepted the beautiful flower. We slowly walked back to Blake's car. By now, the sun was setting, and the air became a little nippy.

Blake leaned against the hood of the car and motioned for me to join him. Unexpectedly, he pulled me into his chest so I was standing in between his legs and leaning my back against his chest.

"I had fun today," Blake's nose lightly trailed up and

down the side of my neck. When his mouth reached the hollow of my neck, he skimmed his lips over the sensitive spot. "I hope you did too."

Unable to form a coherent answer, I "mmhmm-ed" in response. Surprising myself with a boost of confidence, and probably catching Blake off guard, I turned myself around so that our faces were only a few inches apart.

He quickly caught on and smirked. Wrapping his arms tighter around my waist, he managed to pull me closer than I thought was possible. He drew patterns on my lower back, making my skin tingle in places that he just touched.

I felt bold and started to lean me head closer towards his. My eyes fluttered closed as he moved his head in slightly, too. As our breaths began to mix, the butterflies in my stomach were about to burst. His lips gently brushed mine at first, and he slightly pulled back. I tangled my fingers into his hair to make sure he couldn't move back any further.

Not thinking things through, I firmly pressed my lips against his. Probably caught off guard for the second time, it took him a few seconds before his lips responded to mine. His hand travelled to the back of my head and tilted it so that he could have better access to my mouth. The kiss grew deeper after a minute or so, but just as abruptly as it started, he pulled back.

Looking into his eyes in confusion, I saw guilt. "What's wrong?" I asked hesitantly, the words barely coming out in a whisper.

Taking a deep breath, he pulled back and slightly pushed me back so that we weren't as close as before. My heart sunk, as the whole situation came into perspective in my head. "I'm so sorry, Mel. But I can't do this to you anymore."

"What are you talking about?" My voice was weak, and I knew that I wouldn't want to hear what he was going to say. But my curiosity got the better of me.

"This. The whole romantic thing," He gestured with his hands. "I really, really like you, Mel. And I really want to do this and see what we can become, but it all feels like a lie. And every time I kiss you, I just feel guilty."

"Why?" I asked. It felt like he wasn't giving me a full answer.

"Well…because," He paused, obviously not wanting to talk anymore. I continued to stare at him, and I could tell that he was going to tell me eventually. So I waited. "You know how you would have to marry the successor to the company?"

"Uhm. So I'm sure that when you talked to Chief, he mentioned something about how he will take your relationships into consideration when he chooses a successor?"

I nodded, and I didn't think my heart could fill with more dread. I already knew what he was going to say. Not looking me in the eye, he continued, "Well, I'm pretty sure Chief told you that I was the one who wanted the business the most, too. So…uh…yeah. I like you a lot right now, and I really wish I never used you in the beginning. I was blinded by my ambitions of getting the company that I didn't realize how great of a person you are."

As he said the last part, he confirmed my suspicions. My heart broke, and I tried to hold back the tears that were forming in my eyes. So the only reason why people like me here is because I am the granddaughter of Ralph McKinley. A tear rolled down from my eye, and Blake stared at me helplessly, not knowing what to do.

"I am so sorry, Mel." He whispered again, and again. Hesitantly, he took a step toward me and cupped my cheek in his hands. Using his thumb, he wiped away the tear that managed to escape. "I am not lying when I say that I am really, truly falling for you right now. And I hope you will forgive me someday and give me a second chance."

Instead of comforting me and making me melt back into his arms, those words made my sadness turn into wariness. Taking a step back from him, I saw that he winced. "Blake, I don't know if that can happen." I said truthfully. "I can't forgive you that easily right now. I think I need some time to think things through."

He looked down at the ground, "Do you think you will ever forgive me?"

I sighed as I thought about it. After a long pause, I responded, "I am grateful that you told me, instead of leaving me in the dark. So because of that, I think I will eventually forgive you. But I don't know how long it will take."

Finally looking up into my eyes, he stated, "Good. Because I don't want to lose a great person like you as a friend."

And with that, he walked over and opened the car door for me. After we both climbed in, he started the car, and we began the silent ride home. I turned my head towards the window and stared out at the passing fields and buildings. The landscape blurred, and I'm not sure if it was because of the speed Blake was driving at or because of the tears that began to fill my eyes again.

Silently, I cried over this whole situation, and wished I could go home. The mansion was filled with secrets, and truthfully, I was getting sick of the place.

Chapter 13

As the rays of light hit me in the face the next morning, I realized that something didn't feel quite right. I opened my eyes, momentarily disorientating and blinding myself. Then, I remembered last night. As the memories of Blake's rejection replayed in my head, I felt a piece of my heart break.

It's not supposed to feel like this, I kept telling myself. I never really liked him in the first place. I just thought that he was the only nice, sincere person here.

I just lay there in my bed, sorting through all my confusing emotions. As the thoughts got even more mixed up in my head, I could feel pressure building up on my chest. Refusing to cry, yet again, over Blake, I forced myself to get up and take a nice, relaxing shower.

I slowly walked into the bathroom, feeling its calming effects on me. Call me a weirdo, but I found the whole atmosphere of my bathroom very feng shui and relaxing. As

I stepped into the shower, the warm beads of water gently rolling down my body, made me feel a whole lot better.

Of course, water couldn't relieve me of the overwhelming stress of my situation. No matter how long I talk to it (not that I did), it won't give me a response. So after my long shower, I decided to give Jess a long and overdue call.

"Hello? Who's calling?" Her familiar voice answered the phone, immediately making me feel comforted. I could tell the conversation was going to interesting.

"It's me, you dummy!" I laughed.

"Who is me?"

"Melanie!!" I exclaimed, slightly amused.

"Melanie? Sorry, but I don't know a Melanie." Jess paused. "Oh wait! I think I do know one!! But she probably forgot all about me, because she just moved to California. She's probably too busy flirting with all the hot guys over there."

"Oh, shut up!!" Although she touched a sensitive topic about the guys, it didn't make me want to cry. "You know it's me. Anyway, if you keep on going with this, you're going to miss all the juicy gossip I'm going to tell you."

"Okay, okay! I'm done! Yeesh." She sighed, laughing. "I want to know everything. Make sure you don't leave anything out."

"Well…if you want to know EVERYTHING," I emphasized that word, "it might take a very long time to tell you."

"I don't care!! I just miss you so much and I want to know what's going on in your life!!"

So after telling her to find a comfortable place to sit, I began to tell her the story, starting with the night of the ball. And not stopping until I got to the part when Blake "broke-up" with me last night. For the whole story, she silently listened to every word I said.

"Are you serious?" she whispered at the end of my long monologue, "He was just using you?? That is probably one of the jerkiest moves I have ever heard of."

Sighing, I agreed with her.

"And what's up with Pierce?" She asked, not necessarily directed to me. She was just probably thinking out loud. "There has to be some kind of explanation to his actions. Maybe it has to do with his hot and cold attitude towards you."

"Yeah, that's about all I figured out so far." I sighed, wishing that the people living here would stop messing with my brain.

"At least Karter seems normal right now. You could always hang out with him." She suggested, probably hoping that I would somehow end up with him.

"But Jessie, I will never know if they like me for who I am, or because of this whole stupid company arranged marriage thing!!" I yelled, slightly exasperated.

"Who said anything about romance between you and Karter??" she said innocently. Changing her voice to a more serious tone, she added. "But I'm not kidding when I say that you should talk to someone more. It's really not good if you have all this emotion and confusing building up inside of you."

Sighing, I realized that she was right. Last night, I realized that I had become an emotional wreck…mainly because I wasn't talking to anyone about what I was feeling.

"I understand that you probably can't call me every day,

so you should at least talk to someone else, like Karter, once a day or something." Jess continued.

"Thanks for your advice, it means a lot to me. I'll think about it. And if all else fails, I have no problem calling you every single day." I laughed at the end.

"No problem," I could hear the smile in her voice. "Ahh!! I'm at work right now, and boss is giving me the evil eyes. Gotta go!! Promise you'll call again soon??" She quickly asked.

"Of course. Have fun at work!! I love you."

"Love you too, darling. Bye!!" And with that, she hung up. My connection to my past life was gone, and once again I was back in the mansion, all alone.

By early December nothing much had changed. Pierce was as elusive as ever, and I barely ever see him around in the mansion. Only God knew what he was doing with all his free time. And Karter was just Karter. He was always the funny, laid back guy who I could always turn to. But nothing really came out of that relationship, other than friendship. Whenever I saw Blake, I still felt a slight pang of hurt. We never really had a full conversation after that day in October.

December in California still meant the temperature cooled considerably, and it was a little chilly. I was already used to the stereotypical California weather, where it was all nice and warm, so the cold was a little weird. But it was still nothing compared to the temperature in New York.

By this time, I just wanted to get out of the mansion as soon as possible. Every day felt like a boring routine, and it was getting really tiring. Since it was December, it meant that there was only about a month and a half until I got to go back to New York.

That also meant that there was only a month and a half until I found out who my future husband was going to be. But I was just not thinking about that right now, and pretending that won't happen.

As I walked to the lounge area to meet Karter after dinner (part of my daily routine), I realized that all the guys were sitting there with him.

Okay, this is weird. I thought to myself as I made my way into the room. "Hey guys, what's up?" I asked hesitantly, only looking at Karter.

"Well, we've been thinking…" Karter started off. "Since it was your birthday last Tuesday, we decided to go out and celebrate it tonight, seeing as it is a Saturday and all."

I looked at him skeptically, "What are you talking about? We already celebrated my birthday with Chief at that fancy restaurant! I don't need to do anything else."

"Actually, yes you do." Blake spoke to me for the first time in the past few days. "We're your friends. And we noticed that you haven't been very happy for the past few weeks."

"So we decided that we are going to kidnap you and bring you to a bar!!" Karter finished what Blake was going to say. Just as I was about to protest, Karter butted in, "It's perfect because you just turned 21 this year!! And a bar is not something super fancy!! Come on, it's just a club."

I realized that he had a point. Turning 21 was supposed to be a big deal, and I was ready to get out for just one night and forget about everything.

"Fine. I'll go." I said before I could think about it anymore.

"YES!!" Karter pumped his fist in victory. "Now go and change into something more…sexy." He winked at me.

Slapping him, I retorted, "You too."

"Sorry guys, but I don't think I can go," Pierce's voice interrupted from the back of the room.

"Why not? You were all for this plan yesterday!!" Karter whined.

"I have to study and do other stuff," Pierce shrugged his shoulder nonchalantly.

"Can't you put that off for just one night?" Blake asked.

"No can do, sorry Melanie." Pierce apologized, obviously not too sincere. And with that, he walked out of the room.

"Geez. What's his problem?" Karter asked both me and Blake. We both shook our heads. "Oh well. It'll be more fun without that party pooper," Karter joked.

About an hour, and thirty outfits, later we finally left the mansion and drove to the club in Karter's flashy car. I was immediately hit with the smell of sweat and alcohol as we entered the building. I looked to the dance floor and saw hundreds of bodies pushed together, all grinding with one another.

Trying to hide my disgust, I decided to head over to the bar area first. "Hey, where are you going?" Karter asked me.

"I need to get some of that in my system," I said as I pointed to the rows of drinks lining the wall. "Before I can even think about going there." I nodded me head in the direction of the dance floor.

Karter laughed, "Suit yourself. After you are less uptight, join me on the dance floor." And with that, he was gone. I could barely see him as he weaved his way through the throng of people. I turned around to find Blake, but he was already gone.

"Great," I muttered to myself. "Thanks for ditching me on my birthday celebration night." I said to no one in particular. Obviously, I was a little bitter.

I sat down on one of the barstools, feeling lonelier than ever. "Hello, cutie. What can I get for ya." The bartender gave me the once over.

"What's something you'd suggest?" I asked, naïve in the aspect of drinks.

"Well for you, my lady, may I recommend the Long Island Iced Tea?" the name seemed innocent enough. There probably wasn't a lot of alcohol in it anyway, so I decided it was safe enough.

After the bartender mixed it up with his sweet moves, he placed the glass in front of me. Garnished with a lemon and a candied cherry, I took a sip out of the pink straw. Surprisingly shocked, I realized it only had a hint of an alcoholic taste.

Turning around in my chair with the drink in my hand, I looked out onto the crowd where people were literally on top of each other. As I scanned the crowd for Karter or Blake, I realized that I had finished my drink.

I placed the empty glass down on the table and the guy working smiled at me. "Hey, you want some more?"

I shrugged. "Sure, why not?" I couldn't tell if the magic drug was doing any wonders on me, but so far it didn't seem like it. But after I finished my second, I began to feel a lot more confident.

"Thanks for the drinks. I will be back later." I giggled as I slid the money over to the guy; whose name I learned was James.

"No problem. See you soon," he winked at me, making me go in another fit of giggles. Standing up, the floor seemed to spin a little. After I regained my balance, I moved to the crowd of people. I couldn't find Blake or Karter, so I decided to dance by myself in the center of the floor.

The dark room was illuminated with flashing lights that reflected off the glitter in the floor. It made the room seem almost magical and surreal. As I swung my hips to the beat, I felt a person grab my waist from behind me. I turned around and didn't recognize the cute stranger's face. Seeing no harm in dancing with him, we continued to grind up against each other.

I giggled as I wrapped my arms around his neck, my back pressing into the front of his pants. After dancing for what feels like an eternity, we made our way to the bar to refresh ourselves again.

"Hey, James!!" I squealed. "You know what I want." I winked at him, feeling bubbly and secure.

"You betcha. Coming right up!!" he grinned. He turned to the man sitting next to me, who ordered some obscure drink with a crazy name.

After drinking several rounds with each other, and completing a game of truth or dare, I could officially say we were both drunk beyond belief…which sort of explains what happens next.

When we both fell silent and run out of words, we slowly moved our faces closer to each other. Our lips met in a sloppy, wet kiss as he started running his sweaty hands up and down my body. Since we were still sitting in our chairs, the kiss was slightly awkward. But that didn't stop him from deepening and continuing the kiss.

"MELANIE CARTWRIGHT. WHAT THE HELL ARE YOU DOING??"

I immediately pulled back from the kiss and wiped my mouth off with the back of my hand. I turned around to face the source of the angry voice.

"I'm doing whatever the hell I want to do, Pierce!! You have no right to interfere with my life." I warned him as a rush of adrenaline overcame my body. It didn't occur to me that he wasn't even supposed to be here in the first place.

He threateningly walked closer to me. "How many of those did you drink?" He suspiciously eyed the empty glass in front of me.

"It's none of your business," I turned around so I could continue to talk to the nice man from before. Sadly, I was greeted by an empty chair. "Now look what you've done!!" I shrieked at Pierce. I'm sure I was slurring by then. "You made him run away!"

He was still a few steps away from me, so I decided to stand up and directly confront him. But my plan didn't go as I wanted it to. Right as I stood up, the world started to spin, and I saw the glittering floor coming closer to my face. The last thing I remembered was a strong set of arms that wrapped around me. Then everything went dark.

Chapter 14

I groaned as I opened my eyes in the morning, or more like afternoon to be exact. My head pounded and my stomach didn't feel quite right.

So this is what it feels like to be hung over, I thought to myself skeptically. It was probably the worst feeling ever, and I don't know why anyone would drink if they had to go through this.

As I tossed my covers aside, I gingerly sat up and noticed my outfit. I was wearing my pajamas, but I don't remember changing into them. As a matter of fact, I don't even remember coming back to the house.

Oh, shit. I swore under my breath as I had a revelation. Pierce was the last person I talked to that night. As a matter of fact, I think he was the one who was there to catch me when I blacked out. But did he drive me home? And change me out of my clothes? I shivered at the thought of Pierce seeing me almost naked. That's just wrong.

And why was he even at the club in the first place? He said he had a lot of things to do. He's just an egotistical jerk who just cared about himself. I thought bitterly. But the little voice in the back of my head had to butt in. He couldn't be that selfish if he did save you from that club...

Shrugging it off, I tried to stand up. The ground tilted itself a little, but it eventually righted itself out. I slowly walked to my bathroom and took a relaxing shower. Not wanting to get too dressed up, I threw on one of my big t-shirts and some comfy jeans. Messily gathering my hair up in a loose bun, I made my way down the hall to the stairs.

But as I turned to go down the stairs, I saw someone bounding up the stairs. Putting my hands up to protect my face from the collision, I felt a strong chest crash into them. He reached out to steady me when I almost fell backwards. I looked up only to meet a pair of silver eyes. Subconsciously, my heart fluttered with adrenaline. Probably because I was nervous about asking him questions that had to do with last night.

Just as I opened my mouth to ask Pierce about what happened at the club, he quickly muttered, "Sorry, Mel. See you later." And with that, he let go of my arms and brushed past me to walk to his room.

"What is with him?" I whispered to myself, as I was left standing there with my pounding heart. Taking deep breaths to calm down, I made my way downstairs. Not knowing what to do with myself, I wandered around the house. I wasn't hungry for anything, so I just walked past the dining room.

I remembered my parents' room, and decided to go

there. It was perfect because I needed a quiet, serene room to spend some time alone with my thoughts. I tended to do that a lot these days. But it's not like doing anything else will be any better.

As I climbed up the marble stairs for the third time since I had arrived at the mansion, I looked around this part of the house. I could never get used to the grandeur of the place. But it made me a bit sad thinking about how abandoned it really was. Underneath the splendor of the house, it was really lonely and desolate. This is why I can never live in a mansion, I thought to myself.

I slowly turned the handle to my parent's room and took a step inside. Although the air seemed somewhat stale, it felt like the homiest part of the mansion. The sun hit the sheer golden curtains in a way that casted a warm and friendly light on the room. In the rays of light, you could see little particles of dust dancing around.

Walking around the room and trailing my fingers on the slightly dusty furniture, I felt my mind relax and feel somewhat sane again. When I reached the picture of my parents on the night stand, I gingerly picked it up and traced my index finger over the engravings as I lowered myself down onto the bed.

Staring at the happy couple smiling at me, I sadly whispered, "I wish you guys were here. Even though I never really knew you, I feel like you would be here for me, making everything feel like it's okay."

I ended up talking to a picture for a whole hour. No matter how crazy it seemed, it really took a huge load off my chest. Still sitting on the bed, I leaned over and placed the picture back on the table, in the exact same place I took it from.

My headache was slightly better, but the dull ache made me really sleepy. I laid back on the bed, lightly resting my head on the pillow, probably the same one that my parents slept on. Feeling a little comfort in that thought, I eventually fell into a light sleep.

In my unconsciousness, I heard a soft click of a door. Turning my head to the door, my eyes fluttered open. It was nighttime already, and the room was dark, so I could only make out the outline of the figure standing in front of the door. They slowly closed the door behind them, obviously unaware of my presence in the room.

As they reached for the light, a slight feeling of fear crept into my heart. I knew it had to be someone I knew, but I was still scared, nonetheless. I heard a small click of the light switch, and the room flooded with light.

Pierce. My eyes widened in realization. When he saw me lying on the bed, he quickly turned around and made a move for the door.

"Wait," I called out, surprising both him and myself. He froze in mid-step with his hand on the doorknob. "Don't go yet." Pierce didn't leave the room, but he didn't turn around to face me. I could tell he was fighting with himself, trying to make a decision of whether or not to stay with me.

"Please don't leave me alone." I whispered, not knowing why I was saying those words. Maybe it was because I just wanted some of my questions answered. So far, he was the one I knew least about, and I wanted to find out what was making him so mysterious.

The silence stretched out like an ocean, engulfing the two of us. Finally Pierce sighed and slowly withdrew his hand from the doorknob. Still not turning around to face me, he said to the door, "What do you want?" It wasn't in a hostile tone of voice. It seemed like he was hesitant. I may have been overreacting, but I also heard a little defeat in his voice.

"We need to talk." I said carefully, not wanting to chase him away. This could be the moment. This could be when we finally talk to each other. But he still didn't turn around to face me. "Pierce, please look at me." I almost pleaded, with a hint of desperation.

Slowly, he turned around. His eyes confirmed what I heard in his voice earlier. Defeat. "What do you want to talk about?"

"Last night. Your actions. Our relationship. Us." I listed in short sentences. As he began to walk closer to me, I realized that my heart started to pound against my chest. He carefully sat on the floor, leaning against the bed. I adjusted my position so that I was lying on my stomach with my head right next to his.

He didn't respond, so I took the silence as a sign of compliance. I decided to start out with the easy, straightforward questions. "Did you drive me home last night and change me into my pajamas?"

He gave a slight nod. I smiled a little, glad that he was answering my questions. I continued. "Why were you at the club last night? I thought you said you were busy."

After a slight hesitation, Pierce responded slowly, with pauses in the middle. I listened to him patiently. "I was busy. I had my own things to do that night, and they couldn't be rescheduled. But I got out early, and since I was close to the club you were at, I decided to stop by. Little did I know that you were kissing some random guy." He laughed humorlessly. "And drunk to the point where you passed out."

I looked down in shame, my cheeks burning with hear. To say that I regretted that would be an understatement. But I masked my voice and asked with confidence, "Why do you care? Why does it matter so much?"

He fell silent, "I don't know." He didn't say anything after that.

Struggling to keep the conversation going, I thought of another question. "What was so important that you couldn't reschedule?"

"A meeting." He answered, obviously still hiding something.

"A meeting? With who?" I asked pointedly, thinking about Siri.

"It's none of your business," he snapped at me.

The nice person who decided to stay with me was gone. Instead, the normal, guarded Pierce was back. Infuriated, I started to yell at him, "None of my business? How is this none of my business? It is obviously making you guarded and ruining whatever friendship we could have!"

When Pierce still didn't say anything, I snickered bitterly. "But don't worry. I already know who you were meeting with. I know all about your 'dirty little secret.'"

Pierce's head shot up when he heard me use that phrase. I used the exact same words that Siri did when they talked about it in this room almost two months ago.

"What are you talking about? You don't know any-thing," Pierce retorted.

"Want to bet? I know all about your deal with Siri. Your fake relationship. I was in this room two months ago when you guys talked about it. I was right there in that closet," I replied angrily as I stuck my finger out at the closet.

"I do want to bet. You have no idea what the whole story is!" He yelled back.

Intimidated by how angry he was, I almost gave in and apologized for my nosiness. But I couldn't just let him win this time. I needed to know the answers. If I just let it go, I know it will eat me up later.

"Fine! Enlighten me!" I spat in his face.

He fell silent. Not knowing what to do, I simply waited there. My heart pounded once again with all the adrenaline and anger coursing through my body. I was also filled with fear, afraid that he will close up and walk out of the room. But he didn't.

After what seemed like an eternity, he whispered, bare-ly audible, "I have this dream." He paused. "An ambition in life. A goal that is different from what Chief wants it to be."

Completely caught off guard and not expecting his an-swer to be like that, I waited for him to continue.

"A dream that Chief and the guys don't know about. And Siri is using it against me because she is the only one who knows about it."

"What is it?" I murmured in his ear, trying to encour-age him.

"I want to be a doctor," he admitted.

"What?" I asked, not seeing the connection. Wanting

to be a doctor is nothing to be ashamed of. In fact, I would say it is something quite ordinary. But obviously not for Pierce.

He sighed, obviously not wanting to explain. "This whole thing started when Siri barged into the library one day. I was in there studying, not to become the successor of the company, but to become a doctor. She found out that I was pretty serious about this whole doctor thing, and that I want nothing to do with the company."

I sort of understood what he was talking about. "This happened a few days after you arrived at the mansion. Actually, it happened to be on the day of the ball. Do you remember that?" I nodded as he continued. "I begged her to not tell anyone about it, and she said she wouldn't. She was very sweet about it. But at the ball, she came up to me, all giggly and flirty. Then she whispered in my ear that if I didn't want her to tell Chief about my secret, I would have to do something for her."

I remembered how heartbroken I was when I saw her whispering in his ear, pretending to flirt with him. It's all starting to make sense now. Everything was just an act, "So what did she want?" I asked.

"She told me that I would have to pretend to be her boyfriend and that I couldn't talk to you," he didn't meet my eyes. "I don't know why she came up with those terms, but I agreed to them. I thought that it wouldn't be too hard to follow her commands. It actually sort of worked to my advantage."

I raised my eyebrow at him. How was not talking to me an advantage? Answering my question, he said, "If I actually got to know you better, I'm sure that Chief would notice. It would give him more reason to make me the successor of the company, and I don't want that because I want to be a doctor."

It all made sense now. His cold glares, unwelcoming attitude, his fight with Siri. "So does that mean that you actually don't hate me?" I asked uncertainly.

He sighed and turned to face me, "Of course I don't hate you." He placed his palm on my cheek. "From the first time that I met you, I knew that you were a nice person. I really did want to get to know you better, but I'm scared to. I'm scared that Chief will notice and make me do something I don't want to do."

"Then why don't you tell Chief that you want to become a doctor? I'm sure he'll understand." I whispered, silently glad that Pierce felt like he could confide in me.

"We have more in common than you think," he smiled wistfully at me. "I am an orphan too."

Chapter 15

After a moment of silence, I whispered, "I'm sorry."

"It's okay," he looked down, "I'm sort of used to it. And I've accepted that fact. Chief has been so nice to me since then."

I reached out to him and tentatively touched his arm in comfort. After a slight pause I asked, "I'm sorry for being so blunt here, but I don't see how this prevents you from telling Chief that you want to be a doctor."

"This whole thing is really complicated, and sort of really silly." Pierce sighed, "So, when I was a teenager, my little sister was diagnosed with some obscure, untreatable disease. As my parents had to see her grow up and become more frail and weak, they became more helpless. When she died several years ago, it tore my family apart."

I listened silently, not knowing what to say, "I'm so sorry, Pierce. That must've been so hard to go through."

Shaking his head, he whispered, "You have no idea."

His voice cracked a little at the end, but he quickly cleared his throat. It just hurt me to see how vulnerable a guy can be. "Not only were my parents completely walking corpses, devoid of all emotions, we were also in very serious debt. Who knew that medicine and doctors could cost so much money?" Pierce sighed again. "To cope with all the problems, my dad became a drunk. He would come home every day and start screaming at my mother."

"Since my house felt so gloomy and dark, school was the only thing I could turn to. I guess I just took all my frustrations out on school and became sort of obsessed with it. It became my haven, where no drama or family matters could interfere with. But one day, when I came home from school, something wasn't quite right."

"There were two police cars parked in my driveway. And when I walked up to the front door, the policemen told me the news. Apparently, my dad came home early from work and had a few drinks. Then, he and my mother went out for a drive. I guess he was more drunk than he thought, and he swerved into a tree in order to avoid hitting a squirrel." Pierce laughed humorlessly. Then, with a sudden change of emotion, he began to speak determinedly.

"So I thought that my whole life would've been different if my sister never got sick or if we'd had the cure to her sickness. For her, I promised myself that I would strive to become a doctor and save the lives of other kids, so their families won't have to go through what mine did."

I stared at him, completely awestruck. "Pierce, what you are doing is so admirable and caring. You should go for your dream. Tell Chief. I'm sure he will support everything you do."

He let out an exasperated breath, "Melanie, I can't! You don't understand. Chief is not as nice and understanding as you think he is!"

Gasping, I raised an eyebrow at him, wanting to hear an explanation, "Really? Well, now I don't really believe you."

"Okay, so he is a really nice guy, and maybe I am exaggerating a little bit. But when it comes to his company, he is all serious. He will not tolerate any 'funny business.' And I guess I do respect him for that."

"But when Karter, Blake, and I moved into this mansion, we were required to sign a contract," Pierce explained to me. "It basically stated that we would all train to be the successor to the company, and that we will follow Chief's rules."

"Wow, that's sort of intense," I said in disbelief. I guess Chief does really care about the wellbeing of the company.

"About a year after we signed that contract, Karter had this obsession with his guitar." Pierce smiled at the memories that were probably playing out in his head. "He is an amazing singer and writer, and I'm sure he would get a signed record label."

"Really? I've never heard him sing before? And I didn't even know he could even play the guitar!!"

"That's because he decided to go for his goal. He told Chief that he wanted to try and become a singer. He thought that Chief would understand. But you know what Chief said? He said, 'That is in conflict with your contract. If you wish to become a singer, I will have to kick you out of this house.' And we could all tell that he wasn't kidding." Pierce shook his head.

"And so Karter never played the guitar again?" I asked.

"Nope," he shook his head, "He's always been too scared to. I guess that he wanted to stay in the mansion and become a successor more than he wanted to become a famous artist. Since his future here was already stable and guaranteed, I guess he didn't want to take the risk."

"Well, why don't you just take that risk? I mean, if you do get kicked out of the house, what so bad about that? You're still reaching for your dreams." I suggested, hoping it would offer some help to Pierce.

He smiled at me, "I've already thought about that. I've thought about almost every option. But what I realized is that if I do get kicked out, I won't be able to do anything. I have no family or house to go to. I don't have any money, so I can't really go to medical school. Living here is still the best option for me."

"Oh, Pierce," I sighed as I saw his predicament in a new light. I thought that I felt trapped in this mansion. But in reality, I was free compared to him. He literally had nowhere to go. "I'm so sorry." As I said those words, I noticed the water in his silver eyes reflecting the light.

Feeling helpless, I reached out and gathered him into a hug. At first I expected him to stiffen or push me away, but he didn't. Instead, I felt his strong arms wrap around me a hug me back. His hand gently stroked my hair and supported my head, as if I was the one in need of comfort. I moved my hands in a circle over his back, hoping it would calm him down.

He buried his head in my neck and whispered, almost inaudibly, "I'm sorry I have been a complete jerk to you since you first moved in. I've always wanted to tell you everything, and I'm glad I did. You are an amazing person, Mel."

Both touched and shocked at his unexpected words, I pushed him back a little so I could look into his eyes. I could see the sincerity and remorse in them. As I stared into his eyes, he did the same to me. Soon, his eyes became slightly darker and filled with some other emotion.

My breath caught in my throat as he moved an inch closer to my face. Not daring to breathe, I looked down at his gentle, well-defined lips. Quickly averting my eyes and head in embarrassment, Pierce caught my chin in his hands. Forcing me to look back into his eyes, his other hand lightly brushed over my warm, pink cheeks, causing my stomach to tickle like none other.

Letting go of my chin, he suddenly looped an arm around my waist and pulled me on top of him, so I was sitting on his lap. The sudden movement caught me off balance as I wrapped my hands around my neck to steady myself. As I regained my balance, I began to let go of his neck.

"Don't," he whispered, almost too softly to hear. His quiet word made me freeze and stare at him. "Please." After hearing him say this, I relaxed a little.

"I don't want to lie to you anymore, Mel. You asked me if I hated you. And the truth is, I never have. When we shook hands the night you first moved in, I felt this strange connection and shock. After that, I wanted to get to know you better and possibly get to do this…"

His arm held up the small of my back as his other hand supported the back of my neck as he brought his head closer to mine. Even before our lips actually touched, I saw sparks fly on the inside of my eyelids. At first the kiss was gentle and almost like our lips weren't actually touching yet. I could feel the hesitation on his lips, and I'm sure he could feel it in mine too. It was as if we both wanted to remember this time and feeling forever.

When it got a little deeper, the kiss was like fireworks. His hands rubbed up and down my back, and I felt my whole body heat up. My hands made its way into his hair, and I entangled my fingers into his brown locks. I felt his tongue dance around on my lips and I smiled in response. Taking advantage of the situation, he slipped his tongue into my mouth. He gently teased mine with his, and my stomach was tingling like no other.

Right when it felt like I was getting wrapped up in the kiss, he gently pulled away, tugging lightly on my lower lip with his teeth. When I felt a gaze on me, I opened my eyes to look into his. I noticed my stomach didn't feel any better. Instead of the tingling butterflies, it felt slightly hollow… probably from wanting to kiss him more.

"I've wanted to do that for quite some time now," Pierce teased, breaking the tense atmosphere.

"Oh really?" I grinned, smiling like a fool.

"Really," he confirmed, bending down to nibble on my neck, making me giggle. "When I saw Blake kissing you that day at the beach, I almost died inside. But I couldn't do anything about it. I still had that deal with Siri."

When he mentioned Blake, I winced a little. Not because we broke up (not that we were actually officially dating), but because of the way he used me. After him, I didn't think that I could trust any of the guys here in the mansion because they would be using me to become the successor. But I was wrong. Pierce was almost the opposite of that. He didn't want to get to know me because he wanted to be a doctor.

But he likes me. And I admit I have a small thing for him. I can't say that I am in love with him already, but he is definitely growing on me. With Blake, I had the romantic, sweet moments. But with Pierce, I could feel something was different. I don't know how to put it in words, but it seems like he is more…mysterious, passionate, exciting. Actually, I do know one word that describes our relationship perfectly: complicated.

"So does that mean you are still going to pretend to be dating Siri?" I asked.

Pierce ran his hands through his hair, messing it up slightly, "Mel, I have to. At least I will until I figure out something I can do. Chief can't find out about the doctor thing, and Siri can't find out about us."

While taking a deep breath, I leaned my head against his chest and began to absentmindedly draw circles into it, "Us? Are you implying that we are…" I let my sentence run off, not knowing what to say without embarrassing myself.

His chest rumbled underneath my head as he let out a chuckle, "Only if you want us to be."

Smiling slightly to myself, I nodded my head once, knowing that he would feel it. "It's like Romeo and Juliet… with the whole forbidden thing." I mused, drawing a random connection to our relationship.

"And without the tragic ending," he added on, stroking my hair. "We'll make it all work out. I know we will."

"I trust you," I muttered in response, honestly believing him. It all seems very simple: keep the relationship a secret and figure out a plan to help Pierce become a doctor.

But you know how the saying goes…easier said than done.

Chapter 16

The weather outside was amazing. The sun was shining, and it wasn't too hot or too cold. Usually, I'd be freezing my butt off in the New York weather, but here in California, I didn't even need to wear a jacket in the middle of December.

And that's why Chief came up with the brilliant plan of going whale watching today. I don't really mind the whole whale watching thing, but it's the people I mind. My relationship with everyone here is really screwed up, and I don't think I'll be able to last a day with this group of people.

First, there's Blake. Sadly, he's acting like a little kid and still not talking to me. There is the occasional, awkward "hey" and "what's up," but other than that, we haven't had a substantial conversation in a while.

Second, there's Pierce. I think we figured out the whole deal between us, but not talking to him and pretending everything is the same will be hard. Especially if Siri is around….which she will be.

This brings me to her. I don't know what to think about her, but I have a feeling that she's up to something. I don't know what, but I have this wild guess that it's not good. And she does seem like a sneaky little…yeah. I'll stop there.

I guess I could hang out with Karter. I mean, he's the closest person here I can call a friend (and nothing more). I really like his company, but sometimes, his nonstop talking can get on my nerves. But I guess that's the whole point. Friends get on each other's nerves.

And of course, Chief will be there…observing every single move that I make and every interaction with the other people. Don't get me wrong, I love Chief, but sometimes, it feels like he is judging me. And there is only so much you can talk about with your long lost grandfather.

But other than all the people, I was excited for the trip. I've never seen a whale in my life before, let alone seeing it from a private boat that my grandfather owned.

When we first arrived at the pier, the smell of the ocean spray filled my lungs. The mix of salt and seaweed was actually quite calming, and it relieved my uneasiness about how the afternoon would turn out.

As the rays of light danced across the surface of the water, I smiled to myself. It was always refreshing to look at water. I know it sounds weird, but just looking at the reflections of light and listening to the soft crashing of the waves never failed to make me happy.

The boat caught my breath as I boarded on the side. It wasn't quite as luxurious as a yacht, but it was close for a whale watching boat. It was quite large and mainly white.

Blue streaks ran down its side like water, and the name of the ship was written in flowing letters. But the name certainly did not match the elegant boat.

Snorting as I read the name, I exclaimed, "Feelin' Nauti!?!? Who named this boat?"

"What? You don't like it?" Karter teased as he walked on deck behind me.

"I love it, but did Chief come up with that??" I asked incredulously.

"Of course not!" Karter laughed, "It was obviously my idea."

"Actually, it was mine," Pierce interrupted casually as he walked past us, making his way to Siri. She was casually leaning against the railing on the opposite side of the boat.

"We all came up with this idea," Blake added while stopping to stand next to Karter.

"Fine. We all sort of talked about it, and we just happened to think of it. And surprisingly, Chief agreed with the name. I guess he was in a very good mood that day," Karter nodded towards Chief, who was walking towards the cabin to set his bags down.

"I heard that!" Chief yelled over his shoulder, "I'm always in a good mood. And I'm not an ancient guy who doesn't appreciate puns."

Shaking my head in disbelief, I smiled to myself. I guess it doesn't matter how old guys are…they always have a sexual innuendo on their mind.

"Are you guys ready to set sail?" The captain's voice blared over the ship PA system.

"Aye, aye, cap'n!!" everyone yelled, except me. I guess

it was a tradition that they always did before they left the pier.

As the boat left the harbor and moved into the ocean, I felt the salty water lightly spray my face. I made my way to a silver railing on the side of the boat and carefully leaned over the side, looking down onto the water.

"Enjoying yourself?" Karter came up from behind me and stood next to me.

"It is really nice getting out on the ocean in the middle of winter!!" I laughed feeling slightly giddy.

"Of course. New York weather is so nasty compared to this," Karter spread his arms out and tossed his head back, exposing his face to the sun.

"Mmhmm," I agreed, relaxing myself as much as possible. I closed my eyes and heard the soft crashing of the waves. This was the perfect way to forget about everything.

Karter and I stood there in silence, soaking in the sun for a long time. I guess neither of us really wanted to talk. Sometimes, it is nice to have a little silence.

"EH MI GAWD!! PIERCE!! LOOK AT THAT!!" the little devil's screech shattered the silence.

"What?" Pierce answered, almost too sweetly.

"I swear I just saw a whale!!"

"Siri. We're still not far out enough for us to see whales. We need to get a little farther out before we can even get into 'whale territory,'" Pierce sounded like he was talking to a little kid.

"Hmph," Siri stomped her feet, "But I swear I just saw one." When she was greeted with silence, she grumbled, "Fine. Don't believe me."

Stalking away like a two year old, Siri made her way to the cabin where Blake and Chief were talking.

"Does she always act like a little kid?" I whispered to Karter.

* * *

"So…" I whispered into Pierce's ear and traced the tip of my nose up and down his neck. "Now we're resorting to kidnapping?" I giggled.

"If that's what you want to call it…" he smiled and looked down into my eyes. "But I'm sure you want to be with me anyways. So it doesn't count as kidnapping."

I laughed and looked around the cramped closet. We were squished between two large fur coats and several men's winter jacket. "Okay. So I wouldn't mind being with you. I just mind that we are in a closet. So what's with this whole secretive act??"

He put his finger up to my lips to silence me, "Shhh. Don't talk too loud or else they will hear us!"

"They?" I raised an eyebrow at him. It's rare to see him in such a light-hearted, jovial mood.

"Yes. The other guys, Chief, the servants," he whispered. I still looked at him questioningly, waiting for him to answer my first question. "Oh right. Uhm, we're here because I want to talk to you. But Siri is in the house somewhere, and I don't want her to find or hear us."

I smiled. It was always reassuring to hear that he was hiding from his "girlfriend." It made me feel slightly better and more secure about our…relationship. If that's what you wanted to call it. "So for all that, you literally had to whisk me away in the middle of the hallway and go all James Bond? You could have at least brought me to a more comfortable place."

Now, it was his turn to raise his eyebrow. "Do you have a specific place in mind?"

"Uhhh. No, not really," I admitted, shaking my head.

"How about the first place we met and got to know each other?" He winked at me.

"The library?" I asked, remembering the first night that I arrived. That was such a long time ago, and it felt so weird to be looking back. "That's hardly a secretive place. Anyone can go there, and I bet Chief is sitting in there right now."

"No, silly." He rolled his in exaggeration. "Your parents' room. That's where we talked and had that deep conversation."

"Of course. That's also where I overheard you and Siri arguing that one day." I muttered softly.

Pierce looked into my eyes and saw my hesitation. "I know you don't really like my relationship with Siri. And I'm trying to get out of it without dragging other people into it, but she is one stubborn and selfish girl."

I sighed in response and he engulfed me in a hug, "It's okay," he stroked and played with the ends of my hair. "I promise today will be a Siri free day. It's just going to be you and me."

I nodded my head in his chest and slowly pulled away. Silently, he opened the closet door just a crack and peered outside. Seeing no one, he took hold of my hand and quickly pulled me out of the closet and towards the abandoned part of the house.

After we made it up the stairs and into the room, I

walked over to the bed and sat down. Pierce sat down on the floor next to the bed, just like what we did when we had our first talk a week and a half ago.

"So. Is this going to be like a weekly heart-to-heart session?" I joked while positioning my head so it was closer to his.

He looked up at me, "Only if you want it to be."

Shrugging my shoulders, I said, "I guess it's nice. I would love to get to know you better. It still seems like you are a mystery to me."

"Isn't that the whole point? I heard that girls like mysterious and sexy guys." He winked at me.

I slapped his arm and felt my face heat up. "Cocky much?" It was sad how right he was, though. I looked away so I could hide my blush as best as possible. But I'm pretty sure that he still saw it because he chuckled to himself a few seconds later.

"Anyways, so what is it that you wanted to talk about?" I asked.

"Nothing specific, really. I just wanted to talk to you. It felt like it's been a while, and we need to catch up." He admitted. I stared at him. It was surprising that he was acting this way. The way he talked sounded like he was as close a friend of mine as Jessica is.

"Okay. So, how was your day?" I tried to make small talk, hoping it would lead to a deeper conversation.

He sighed, "Not good. Chief talked to me today and told me that he was really proud of how I was doing." Rubbing his face, he continued. "I mean, I guess it's a good thing, but I really don't want to deal with this whole thing right now. And I don't know how to break the news to him. I'm really afraid that he won't be happy."

"Just take it one day at a time. I'm sure it'll be okay." I reassured him, slightly reaching out to pat his shoulder.

Reaching up to hold my hand on his shoulder, he whispered, "But I don't have a lot of time left. He's going to be announcing the successor to the company in a few weeks."

"How do you know?" I asked, genuinely curious about how he knew.

He looked at me like I was stupid, "Mel. You've been here for nearly three months. Don't you remember what Chief said?"

I completely forgot about the whole agreement with Chief. "Oh my god! It's already been three months? How did you remember that?"

He nodded, "Yeah, which means you only have four more weeks here. And before you leave, Chief would have announced the successor. I remembered that because it's when you are leaving…of course I would know that."

"I completely forgot about that," I whispered, in shock. Because in less than a month, I would find out whom I would marry. It would either be Karter or Blake, since Pierce didn't want to be in charge of the company. As I thought of a future with either one of them, I paled. "But this is so wrong. I don't like the other guys like that! You're the only one that I like in a romantic way!" I blushed again as the words left my mouth. I didn't mean to say that out loud.

Instead of making fun of me, realization set into his eyes. I guess he never made the connection that we could never be together if he decided to go for his dream. "I can't stay, though. As much as I like you, I can't break a promise that I made to myself." He whispered, looking down at the floor.

I placed my hand underneath his chin and pushed his head up so that I could look into his silver eyes. "I know, and I completely understand. Don't worry. I'm sure we can make something happen."

Smiling wistfully at me, he slowly stood up and sat on the bed next to me. "You know what?" he whispered into my ear, "Sometimes, I think that you are too good to me. First I act like a complete douche to you, yet you still forgive me. And now…"

I didn't let him finish his sentence. Cutting him off with a light brush of the lips, he quickly understood my message to shut up. He grinned slightly and quickly took hold of my hair behind the crook of my neck.

"Mel," he whispered my name in an almost desperate tone before crashing his soft lips onto mine. Letting him take control of the kiss, I felt his tongue skim across my bottom lip. After letting him gain access, he quickly started kissing around my face. I felt his lips brush against my neck while his hands roamed my body.

The trails that his fingers and lips left lit my body on fire. With each touch, I wanted to be with him more. "Pierce," I whispered, surprised by how husky my voice sounded. I moaned when his lips found mine again.

Instead of the sweet kisses we just shared, this one was more fiery and passionate. Desperation gnawed at my insides, and I had to get closer to him somehow. Quickly, I straddled him and leaned over so he could have better access to my mouth.

After a few minutes, he pulled back a little and rested his forehead against mine. "God, Mel. If you don't stop, I don't think I can control myself."

I blushed and pulled back a little further, so I could see his face properly. Sighing, I said, "I'm sorry."

Looking into my eyes, he quickly responded, "Don't be sorry." Awkwardly, I climbed off of his lap and sat next to him again. "Aww, don't be like that!" he smiled and wrapped his arm around my shoulder.

I sighed and leaned into his chest. "Much better," he grinned.

"You know, the closer we get, the harder it will be to separate." I pointed out, ruining the moment. However, it felt necessary. After my "break-up" with Blake, I moped around for a few weeks. But if I had to do that with Pierce, I didn't know how I would cope.

"I know," he exhaled. "I really don't want to think about it now. And I keep on telling myself that we will find a way to be together if we wanted to be."

"How will that ever happen?" I ask, hoping he had an idea.

"I don't know."

"Well, what if Chief does kick you out of the mansion? Where will you go?"

"I don't know."

"Okay...uhm. Well, what if he forces you to be the successor?"

"I don't know." He was starting to sound like a broken record. I could hear the hint of frustration creeping into his voice. We sat there for a few moments in silence before I came up with an idea.

"Come with me," I pleaded.

"What?" he looked puzzled, "What do you mean?"

"If you do get kicked out, come to New York with me."
I explained. "You can live with me and my mom."

"Are you sure?" he looked at me skeptically.

"Well tell me if you have a better idea!!" I sighed
exasperatedly.

"Fine. Fine." He finally agreed after thinking about it
for a while. "And what about you? What will you do after
you find out who you will marry?"

This time, it was my turn to say I don't know. "But I'll
figure something out. Chief is my grandpa, so I'm sure he
will understand…sort of." Under my breath I muttered, "I
hope."

"I really want this to work out," Pierce admitted, as he
cupped my cheek in his hand.

"Same here," I whispered as I closed the distance between us, once again. This time, it was back to the sweet
lip brushes.

Suddenly, someone called out from behind the door,
"Pierce? Are you in here?" Pierce and I quickly pulled
apart, when we heard the door handle turning. Running
my hands through my hair, the door opened and revealed
a shocked Karter.

"What's going on in…" The scene in front of him started to register. And to my biggest surprise, a huge grin split
his face in two. "I KNEW IT!!"

Pierce and I shared the same confused and embarrassed
look, but Karter just walked into the room with the goofy
grin of his.

"I totally called this. I knew it was going to happen!!"

He started to do a little dance around the room. "I am such a psychic!!"

"Uhm. Karter?" I asked tentatively, "Are you okay?"

"Of course! It's just that I knew this was going to happen. When I saw how Pierce treated you during the first few days that you were here, I knew that something was up. And it was just a matter of time before you two lovebirds finally came together."

He continued, "Truthfully, I did think it was slightly weird that you went out with Blake first, but I guess this was inevitable. You and Pierce. Together."

Still skeptical of his behavior, I wondered why he wasn't upset or anything, "Uhm. Karter? Not to sound conceited or anything, but why aren't you like…upset?"

Quickly sobering down, he looked at me. "Upset? Nah. Mel, I think of you as my sister and a great friend. I never really liked, liked you…no offense." Of course he would add that on, I grinned. "And I've always known that Pierce would take over the company, so it's not like I was losing my chance at being the successor. Truthfully, I was only along for the ride. Who wouldn't turn down the chance at living in a mansion like this for a few years?" Karter winked at me.

I smiled wistfully at him. Oh, if only he knew the truth about Pierce. His whole mindset would change.

Chapter 17

Christmas came and went, bringing holiday and good cheer to everyone in the mansion. It is amazing what the holiday season can do to people. Blake talked to me several times, and we were almost back to a normal friend relationship. I have to say it was more refreshing than avoiding him and being awkward. I guess he liked it better too.

And there's always Karter. He's such a spaz, it's not even funny. After the day he found Pierce and me together, he teased us about it nonstop. Although we made him promise not to tell anyone, he still smiled pointedly in our direction every time he saw us together. I'm surprised that no one else caught on.

"MEELL!!" a screechy voice called out my name. "Are you coming or what?"

Siri's blonde head bobbed up and down in excitement. I didn't know how she managed to get me to go shopping with her, but I felt bad for turning her down, even though she may have had an ulterior motive.

"Yeah. One sec. I just need to get these shoes on," I hopped up and down, trying to stuff my feet into my Christmas present from Karter. These shoes almost topped the dress he picked out for me for that one dance. Of course they were high heels. But on top of that, they were red. I promised that I would wear them today, but I didn't know how long I would be able to last in these things without tripping.

"Hey guys!! I see you are keeping your promise," Karter walked into the foyer right as I was about to leave with Siri. "Why are you guys leaving so early? It's not even noon!"

"We are just going to go shopping for a little bit. We need something to wear for tonight!" Siri winked at Karter.

"Ahh. Right. I almost forgot about the giant company party tonight. Mel, do you want my fashion advice again?" Karter wrapped his arm around my shoulder.

"No way!!" Siri slapped his arm off for me. "No boys allowed today!"

Karter held his hands over his heart and pretended to wince in pain, "Ouch that hurts. It's always comforting to know that I am not wanted."

"Aww, Karter. You know we love you," I pinched his cheeks in affection. In return, he gave me a giant bear hug. "We will see you later tonight!!"

Siri linked her arm with mine, and we walked out the giant front doors.

"Karter is a sweet guy," Siri said very pointedly. I raised an eyebrow at her. "Do you like him? I think you should. He seems to like you a lot."

"Ahh," I shrugged my shoulders. "We're only good friends. It's almost like we're brother and sister. I can't imagine being with him in a romantic way."

"Why not? What about Blake?"

"I don't know--definitely not Blake. I'm not going through that again." I responded. "Why are you suddenly so curious about my love life?" I asked her skeptically.

"Oh, I just want some gossip," she gave me a big smile. "My life has been so boring so far. I don't have anything to talk about."

I just nodded my head and let her answer slide. It sounded almost too convenient, but whatever. We walked up to the limo, and Evander opened the back door for us.

"Thanks, Daddy!!" Siri called out to her father.

"Thanks, Evander." I smiled at him as I got into the car after Siri.

"You girls have fun today! And please don't buy too many things," he joked before he slammed the door shut.

The car ride was tolerable, and we talked about superficial things. Although Siri had a suspicious side to her, she seemed like a decent person overall. It's hard to believe that she was blackmailing Pierce right now.

"Eh my god! We're here!!" She yelped and immediately opened the door herself when we arrived at the entrance of Bergdorf Goodman's.

I didn't think I'd ever get used to walking into such a high end store. Before, in New York, I would walk into a store like this just to gawk at the price tags. I would feel guilty when I checked out.

As Siri literally dragged me into the store, I tried to look like I fit in the store.

"Hello, ladies. Welcome to Bergdorf Goodman's! My name is Nancy. What can I do to help you today?"

"Noth…" I began to mutter. Usually, I would just ignore the store assistants and brush off their help. But I guess not this time, since Siri interrupted me.

"Well, we're actually looking for some dresses for tonight."

"Really? I assumed you would say that. Tonight is the big night. Any new year resolutions?" The lady smiled at us.

"Oh, just the usual. Keep up with my exercise schedule," Siri and Nancy laughed together.

"Same here," Nancy smiled at the both of us. "So, do you two have anything in mind? Any specific color? Style? Neckline?"

"Well, I was thinking of a black dress. Preferably strapless and a sweetheart neckline. Do you have anything like that? Oh and something elegant. Not too formal, though." Siri seemed like an expert in this store. Me, on the other hand, had no idea what to say.

"Of course. I do have a few things that came into mind." Nancy turned to me expectantly, waiting for what I wanted. I hesitated before giving a general answer. "I'm not really sure. Do you have any suggestions?"

She gave me a warm smile, and probably realized I was new to this whole high end shopping thing. "Well. Let's help your friend first and then I'll see what I can do for you."

The two of us followed her around while she whisked up a few black dresses off the racks. When we reached the dressing room, she turned to Siri. "Okay, miss. So I have a few dresses for you to try on. While you are changing, I'm going to help this girl here." She nodded her head towards me.

"Thank you so much! But I'll need your help with which dress to choose after I try the first one on!! I need your advice too, Mel." She smiled at me as she drew the curtain closed to her dressing room.

"Okay. Now for you. So you really don't have any preferences?" She asked me politely.

"Honestly, no. Not really. I'm trusting your fashion sense. It is probably better than mine anyways." I joked.

Nance smiled at me and joked back, "Well. Let's hope I don't make you look like a fool tonight!!"

"I'm sure you won't," I reassured her as we walked around the store. She picked up a yellow dress from one rack and held it up to my body. After a moment of hesitation, she put it away.

"Yellow just doesn't seem right for the occasion…or your skin tone. No offense." She chuckled.

"Not offended," I responded. "That's what I've always known."

She picked up another dress. This one was a bright, electric blue. "Now, this one…may be the one." Once again, she held it up to my chest. "Meh. We're going to have to hold on to this one, but I know there's something else that may be better. But first, go try this on, and we'll see how your friend is doing."

I nodded and made my way to the dressing room. Siri was already outside and twirling around in one of her black dresses.

"What do you think?" She squealed as she saw my reflection approaching her in the mirror.

"That looks cute," I smiled as I turned to close the curtain. I slipped on the bright blue dress. Zipping it up easily, I walked out to meet Siri.

"Ohh!! Mel! You look gorgeous!! You should totally get that one," she squealed. "Where's Nancy! I need her advice on this dress."

"Well, I think that dress is really cute on you," I offered some advice. "It is very cutesy with the bow and stuff." A giant bow formed the neckline to the dress. Honestly, it looked good on her, but I guess anything would. She had the body that all girls are jealous of.

"Cutesy? No way. I'm going for the elegant look tonight." She shook her head as she went back to the dressing room.

"Hey, you!" Nancy came running to me with a new dress. "I just found the perfect dress. You have to try this on…right now."

She handed the dress to me and then pushed me into my dressing room I looked closely at the dress before I put it on. It was a red dress, which is almost too bold for me. But it was also a deeper shade of red, which made it sophisticated at the same time.

The way the material slipped on was amazing. And it felt like it was made out of silk. Stepping out from behind the curtain, I heard Nancy gasp. I turned around and looked at myself in the mirror. "Oh, Nancy. This is almost too perfect!! Thank you so much!" I went over to her and hugged her.

"No problem, sweetie. It is my job, after all. And who

knew? It matches your shoes too." She smiled at me. Turning around, she looked at Siri. "Oh, my! You look absolutely amazing!"

Siri smiled proudly and did a full turn, "I think this is the one."

I turned around to look at her. Smiling, I said, "I think so too. That is definitely not cutesy. It is classy and elegant."

Siri and I got out of our dresses and changed back into our normal clothes. Making our way to the cash register, Nancy got behind the table. After ringing the two dresses up, she smiled politely, "That would be a total of $1,027.14."

I restrained myself from gasping and forced myself to hand over the credit card that Chief gave to me.

"Thanks so much for shopping here! I hope to see you two around again!!"

"No, thank you! And we will see each other again, sometime soon." Siri smiled back and picked up her bag.

"Yeah, thanks so much!" I smiled as I picked up my own bag. As we waltzed out of the store, Evander met us outside and took our bags for us.

"How was shopping, girls?"

"Amazing! You should totally see the dresses we picked out! They are absolutely gorgeous." Siri responded enthusiastically.

"So. Your usual chauffeur isn't here, so I'm going to be driving you two home. How fun is that?" Evander pointed to a normal, small car.

"That's fine with me. I prefer less gaudiness." I smiled at Evander as I got into the car after Siri.

"So, did you two really spend three hours at that store?"

Evander made small talk after a few minutes when the car fell silent.

"Yeah. It definitely didn't seem that long. But you know the saying…time flies when you're having fun." I noted.

"Of course."

I sighed and looked out the window. We passed lots of roads and houses and stores. Suddenly, I saw a car headed straight towards us. It was going to hit right at the window where I was sitting if Evander doesn't stop the car in a second.

"EVANDER!! WATCH OUT!!" I screamed as I saw the black car come racing to my window. I closed my eyes and braced myself for the impact.

Chapter 18

My body was thrown forward against my seat belt as Evander slammed on the brake as hard as he could. Instead of crashing into my window, the black car hit the front of our car with a loud crunch.

I looked around me and realized that Siri and Evander were both okay. There were no injuries, so I let out a sigh of relief.

"WHAT THE HELL WAS THAT!?!" Evander yelled in fury as he tried to see who was in the black car. "Stay in the car, you two." He quickly got out of the car and twisted his head around, as if to see what was going on.

Red and blue lights quickly flashed around us and the piercing sound of sirens blocked out all other sounds. Siri and I huddled together in the backseat as we saw a police officer walk up to Evander. After several minutes of talking, Evander motioned for us to get out of the car.

"So Chief was notified about this a few minutes ago,

and he sent Pierce over to come and pick you two up. I'm staying here to fix up this whole mess." Evander walked to the back of the car and popped up the trunk. "And don't forget your dresses. I will see you two tonight."

Right as he finished his sentence, Pierce's car screeched up next to us. He quickly ran out of the car towards us. Looking at his expression, I could tell that he was worried. But when we finally made eye contact, his body noticeable relaxed. We shared a brief smile, it was so nice seeing him here.

"Pierce!! Baby! I'm so glad you are here! You have no idea how scared I was." Siri ran up to him and snuggled into his chest. Pierce wrapped his arms around Siri after a few moments of hesitation. He met my eyes and gave me an apologetic look.

Even though I knew his actions for Siri were fake, I was still hurt by the sight. Not knowing what to do, I made my way towards his car.

Jokingly, but with a hint of jealously I called out, "Can you please unlock this car, you two lovebirds?"

Pierce quickly pulled out of the embrace and turned to unlock the car. I climbed into the car immediately, without looking back at him.

The car ride was silent, and Siri sat in shotgun, next to Pierce. The whole time, I sulked about how I couldn't even talk to Pierce....not that I had anything to say to him anyways. When we finally pulled up to the mansion, I grabbed my shopping bag and fled the scene. I'm sure Pierce gave me a weird look, but he's going to have to deal with that. I was not in the mood to accept Siri's flirting.

I ran up to my room and opened the door with too

much energy. The door slammed on the inside wall, which make a giant sound.

"Aww. Someone isn't in a good mood today," a voice cooed from inside my room. "Little diva, are you going to tell me what's wrong?"

"Lukas!!" I yelled and ran into his awaiting arms. "I missed you!! I haven't seen you since the last dance, which was about three months ago!"

"I know, darling. I know. It has been too long." He waved me off as he walked about the room, leafing through my stuff. Finally he came back and started to inspect me. "And I can tell that your hair misses me too…almost too much." He picked up a handful of my limp, style-less hair and let it fall back into place again.

"I missed your sass too." I teased.

Lukas brushed off my comment like nothing, "Shut up so I can get to work. There is so much that I have to do and so little time! How am I supposed to get you ready for that party tonight! It is only four hours away!"

"Should I take that as an insult?" I raised my eyebrow at him.

"Take it however you want to." After hearing no response from me, he continued. "What's in that bag? Please tell me that it is something suitable for my taste."

"I think you will be impressed," I smiled smugly as I pulled the dress out of the bag.

"Oh my word. Honey. That is gorgeous. Where did you learn how to get so fashionable so fast?" Lukas stroked the material of my dress adoringly.

"It's a secret."

"Mel, dah-ling. You don't have to keep secrets from me.

I want to know everything. I need to get caught up on the 411 of your life."

"Even all the dirtiest and darkest secrets that I can't tell anyone else?" I asked.

"Of course. I missed you. And we need something very long to talk about while I fix up your mane." He commented, obviously referring to my hair.

"Fine. But you are sworn to secrecy. Promise?" I faced him so he could tell I was being serious.

With an equally serious expression on his face, he lifted up his hand. Only his pinkie was sticking up. "I have never broken a pinky promise in my whole entire life."

I smiled and hooked my pinkie with his, and then began telling him the whole story…starting with Pierce and Siri. Lukas always managed to keep the conversation light, and we laughed about almost all the serious stuff that I was worrying about earlier.

"My masterpiece is finished. Your hair is now beyond acceptable. It qualifies as gorgeous and borderline perfection right now." Lukas put the finishing touches on my hair.

I looked into the mirror and beamed at Lukas. "Once again, I must complement you and your magic hands."

Lukas winked at me, "I know a certain someone… ahem Pierce…who won't be able to resist you tonight!! Come on, Mel. Show me that puma inside of you." As he finished his sentence, he made his hands into claws and meowed at me.

Laughing my head off at the sight, I managed to choke out, "I don't know who came up with the phrase 'diamond is a girl's best friend'. But they are so wrong. You are a girl's best friend."

In response, he did the weird meowing thing again. "Okay. Enough funny business. Let's get down to starting my second masterpiece. Your face."

I smiled as he turned the chair away from the mirror. He wanted the full "transformation" effect when I saw myself again after he's done. It reminded me of the show *What Not to Wear*, especially the makeup part, which happened to be my favorite part.

After about half an hour of hard work, Lukas finally stepped back to observe my face. "I think my work here is done." He sighed with an accomplished look.

I turned around to take a look at myself in the mirror. The surprised look on my face wasn't exaggerated, and it never failed to surprise me how great of an artist Lukas really was. "Oh, Lukas. You are amazing!!"

"Shh. I know. Now go and put on that red dress. I want to see those sexy legs!" He pushed me towards the dress that was lying on my bed.

The dress looked even better on me than when I was at the store. With my hair put up and my makeup on, I could barely even recognize myself. The dress hit about mid-thigh, but it wasn't slutty at all.

"You look like a real puma." Lukas clapped his hands together in excitement. "Go out there and break some hearts tonight!"

"That will be a positive change from the last time there was a dance," I smirked at him.

"Now that's the right attitude." He looked at his watch

before pushing me out the door. "It's time for you to shine, Cinderella."

"Cinderella. Really?" I looked at him skeptically.

"Just make sure you don't come back before midnight. And don't lose one of your gorgeous pumps. And please don't turn into a rat…or a fat pumpkin."

"Trust me. I won't." I reassured him as I walked out the door. As I walked past the lounge, I saw the three guys sitting there with their tuxes on, playing a video game. The overall sight was so amusing that I started to laugh out loud.

"You guys are such big babies," I nodded my head in their general direction.

Karter turned around and gave me the 'up and down'. "So I guess that makes you the hot baby."

"That didn't even make any sense, and you know it." I grinned at his lame attempt at a pick up line. "You're going to have to pick up your game for later on tonight."

"She's right, Karter." Pierce added on. "Anyways, it's time to go." He walked over to the TV and turned it off.

"BUT I WAS JUST ABOUT TO WIN!!" Karter let out a murderous scream.

"Oh, shut up and take it like a grown man," Blake tried to give Karter a noogie.

Karter dodged from his reach. "Don't you dare touch my hair. It was tousled very carefully so it would look like perfection."

I grinned as we made our way down to the giant foyer and the connecting room. There were already several guests there, including Siri.

"Come on, Pierce. We'll spend the New Year's together." Siri ran up to him and dragged him away with his arm.

"Don't worry Mel. I'll stay with you for the New Year," Karter winked at me. "Or I'll distract that clingy girl when it just to happens to be midnight."

"Thanks, big bro. You're so sweet to me." I gave him a quick hug. Big bro had been his nickname for quite some time…mainly because he so closely resembles one.

"That's what I do for my baby sis." He hugged me back.

For most of the night, I hung around Karter and Blake. This time, they didn't run off with other girls, although several other girls came up to them.

"Blake. Karter. You guys have to like some of the girls here. They're all so pretty. I don't want to weigh you two down. I think I can handle myself around here." I told them after they rejected the sixth group of girls.

"Are you sure, Mel? I honestly don't mind staying with you. I was serious about staying with you until midnight." Karter told me.

"Nonsense. Go out and have fun." I gave him a parting hug. "You too, Blake." I turned to hug him too.

Once the two of them left, I made my way to the punch bowl. Sipping at the red juice and staring out into the crowd, I suddenly felt really lonely. Everyone was having such a good time tonight, and I was standing alone, with no one to talk to.

As the feeling of loneliness and nostalgia sunk in even more, I decided to make a quick stop at my parents' room. There was still a good half-hour before midnight, so I could easily make it back in time.

Slowly making my way to my parents' room, I paused

in the middle of the corridor. I took small, quiet steps, and I was barely able to make out hush whispers coming from around the corner. I kept on walking and peeked around the corner. Two men were talking, and one of their backs was facing me. I didn't know who he was, but I knew that the other man was Evander.

"What the hell happened today?" Evander yelled as loudly as he could while whispering.

"You told me to do it," the mystery man responded.

"But I was in there! And so was my daughter! You could've killed me too!"

"I was just following your orders, sir."

"That is not what I meant when I said…"

Suddenly, a large hand came down on my shoulder and clamped my mouth shut so I wouldn't scream. Right when I was about to bite the person's hand, they whispered in my ear.

"Shh. It's me. You're okay."

My body melted back into Pierce's body. The adrenaline finally wore off, and I felt a wave of fatigue hit me. Slowly, we made our way to another empty corridor right outside of the party room. I leaned my back against the wall and slowly slid down so I was sitting on the floor. Pierce did the same thing. After a long time a gathering my thoughts, I broke the silence between us.

"You scared me to death! What if it wasn't you? How the heck did you know where I was?" I demanded the second I could talk. To say that I was angry would be an understatement. It didn't help that I was still mad at him for his disappearing act with Siri.

"I saw you leave the room by yourself, and I was worried. So I managed to escape and follow you," he explained, not surprised by my angry tone. In the background, you could hear the crowd chanting down the seconds until midnight. 8...7...6...

"I don't know what your plan is, but I am certainly not happy. Especially with you and Si..." before I could finish my mad rant, Pierce mashed his lips against mine. It was either to silence me or because it was officially the New Year.

The feel of his lips made the anger inside me melt away for that instant. His soft lips gently pulled back after a few seconds. "Happy New Year," Pierce sighed breathlessly.

"You too," I muttered, looking down.

"This year will be very interesting..." Pierce whispered, probably alluding to the whole marriage business thing.

"I guess only time can tell what is going to happen."

Chapter 19

The table was silent. All you could hear was the occasional sound of silver forks and knives hitting against the delicate china plates. Someone chewed loudly, and the sound of swallowing disgusted me a little. What a typical morning. Nothing really exciting happened in this New Year so far. I guess some things never change…like our usual silent morning breakfast…

…Or so I thought. Chief slowly stood up and gave all of us an expectant look. Karter, Blake, Pierce, and I all stopped eating and met his gaze with the same questioning look on our faces.

"I know we haven't talked about this in a while, so it may be a shock for you guys," Chief warned us before going on. "But this Friday is the four month anniversary of Melanie's arrival."

At first, I had no idea what he was talking about. A few seconds later, realization dawned on me and it showed in my expression. I looked at the other three guys. Karter and Blake didn't seem to know what was going on, but Pierce's face was clearly paler at this point.

"Chief…no. Not now." I whispered, hoping he would stop giving his speech.

Ignoring me, he continued, "I promised Mel that on Friday, I would announce who was going to be the successor to the company. She only had to live here for four months before I made the final decision."

"Chief. Do we have to do this?" I asked in a small voice, looking over to Pierce. He looked so broken right now; all I wanted to do was to give him a hug.

Pierce had still never told Chief that he wanted to become a doctor because he didn't have a plan of what to do after he got kicked out. But it seemed like his time had run out. It was now or never.

Instead of speaking up like I thought he would, he clamped his mouth shut and stayed silent. I shot him a questioning look, but he avoided eye contact with me.

Chief kept on talking as I tried to get Pierce's attention, "You are expected to meet me in the foyer on Friday at 9 in the morning. Please don't be late." With that, he casually left the room, leaving the four of us in shock.

"So…Are you excited for your wedding?" Karter asked me jokingly after a long moment of awkward silence.

I gave him a death stare. Sarcastically, I answered, "Oh yeah, for sure. The only problem is that I have no idea who I'm getting married to."

Karter gave me a pointed look and shifted his eyes toward Pierce. Obviously he thought he knew who the successor was going to be. However, he couldn't be more wrong, which broke my heart.

The only person that I truly liked was the only person that I couldn't have. I shook my head slightly at Karter and walked out of the room. Hoping to find an escape, I decided to take a jog. The air was slightly cold, but it was refreshing. The sound of gravel under my feet quickly eased some of my tension, and I already felt a little better.

Breathing at a steady pace, I was able to calm down and think about my situation clearly. I was going to go back home to New York in a matter of weeks, or even days. Chief promised that I would have a year back at New York before I had to come back and marry the successor.

I tried to deny the fact that Pierce was going to be chosen as the successor, but all odds were pointing to him. Apparently Chief liked him the best because of his personality and work ethic. Along with that, Chief probably found out that I was "going out" with Pierce, which didn't help his cause at all.

Also, Pierce didn't speak up at breakfast, which showed that he probably wouldn't talk to Chief at all about the doctor issue. He would be named the successor, and I would be forced to marry him. But I wouldn't be able to bring myself to marry him knowing that he didn't want that for his future.

Getting tired, I wiped the sweat off my brow and made my way back into the mansion. I slowly dragged myself up the stairs and into my room. Although it was only the early afternoon, the sky was cloudy and dark. I sighed and collapsed on the bed, already wishing the day was over.

The next few days passed by quickly, and it only felt

like hours before Friday rolled around. Pierce and I got together a few times, but it didn't feel the same. There was obviously a giant elephant in the room, but neither one of us wanted to address the problem.

"Mel!" I heard a girly voice coming from behind me.

"Hi, Siri." I greeted her without enthusiasm. I was not in the mood to be fake, nice, and cheerful. We were on our way to the foyer, where Chief was going to announce the big news.

"Soo…" Siri dragged out her o's. "You're finding out who you're going to marry today!! Are you excited?"

"Yeah, sure." I gave a curt response.

"Well, I would be excited if I were you. I know this meeting will be interesting." Siri seemed like she had something in mind, but I didn't feel like questioning it. Instead, I ignored her and kept on walking.

She kept on walking alongside me, obviously going to the meeting too. As we came to a stop in front of Chief, I saw that all three guys were already there.

"Good morning, Melanie and Siri." Chief greeted us when he saw us. "I'm glad all of you got here in time. I guess you are all curious as to who I chose."

None of us said anything. The room was silent, with tension was so thick that even a knife couldn't cut through it.

"I guess I won't keep you hanging on in suspense for any longer," Chief smiled, oblivious to the atmosphere in the room. I almost laughed because it was starting to sound like a TV show. "After a lot of deliberation, I thought that Pi…"

"Sorry, Chief. But can I interrupt?" Siri quickly broke in before he could finish his sentence. All five of us stared in shock, waiting for her to continue.

As she was met no objections, she continued with an air of confidence. There was a slight undertone of malice in her voice, "I think it is a bad idea to force people to do what they don't want to do."

I stared at her wide-eyed, predicting what she was going to say. She was going to blurt out Pierce's secret. I looked across the room at Pierce, and his expression mirrored mine. Suddenly, his face filled with anger and determination.

"Chief. I need to tell you something," Pierce broke in, not caring that he interrupted Siri.

"But Siri was talking. Why don't you let her finish first?" Chief tried to be polite and acknowledged the frustrated girl in front of him.

"Thank you, Chief. So as I was saying..." Siri continued with a little too much sweetness in her voice.

"This can't wait," Pierce interrupted her once again.

"Fine. What is it?" Chief noticed the change in Pierce's attitude. "This better be important."

Under my breath I muttered to myself, "Oh. This is important. You have no idea."

Without beating around the bush, Pierce let out the truth. "I don't want to be the successor of the company."

Chief stood there speechless for the first time. It's rare to see someone so rich and powerful being speechless. In almost every situation, he had something to say. But I guess this was the one exception.

"My dream in life is to become a doctor." Pierce stated matter-of-factly.

"Pierce…" Chief said in a warning tone, subtly telling him to stop talking.

"I'm sorry. I had to tell you that before someone else did." He shot an icy glare at Siri. Strangely, she gave a calm smile back.

"You know what this means?" Chief asked gravely. "You do remember the time when Karter wanted to be a musician, do you not? And you do remember the contract, right?"

"Of course I remember those things."

Chief sighed in exasperation. "Pierce. You are going against the contract that you signed when you first arrived in this mansion. I'm sorry, but I have to take you out of the running and ask you to leave the house."

Pierce looked devastated. He quickly turned and walked out of the room without looking at anyone. I turned to Siri, ready to rip out her throat. My disgust towards her multiplied when I saw the evil, gloating expression on her face.

Before anyone could stop me, I left the room right behind Pierce. I didn't care about what others would think of that. I just couldn't deal with being in the same room as Siri, and I had to find Pierce to see if he was okay.

As I neared his room, I heard his drawers opening and slamming. His footsteps were loud against the floor, and I hesitated outside of his door. A few seconds later, all the sounds disappeared. Curiosity got the best of me, and when I opened the door, I was met with silence.

Pierce was sitting on the floor, leaning against his bed with his head in his hands. My heart broke when I saw him like this, so I quietly walked over and cradled him in my arms. Instead of pushing me away like I thought he would, he silently leaned into me.

"Shh…It's okay." I whispered as I stroked his hair. "Everything will be okay." I repeated this mantra over and over until I almost believed it.

"Pierce, look at me," I pleaded and brought his head up. His eyes were full of loss. He didn't know what to do with himself now that he was homeless and penniless. But behind the look of sadness, I saw a spark. Now that he was free, he could go after his dream. "Go to my house in New York. Book the first flight out of this place and go there."

After a moment, he nodded and slowly stood up. Carefully, we walked around the room, and I helped him pack a little. We stared at each other when the room looked bare except for the furniture.

"Thank you, Mel. You have no idea how much you have helped me," He walked over and enveloped me in a hug.

"Don't thank me. It is the least I could do to help a homeless person," I mused, trying to lighten the atmosphere.

Pierce didn't laugh. Instead, he placed a light kiss on the top of my head. "I love you, Melanie."

When I heard those three clichéd words, my heart nearly stopped. Restarting again twice as fast, my heart pounded against my chest as Pierce tilted my head and brought his lips closer to mine.

His lips brushed against mine as he brought his arms around the back of my neck and my hips. Pushing me against his body, he slowly traced his tongue against my bottom lip. A moan escaped my lips as I tangled my hands into his hair. Sparks flew and my whole body heated up like a firework.

When we finally pulled apart, I looked deep into his grey eyes, "I love you, too."

He smiled one of those heart-wrenching grins while playing with my hair, "I'm going to miss you when I leave first, but I can't wait to see you in New York."

I nodded in agreement as I leaned my head against his chest again. Although things looked uncertain and bleak right now, I knew that things could only go up from now. But first, I had to deal with the devil herself who made all hell break loose.

I didn't hear from anyone as I went back to my room. No one came upstairs to get me or Pierce, so I guess the big news sort of put everything on hold. I didn't see Chief for the next few hours, and Pierce left the day after he dropped his secret. The other two guys and I saw him leave, and my heart sagged when his plane took off.

It was only going to be a little while before I got to see Pierce again. But by then, I might be engaged to someone else. I winced a little at that thought and hoped that Chief would change his mind. Hopefully, he would realize how ridiculous this whole situation is. Arranged marriages were things of the past…it didn't happen in modern times.

A week went by without anything happening and the house seemed eerily silent, which didn't help the mood I was in. I talked to Pierce several times after he arrived at New York, but it just wasn't the same. I sighed and stared at the ceiling of the room as I lay on my bed. I jumped a little as my cell phone started to ring right next to me.

"Hello?" I answered, not bothering to check caller ID.

"Hello, lovely!! I missed your voice," a friendly woman cooed.

"Hey, mom. I missed you too." I smiled when I heard her voice. It was nice talking to her, since it has been a while.

"So guess who finally knocked on my door today like a lost little puppy?" I could imagine her grinning on the other side of the phone.

"Pierce?"

"Yes. Honey, you said he was going to arrive a week ago!! I thought he was lost in New York! But when I talked to him, he said that he was living in a hotel. Apparently, he didn't want to be a burden." My mother scoffed at the idea. She was the most hospitable person, and nothing would be a burden for her.

"Awww. Is he there right now?" I asked, hoping that I could talk to him. It has been a few days since we last talked.

"I'm sorry, honey. He is actually out right now. He said something about an interview with a school."

Smiling to myself, I was happy to hear that Pierce had already started to go for his dream. "Okay then. That's fine."

"Oh yeah! Jessica called yesterday and asked me when your funeral was," my mother laughed heartily. "She said that since she hasn't heard from you for a while, she assumed you were dead. I suggest you call that silly girl soon. I like her sense of humor."

I slapped myself in the forehead. I couldn't believe I hadn't called my best friend in weeks. "Thanks for reminding me. She's going to kill me!!"

Someone knocked on my door. After a few seconds,

the door opened and Evander stuck his head in the room. My heartbeat quickened, but I tried to ignore the feeling. He wasn't going to hurt me when I was on the phone. He could easily get caught.

"Excuse me, Miss Cartwright. Your grandfather wants to see you right now in the library." I nodded quickly and waited for him to leave.

When he did, I turned my attention back to my mother, "Sorry, mom. I have to go. Chief is calling for me."

"Okay, honey. Have fun. And come back soon!! I miss your pretty face."

"I love you, bye!" And with that, I hung up the phone. Slowly, I rose and made my way to the door. I hesitated to open it, wondering if this whole thing was some kind of evil plot by Evander. Keeping my phone in my hand, ready to call someone if I needed to, I made my way down the stairs.

I heard voices coming from the big library, and immediately relaxed when I heard Chief's distinct voice. Laughing at myself for being so paranoid, I pushed open the heavy oak doors and made my way into the giant library.

Karter and Blake were also in the room. I paused at the door, hoping that Chief wasn't going to announce who the successor was going to be or anything else that's important.

"Hi, Melanie. Come over here and have a seat," Chief gestured to an empty chair beside him. He didn't seem happy or sad...he was just seemed indifferent. After I sunk into the leather chair beside him, he continued. "After the whole fiasco last week, I had to reevaluate everything."

I gulped, knowing that he was still going to go with his original plan of the arranged marriage. "I'm not going to hide the fact that Pierce was my first choice as a successor. But I think that his confession actually changed my plans for the better."

Looking over at Karter and Blake, I could see that they were trying to keep poker faces on. Karter was more successful…probably because he didn't really care about being the next owner of the company. Blake, on the other hand, had a mix of excitement and disappointment in his expression. The excitement was probably because he had a chance of being the successor and the disappointment was because he wasn't Chief's first choice.

"I can tell that this person is very dedicated to the company, and they want this job the most. So I am proud to announce that Blake will be the successor to RM Productions."

Blake's face lit up and had the same expression as a child's on Christmas morning. At the same time, my world just crumbled down in front of me.

The hope that I had in me was crushed by the realness of the announcement. It just made everything seem more official. I still had a year to be free, but after that, I had to marry Blake. The thought killed me, and it felt like I was already betraying Pierce.

My breathing hitched up a little, and I tried to close my eyes to calm myself down. A single tear betrayed me as it slipped past my eyelids and rolled its way down the side of my cheek.

"Congratulations, Blake." I tried to speak normally, but my voice cracked at the end. "Sorry, please excuse me." I whispered, ducking my head down as I ran from the room. Instead of going to my own room where someone could find me, I went to my parents' room.

Heading straight for the bed, I quickly jumped onto it and landed on my stomach. The puffy covers engulfed me, and filled me with a small sense of comfort. As I buried my head into the pillows, I took deep breaths. My life seemed so out of control right now, and I couldn't make my future what I wanted it to be.

It was like I was on a sinking ship, and I couldn't do anything about it. There was no life raft, and I was doomed to go under. After a few minutes, I heard the door handle turn. Not bothering to look up, I muttered, "Go away."

The intruder didn't listen and made their way to the bed. I felt the side of the bed dip down a little, and I rolled over to face the person. When I saw Blake sitting there looking at me with apologetic eyes, I broke into another fit of tears.

His strong arms wrapped around my shoulders and pulled me into him. As he tried to soothe me, I repeatedly punched his chest and yelled, "This isn't fair! I don't want to marry you."

He hugged me tighter and brought his head down so he could whisper into my ear, "I know. I know. Everything is going to be okay." Eventually, I gave into his calm voice and my heart-wrenching sobs became a quiet sniffle.

"I'm sorry you are put in this type of situation," he pushed me back a little so I could look into his eyes. His green eyes reflected sincerity, "I won't force you to marry me because I don't want you to be unhappy."

I wiped at my eyes, "Thanks. But it's not up to us. It's Chief's call."

"I will talk to him, now that I am the owner of the company. But if he won't give in, we can always get a divorce or something," he tried to come up with different plans. "I know you love Pierce, and I'm not going to get in the way of you two."

"I never imagined that I would ever get a divorce," I muttered lamely. "I always believed in happy endings. It's already awful how one in two marriages ends in divorce."

Blake laughed at my sappiness. I couldn't help but smile as I thought how ridiculous my statement was. "There we go. That's what I want to see. Your smile is beautiful." I blushed at Blake's comment.

He was a really sweet guy, and I'm sure that I might have fallen for him under different circumstances. But I definitely knew that I had already forgiven him for what he had done before. "Thanks, Blake…for being there for me."

As he pulled me in for another hug, I realized that I liked Blake as much as I liked Karter. The two of them were extremely nice and the best guy friends a girl could ever ask for. Finally, we pulled apart and he left me alone so I could reflect by myself.

I collected all my thoughts, and made my way to the door. But before I could reach it, someone else opened the door.

"Evander?" I said, surprised that he came to find me.

"Yes, Ms. Cartwright." He confirmed as he walked in. "May I talk to you for a few minutes?"

"Okay," I said warily as I backed up into the room.

"I know that you are unhappy here, and that you want to go back to New York so you can see Pierce," he noted.

"How do you know that Pierce is in New York? He

didn't tell anyone where he was going," I eyed Evander suspiciously. We didn't tell anyone because we knew that Chief wouldn't like the idea of me and Pierce being together for a year before I married Blake.

"Let's just say that Chief likes to keep up with current events," he responded succinctly. I stayed silent, waiting for Evander to continue. "And that's why Chief will not allow you to go back to New York. He already invited all your friends to stay here at the mansion with you, so you wouldn't have to go to New York to see them."

I took a small gasp. Chief wouldn't do something like that. He isn't that cold hearted…but then again, he's making me marry someone I don't like. "Okay, so why are you telling me this?" I asked Evander.

"I don't like seeing you unhappy," Evander shrugged his shoulders as if it was obvious. "So I have something for you."

"What is it?"

He stuck out his arm. In his hand, he held a small rectangular piece of paper. Hesitantly, I reached out and grabbed it. Looking more closely at it, I realized it was a plane ticket to New York. The flight was for early the next morning at 2 am.

"A plane ticket?" I questioned, still not sure of his motives. "Why are you giving this to me?"

"I just wanted you to be happy. You can run away from all these problems right now and forget about your life as an heiress. You don't have to be the heiress bride anymore."

Everything made sense now. He wanted to get rid of me in a civil manner. If I agreed to this proposition, Siri would be free to marry Blake once Chief realized that I was gone.

I looked up at Evander, "Thank you." I folded the ticket gently and placed it into my pocket. Evander gave me a satisfied smile and led me out of the room.

"I will be waiting for you at midnight, to drive you to the airport." He whispered as I walked past him out the door. I nodded and went straight to my room to pack.

People say that it is always a bad idea to run away from your problems, but in this situation it seemed like the opposite. I gladly ran away as fast as I could.

Chapter 20

The shrill sound of my alarm pierced through the silence of the room. Groaning as I sat up to turn the alarm off on my cell phone, I flipped open the little device. Light flooded into the room.

I sighed as I realized that this was probably going to be the last time I was going to be in this room. Running away meant that I couldn't come back to this mansion...ever. And this was all because of my deal with Evander.

Looking at the time once again, I realized that it was already 11:50pm...ten minutes until midnight. I had packed right after my rendezvous with Evander so I could have a little time for shut eye and rest. I was also hoping the nap would help me stay sane. My nerves were jumping everywhere, and I needed to cool down somehow.

With my suitcase in one hand, I carefully slung another bag over my shoulder. Slowly, I opened the door and made sure the coast was clear. I couldn't afford to run into either Karter or Blake because that would probably ruin my whole plan.

I turned around and took one last look at the room. I smiled as I remembered my first encounter with the one way mirror of my closet. I was definitely going to miss this place. Setting my suitcase down, I used two hands to ease the door closed. It closed with a small thud.

I was able to stay silent as I made my way down the stairs. Making it past the front door was the biggest challenge, though. I tried my hardest not to make a sound as I pushed the handle down, but the door creaked loudly when I tried to open it. I looked around, paranoid that someone heard me. Thankfully, no one was in sight. After a few seconds, I tried to ease open the door again.

"What are you doing?" I whipped my head around at the voice. My heart thudded loudly and then slowed down when I saw who it was.

"Evander! Don't scare me like that," I breathed out a sigh of relief.

"Sorry, Ms. Cartwright. But we're leaving from the back…not the front," he quietly took my heavy suitcase from me. After shutting the front door again, I followed behind him.

Coming to the back of the house, he opened a door leading to a path that wound around the mansion. I used to run laps on this trail with Blake. I sighed and realized that I was going to miss him a lot.

"Hurry, Ms. Cartwright! We will be late!" Evander whispered harshly a few feet in front of me. I shook my head to clear my thoughts. I had stopped walking, so I ran to catch up with Evander. He made his way to a black car with its lights turned off.

"Go and sit in the passenger seat. I will be there shortly after I put your luggage in the trunk," He waved me off and nodded towards the front of the car. I nodded and followed his orders.

Right as I pulled the seatbelt over my chest, I heard Evander slam the trunk shut. A few moments later, he was sitting in the driver's seat. I looked out the windshield as he started the car and began to drive to the main road.

I noticed something at the front of the car. There were two little red flags with gold crescents that stuck out on either side of the car. I laughed out loud when I realized this was the same car I first saw in New York. Remembering its suspiciousness, I thought about how I first met Karter. It was going to be hard leaving him since I've known him the longest. My laughter and smile faded as I thought about leaving the life I had in the mansion. Although the stipulations were ridiculous (arranged marriage?!?!), I loved the people there.

"Do you have your plane ticket?" Evander interrupted my thoughts.

"Yeah, it's right here," I stuck up my hand with the small white ticket in it.

"Good. Do not lose it."

I decided not to answer and looked out the windows again. Houses zoomed by, but they were hard to distinguish in the darkness outside. The city was asleep, and no lights were on. I had this strange feeling of loneliness and sadness, but it quickly passed. I pressed my forehead against the cool glass window and closed my eyes. Drifting off into a light sleep, I heard the soft purr of the engine before I lost consciousness.

"Ms. Cartwright. Wake up! We're here." Evander shook me as I groaned. My eyes were still heavy with sleep, but I forced myself to get up. Looking around, I noticed several other cars at the terminal. I had no idea flights ran this late at night.

Climbing out of the car, I saw Evander standing at the sidewalk with my suitcase already out of the car, "Thank you, Evander." Warily, I reached up to give him a hug. Surprisingly, he hugged me back.

"Have a nice life. I hope to never see you again," he said, almost as a joke. However, I could hear the serious and threatening undertone he had in his voice.

"You too," I meant it sincerely. I honestly didn't want to see him anymore if he was really trying to take over the company by hurting me.

I grabbed my suitcase and turned on my heel. Without turning back, I walked into the airport and boarded the plane to New York.

* * *

"Welcome to LaGuardia Airport. It is now 6:27 am in New York," an overly cheerful female automated voice blared over the loudspeakers. The airport was almost deserted, except for those who were on the same flight as I was on. I groaned from lack of sleep. A little baby sat in the seat directly behind me. At first I thought she was super cute. But as the flight went on, I changed my mind. The baby cried the whole time, and I was nearly ready to change my mind about wanting kids when I grew up. It seemed like such a hassle.

As the sun just peeked over the buildings in the horizon, it illuminated the sky so that it was a beautiful pinkish red. I sighed at the sight as I dug into my pocket for cash. Looking down at the crumpled bills I managed to find in my pockets, I realized that I probably had just enough for a bus and taxi ride.

The bus was incredibly shaky when it started to move. I had no experience riding busses, so I nearly fell on top of a young man who was reading the newspaper.

"Excuse me! I am so sorry!!" I looked at the man I had elbowed in the face.

Grunting at me, he only glanced up and looked back down. I quickly made my way to an empty seat in the row behind him before I could hurt anyone else. I sighed and leaned my head against the window. This was going to be a long ride.

A few minutes later, I saw the guy in front of me turn around. He gave me a weird look and faced the front of the bus again. Self-consciously, I raised my hand to my face to see if there was anything wrong with it. I faced the window and used the reflection to check if I had anything in my teeth. Nothing.

The guy turned around again for the third time, and I gave him a dirty look. He quickly averted his eyes and looked down at his newspaper again. I couldn't hold back my curiosity. Going against my hatred for confrontation, I tapped him on his shoulder.

He turned around with a shocked face. He wouldn't look me in the eye, "Yes?"

"Excuse me, but do I have something on my face?" I asked in an accusing manner.

"What?" he looked at me like I was crazy.

"You heard me," I sighed in annoyance. "Why did you keep on turning around?"

"Are you…" he paused as he looked down at his newspaper again, "…Melanie Cartwright?"

"Yes," I became suspicious, "How did you know?"

"I knew it!" The man held up his paper. Splashed across the middle page of The New York Times was a giant picture of Blake and me. It was taken when we went to the haunted house and corn maze. I hadn't known people were following us! Forgetting all my manners, I snatched the newspaper from the stranger's hand. Quickly, I scanned the title and the text underneath.

RM Productions: Now known as BM Productions?

Yesterday, the multibillionaire Ralph McKinley announced the new CEO of RM Productions. Twenty three year old Blake Miller was chosen as the successor to this very prestigious company. With strong features and determined blue eyes, Miller proves that RM Productions will be left in good hands…and so will Melanie Cartwright. Cartwright is the long lost granddaughter of McKinley and she has fallen in love with the new successor. It is a match made in heaven, and their wedding is scheduled to be at a private beach in California in one year.

My mouth gaped while reading the article. The blood in my body began to boil as I read more about Blake. How could they say that I fell in love with him? I was in love with Pierce!

The man gave me a strange look. He nervously congratulated me. "Good luck with the wedding and everything…"

I threw the paper back at him and stared angrily out the window for the rest of the ride. Obviously, the man was too scared to talk to me anymore, but I couldn't care less. I didn't know this whole thing was so publicized. But I should have known better. RM Productions was a big part of American business. Of course people would want to know what was going on. Chief had done a good job holding back paparazzi...I was actually unaware that there were any at all.

At 8, I was finally standing at the doorstep to my old house. My stomach grumbled as I smelled the scent of fresh bread in the oven. Tears sprang into my eyes, and I batted them away. My heartstrings were pulled at the sight of my small, cozy home. I never realized how lonely and cold the mansion was; just looking at the house made me feel whole again.

I pushed opened the door while yelling, "Lucy! I'm home!"

I heard scrambling feet at the top of the stairs. As I pulled my suitcase into the house and slammed the door shut, the rotund little lady ran towards me.

"Melanie! This is such a nice surprise!! We weren't expecting you for a week...at least!! I missed you so much, honey." She threw her arms around my shoulders. I smiled into her head and wrapped my arms around her too, squeezing her until she was out of breath.

"Do you want to kill me??" my mother scolded me as she pulled back, "Why don't you save all your energy for Pierce?"

My heart beat faster after just hearing his name. I looked at my mom and noticed that she was looking down the hall. Following her gaze, my eyes landed on the most handsome person alive. My breath caught in my chest as he walked towards me and pulled me into a hug.

He lifted me off the ground and spun me around in one fluid movement. As he set me gently back on the ground, I noticed that my mother left the two of us alone. Pierce took his hands and directed my head so I was facing him.

"I missed you a lot," he whispered as he bent his head down over mine. I forgot how tall he was, and how right it felt to be in his arms. He cocooned me into a protective nest with his body.

"Me too."

He brought his lips down and I met him halfway. The fireworks exploded as we shared a sweet kiss. His lips moved against mine, and I kissed him back with equal fervor. All too soon, he pulled back.

"What will your mother think if we get too carried away?" his gorgeous grin made me breathless. Smiling back at him, we walked into the kitchen together hand in hand.

Greeting my mom again, we sat down at the small, wooden dinner table. Pierce sat across from me and hooked my leg with his. I grinned as my mother brought a new loaf of bread to the table. I could get used to this whole new world…away from all the glamour and money.

* * *

"Mel," I heard my mother call from downstairs. "Someone is here to see you!"

My eyebrows furrowed in confusion. Who would visit me at this ungodly hour?? I groaned as I looked at the alarm clock next to my head. The red digits read 6:00am. Pushing myself up with my two hands, I sat up on my bed. My brown, curly hair fell into my face and I pushed it back while standing up.

Before I could put any decent clothes on over my skimpy tank top and cloth shorts, a person barged into my room. I saw a frenzy of red hair a second later, and I was pushed down onto the floor with a surprising force.

"Melanie Cartwright!! You are so dead to me!!" Jessica's voice screeched out on the top of her lungs.

After getting over the initial shock, I started laughing out loud. However, she was crushing me, since she landed on top of me. I tickled her in order to get her off of me, but I earned a punch in the face because of her flailing.

"OH MY GOD!! I AM SO SORRY!!" Jessica jumped off of me and pulled me to my feet. "Did I give you a black eye? Bloody nose?" Her hands fluttered over my face, making sure I wasn't hurt.

"Calm down, Jessica! I can't even keep up with your talking anymore!"

Suddenly, Pierce comes running into my room. We looked at each other in confusion for a second before bursting out in laughter. Jessica, on the other hand, was speechless.

"I thought I heard someone screaming and a loud crash in this room," He raised his eyebrow at Jessica after he finished laughing. "Now I understand. I'll leave you two alone." Flashing his signature grin, he left the room and closed the door behind him.

Jessica didn't move since he came into the room. Her

mouth gaped open, and I could see drool coming out of it. Happily, I slapped her upside the head.

"Whaa…?" She slowly fell out of her daze.

"Eyes off. He's mine." I joked with her.

"Are you kidding me??" Jessica finally met my eyes. "Did you seriously live in a mansion with THREE guys who are beyond gorgeous??"

"Well…I guess so," I shrugged nonchalantly. "You know what Karter looks like, and you now know what Pierce looks like. You can just imagine what Blake looks like."

She gave me a death glare, "Why does everything wonderful happen to you??"

"Well…it all comes with drama. It's not as great as you think." I sighed as I thought about the newspaper article from a few days ago.

"Aww. I'm sorry," Jess pulled me into a hug. I smiled as I realized how much I actually missed this girl. "Anyways, I have to go."

"What? But you just got here!" I pouted.

"Some people here still have to work. That's why I'm here so early! We're not all heiresses of multibillionaires," she winked at me as she walked out of the room. "I will be here right when work gets out, so I'll see you later."

"Bye!! Love you." I collapsed on my bed after she left. Sleep overtook me again when my head hit the pillow facing the wall.

Falling into a deep sleep, I was able to rest completely. However, I felt a little tickle in my leg as I slept. I pulled it back underneath the covers. The tickling sensation continued on my shoulder. Turning around, I moaned a little.

There it was again…now on my other shoulder. I realized the feeling was too vivid to be a dream. I cracked open one eye, only to find Pierce leaning over me as he sat on my bed.

"Don't!" I whined in a sleepy voice as I closed my eyes again.

"I'm bored," he brought his lips to my shoulder again. His breath tickled and I giggled at the sensation.

"Find someone else to bother…," I muttered as I met his silver eyes again. "…like Jessica. She seems to be smitten with you."

"I don't want to," he whispered as he lay down on the bed next to me. He dragged his fingertips up my leg and waist. My heart almost stopped in my chest.

"How do you have this effect on me?" I meant to just think that, but managed to say it out loud instead. Blood rushed up from my neck and pooled in my cheeks.

He simply laughed at me and continued to do what he was doing. Feeling insignificant, I realized that I didn't have the same effect on him. He seemed unfazed by my presence. Completely the opposite for me -- just looking at Pierce made my heart melt.

My mood completely changed after that. Pushing him off of me, I used my arms to create space between us. Pierce just looked at me in surprise. Instead of leaving him and the bed, I did the opposite of what he was expecting.

Sensually, I placed my hands on his abs and pushed them up towards his chest. His shirt bunched under my hands, and I crinkled my nose. That wasn't supposed to happen. Readjusting my game plan in my head, I replaced my hands underneath his shirt.

While tracing the contours of his abs, I slowly looked up at Pierce through my eyelashes and buried my head in the crook of his neck. I ran my tongue up against his smooth skin and nibbled on the same spot afterwards. Slowly, I brought my hands up to his bare chest. When I felt his heartbeat under my right hand, I smiled in victory. His heartbeat definitely quickened under the palm of my hand.

Pierce felt my smile against his skin and muttered, "What is all of this for?" If I was right, it seemed like he was a little breathless.

"I just wanted to check something," I looked up at him and then got out of the bed. I wanted to make sure I could have the same effect on him as he did me. While walking to my bathroom, I added extra swing to my hips.

The cherry on top of this whole experience was when I heard Pierce mutter a curse under his breath.

An hour later, my mother, Pierce, and I were sitting around the dinner table. We were all enjoying some of my mother's bestselling honey bread with honey butter. It was delicious. My mother ate a slice with one hand while holding a newspaper in the other.

"Melanie! Look at this!" She suddenly dropped the newspaper on top of the table, completely covering the bread.

I looked down at the large, gray piece of paper. Blake's face once again took up most of the page. But this time, my face wasn't next to his. It was just him.

"This is your friend, right?" my mother questioned as she looked between Pierce and I. We didn't respond as we read the headline.

RM Productions on its way down?

New CEO Blake Miller seems to be cracking under the pressure that comes with running the company. On several accounts, we have heard Miller ignoring phone calls and pitching unrealistic ideas for the company. What will happen after Ralph McKinley completely steps down from his reigning throne?

Pierce and I shared a look after we finished reading the article. This was not good. Maybe it wasn't a good idea to leave him alone at the mansion.

"This is not good," I whispered as I whipped out my cell phone. Pierce already beat me to it when I realized he already had his phone pressed up against his ear.

"Blake, man. What's up?" Pierce greeted him in a normal way. He knew that if he immediately brought up the newspaper article, Blake would shut down. He probably didn't even know that he was being criticized by The New York Times.

I didn't even know about half the articles that were published during the four months I was away. But my mother saved every single one. At first, she cut them out and put them on the fridge, but as it became too crowded, she moved it into an album. It was weird to see how people were viewing my life from the outside. And now that I am on the outside, I realized that it wasn't so great.

"Look. I know this may seem random, but Mel and I just read an article about you in the newspaper." Pierce paused for a second as Blake responded.

"Put him on speakerphone for heaven's sake!!" I punched Pierce in the arm. My mother looked at me and I gave her a look. She nodded and left the room.

"...stressful over here," I heard Blake's voice blast through the tiny speakers on Pierce's phone.

"Aww, I'm sorry Blake!" I cooed, "But I know you are strong. You can get through all the stress. Be sure you prove the newspaper wrong."

"Exactly what did the newspaper say?" Blake asked. Pierce shot me a hard look. Whoops. I guess I wasn't supposed to mention what was in the article.

"Well, it was some random gossip trash saying that you are cracking under pressure," I tried to play it off like it was no big deal at all. I could never have a career as an actress.

My heart broke a little as I heard Blake let out a sigh. I could hear him rubbing his face in his hands, "It is just so lonely over here. I feel like there is no one to vent to."

"You can always go to Karter, even if he is annoying..." Pierce suggested.

"I know! And I would've..." Blake sighed and paused again, "...if he hadn't left the mansion the day after Melanie did."

"He did WHAT?" I nearly screamed the last word.

"He left a day after you did. I guess he thought that your absence meant that he was free to leave too." I felt a pit form in my stomach. I wouldn't have left if I had known this would happen...okay maybe I still would have, but it probably would have been harder.

"So where is he now?" Pierce asked the question that was nagging in the back of my mind.

"Last I heard, he is now some big shot at a café down in Santa Barbara," Blake almost laughed out loud. I couldn't help but crack a smile. I looked up at Pierce and saw him grinning while shaking his head.

"Of course he would," I said. I remembered the time when Pierce had told me that Karter wanted to go into the music business. He was also going for his dream now -- just like Pierce and Blake.

As I thought about the situation for a little longer, I realized that my move out of the mansion was for the best. Although we were all split apart, we were all going after our goals. We just needed to get through the hard times first... like help Blake through the rough transition.

"Blake. Do you know what this means?" I asked with a lot of hope in my voice.

"What?"

"We're all doing what we want to do!" I chirped excitedly, "I know that after you get through this hard time, we will all be a lot happier."

"Yeah," Pierce added on. "We're all going to be there for you. Just remember not to crack under pressure."

"Thanks, guys." Blake said sincerely. I could almost hear the smile in his voice.

"Blake. Come here, baby. I need you," a muffled female voice called from the background. Blake groaned into the phone.

"Is that..." Pierce began to ask.

I interrupted him, "Siri?"

Chapter 21

I held my breath as Blake began to explain himself to Pierce and me. I hoped to God that he wasn't going out with Siri because it would make me really mad. No one should be manipulated by that little devil.

"It's not like that. I promise!!" Blake whispered in a hushed voice. I heard some shuffling in the background. "Siri, can you please get out of this room? I'm making an important business call!"

"But, Blakey-poo. I'm bored!!" I could barely make out what she said through her whining.

"Please," Blake's voice was muffled. He probably put down the phone to deal with the blonde bimbo, "…just leave."

We heard a door slam. I looked over at Pierce and raised my eyebrows. It seemed like Blake really didn't like Siri, and I let out a sigh of relief.

As we heard someone pick up the phone again, Pierce

asked, "So, what was up with that? Why is Siri hanging on to you like a little flea?"

Blake chuckled at the description, "Flea? Well honestly, I have no idea. She never really liked me before. Right when Melanie and Karter left, she decided to hang out with me a lot. And I just began to realize how truly annoying she is."

"Oh," I laughed humorously, "You JUST realized?"

"Okay, fine…maybe not JUST realized. But you know what I mean," Blake sighed in annoyance, "Having Siri following me around everywhere does not help my situation. If anything, she actually adds more stress to my life."

As Blake expressed more of his hatred towards Siri, Pierce and I just laughed. It seemed that now that Blake was the new owner of the company, he had been getting more attention from Siri. We agreed that we all thought she is just using him -- just like she had used Pierce. I felt bad for Blake, but I'm sure he would find a way to get rid of her. He was smart enough to accomplish that!

After an hour long conversation with Blake, Pierce and I went out for a bite to eat. It was only 9am on a Friday, so we made our way to New York City. We had plenty of time to spare and to explore the city before Pierce had to attend his afternoon classes at NYU.

Yeah, he's going to school at NYU. He actually had found a way to get into the school that late by meeting with an admissions officer. Apparently, he persuaded the registrar to admit him to the school. I was not too surprised about that because I knew his magnetic personality. But he was also well qualified to go there. I wasn't exactly sure how his classes worked out, but he was in the premed program and training to become a doctor.

I sighed in contentment as we walked down the bustling street of New York. No matter what time of day it was, people were always crowded on the streets.

People walked briskly past us; half of them on their cell phones. They all seemed so official and businesslike. Not much of a surprise though, since we were in the business district. Nothing much had changed from how I remembered it. It was sort of weird seeing how the world could go on around you while your life took a 180 degree twist. Now that I was technically a multibillionaire/celebrity because of Chief, I definitely viewed things a bit differently.

I sighed as I thought about Chief and the business again. Although I ran away, it felt too good to be true.

I had a sinking feeling in the pit of my stomach. There was no way that Chief would not be able find me again and somehow return me to California. I wondered what he was going to do with me. Maybe he would realize that I really did not want to be a part of the company.

I felt Pierce's arm wrap around my waist as we walked down the sidewalk, and my mind was pulled away from my worried thoughts. I leaned back into his chest and took a deep breath. His cologne filled my lungs, and I calmed myself down. Looking up to him, I found him staring down at me with a gentle smile.

"Hey," his eyes were filled with worry. "What's wrong?"

"I was just thinking about Chief and the business again," I muttered quietly, hoping he didn't hear me. I didn't want to ruin a perfect day.

"Don't worry about that. Didn't Evander say he would take care of everything? No one will come here to look for you," Pierce gave me a small squeeze. I sighed. He's right. I should enjoy my time here and not be so paranoid.

"Okay," I pulled away from him to face him. We stopped walking, and other people started to go around us. "What do you want to do now?"

"How about a nice brunch. Do you know a place that's good?" He took my hands into his.

"Hmm," I paused to think. "How about Veselka?"

"Sounds good. I still don't know what restaurants are good, so I trust your expertise." He lightly tapped my nose with his index finger.

"C'mon. Let's go then!" I dragged him behind me as we made our way to the subway.

The day passed by quickly, and before we knew it, Pierce had to go his classes.

"Do you really have to go?" I asked while pulling him into a hug.

"Yeah," Pierce kissed the top of my head. He pulled back a little and cocked his eyebrow. "I thought you were supposed to support my dreams!"

"Ha-ha, very funny," I said sarcastically. After a small pause, I made my voice more serious. "You know I do."

Gently, he pressed his soft lips against mine. Too soon, he pulled away, leaving my heart beating like a hammer inside my chest. He slowly turned around and walked away.

"Bye," I sighed as I waved goodbye to him.

Running my hands through my hair, I was at loss of what to do. Suddenly, I felt my phone buzz. The screen lit up, signaling a new text.

I forgot to tell you something: I love you. Meet me at the steps in Times Square at 7 tonight. Dress nicely.

I nearly melted at the sight of that message. How can four sentences turn my legs into jelly? I smiled to myself as I quickly put my phone away into my pocket. I didn't want to text him back and disturb him in the middle of class.

I looked down at my clothes. I was wearing dark wash skinny jeans with a pair of flats, a loose top, and a scarf. Hmmm…I guess I'm going to have to change for tonight. As I looked at my watch, I noticed it was already 3. I only had three hours. Realizing it wouldn't be worth it to go home, I decided to go to Soho and spoil myself a little.

My eyes landed on the giant, white D & G Banner right above my head. My mouth started to water as I looked at the window display. Unable to resist the temptation, I pushed my way into one of the most expensive stores on the street.

"Welcome to Dolce and Gabanna. How may I help you?" a sales attendant dressed in all white greeted me. I looked around and noticed all the clothes were crisp, and white.

"Um…I'm just looking around," I said softly. I doubted I would be able to afford anything here on the racks.

The sales assistant turned her nose up at me, realizing that I wasn't actually going to buy anything. With a fake voice, she responded, "Well, have fun just looking. If you ever need my help, feel free to find me."

After she walked away, I rolled my eyes at her back. I didn't think there could be more Siri's in this world, but obviously, I was wrong.

Right as I was about to leave the store, a flash of red caught my attention. I turned around to find the most beautiful dress staring at me. I walked towards it, and let the fabric slide between my fingers.

"That's five hundred dollars," the sales lady came back. "Please be careful and don't ruin it. The dress is made out of silk chiffon."

"Mm hmm," I murmured, still mesmerized by the red dress. Suddenly, what she said hit me like a train. Wheels turning in my head, I decided to spite her. "Oh, don't worry. I won't. Do you think I could try it on?"

"Are you thinking about buying it?" she said haughtily. I couldn't believe my ears. How did this lady even get hired?

"Does it even matter? I would like to try it on," I shot back at her. Now, it was more than just trying on the dress. I needed to give that woman a wakeup call.

Sighing and rolling her eyes in front of my face, she roughly pulled the dress off the rack. Not even waiting to check if I was following her, she briskly walked towards the changing room and dropped the dress on the bench, "Here you go."

"Be careful and don't ruin it. Remember? The dress is made out of silk chiffon," I gave her a fake smile as I threw her words back at her. I had no idea what turned me into a complete bitch, because I was normally never like this, but I would like to put some of the blame onto her awful personality. She aggravated me.

I realized she quickly disappeared from the room, which left me alone with the dress. I looked at it more closely. It was one shouldered with a black belt at the waist. The bottom of the skirt looped upwards to the shoulder, so it looked like it connected to the top of the dress.

I put on the dress quickly and looked at my reflection. It was extremely flattering, and it easily looked like I was a size smaller than I really was. The red color complemented my skin tone and hair. There was no way I was letting this dress go.

I reluctantly took the dress off and willed myself to look at the price tag. My eyes nearly bulged out of my sockets. The lady was not exaggerating when she said it was $500. Well...maybe a little, but not by much. It was a grand total of $468. Groaning, I realized I couldn't possibly afford it.

Not wanting to put it back on the rack and have the lady laugh at me, I stayed in the dressing room for a bit. I took my time putting on my street clothes. When I couldn't delay any longer, I hung my head and walked out the room without the dress.

The lady was waiting for me outside, "What? Didn't fit? Too expensive?" She snarled. I guess I deserved that. I was a pretty snarky to her earlier.

Suddenly, someone called out my name. Whipping my head around, I looked for someone I recognized. There were only a couple of people in the store, but I didn't know anyone there.

"Melanie Cartwright?" the voice called out again. I turned around to face a middle aged woman with fake blond hair. It looked too light to be her original hair color and her lips were stained with dark red lipstick. She was the epitome of a rich housewife.

"Yes?" I answered cautiously. I had no idea who this woman could be.

"Oh my god! It is you!! This is amazing. It's the first time in my life that I have ever met a celebrity!" The lady gushed as she put her hand on my arm. I looked at her as if she sprouted two antennas from her head.

I looked around, not believing what was happening. The sales lady gave me a baffled look as I turned to face the housewife again. "Celebrity?" I asked.

"Of course! I saw you're picture in the paper the other day. You're Ralph McKinley's granddaughter right?"

My head finally clicked in recognition. "Oh. Right," I blushed, not liking all the attention.

"Ra-ralph McKinley's granddaughter?" I looked to my left and saw the sales woman stammer. Suddenly, she composed herself and acted civilly towards me. "So, how was that dress? I'm sure it looked gorgeous on you."

I ignored her comment as the housewife brought out a piece of paper and pen, "I know this is extremely awkward, but can I have your autograph?"

"But I'm not famous at all…" I muttered as she pushed the pen into my hands. I didn't even have an autograph for heaven's sake! Quickly, I scribbled my name down.

She squealed. Yes. The old lady squealed as I handed her the piece of paper I signed. "Thank you so much! And here is my business card. I'm actually having a small party for the high society in my upper east apartment. Do you think you can come?"

Is she being serious here? I didn't want to turn her down, afraid I was being rude. She took a business card out of her pocket and wrote down her address and the time of the party on the back of the card, "Here you go, honey. I would really love to see you again!"

"Thanks?" I was left dumbfounded when she walked happily away.

The sales lady interrupted my thoughts, "So, would you like to buy that dress? You could even wear it to her party!" Obviously, she had been listening in to our conversation.

"Um…"

"Great! I'll get it out of the fitting room for you. By the way, my name is Sarah," She kept on talking to me as we walked together to the fitting room I was in a few minutes ago.

"That lady is a regular here. Her husband is a famous doctor." She lowered her voice as if she was going to tell me a secret, "In fact, he's a neurosurgeon. That's how she's so rich." Sarah turned her nose up as she continued to gossip about the housewife. As if I cared about petty gossip.

She grabbed the dress and brought me to the cash register, "Um. I don't know…" I started to protest, but she cut me off.

"I'll even give you a treat. Don't tell anyone, but I'll take 10% off for you, not that you need to save money or anything," she blabbered on.

I had no idea if I had the money to buy the dress. I only had my wallet which was filled with about $25 dollars in cash. Definitely not enough for the dress. I didn't want to make a fool out of myself.

"So the total is now $421. Would to like to pay it using cash, credit, debit, or check?"

It was too late. Trying to calm myself I took out my wallet to check if I had any money on me. I quickly noticed the shiny card that Chief gave me when I lived in the mansion. As I took it out, I chanted "please, please work" in my mind.

She happily took the card and swiped it. We waited…

and waited…and waited. Suddenly a small beep filled the silence between us. Sarah's smile faltered and turned into confusion, "I'm sorry, Melanie. There seems to be some confusion here." She handed the card back to me silently.

I stared at the piece of plastic in her hand. She didn't have to say it for me to know. That small card was denied.

Chapter 22

Denied. My card was denied. I knew it didn't seem like a big deal on the surface, but it had a lot of meaning to me.

Why would Chief cut me off from his life? I understood that I was being childish when I ran away, but I didn't think that it would make him hate and disown me. This just didn't seem right! I needed to talk to him, but I was afraid that if I did, he would force me to return to the mansion without Pierce. I had no idea what to do.

Sarah, the sales attendant, gave me a weird look. Slowly, she asked, "Would you like to try another card?"

I looked down at my wallet again. I thought I had no cash and only a few Starbucks gift cards. Realizing I had my old credit card, I sucked in a deep breath and handed it over. Sarah swiped the card and waited only for a moment before telling me to sign the printed receipt. I tried to ignore the sinking feeling in my stomach as I saw more than

$400 taken out of my meager account. It was the one I had before Chief appeared in my life.

I didn't know why I HAD to have the dress. It was probably because of my pride and desire. As she handed me my card and dress back, I quickly took them and walked out of the store. Feeling suffocated in there, I took in a deep breath of fresh air outside and calmed myself. I would find a way to talk to Chief and figure everything out. This was just so unlike him.

He spent twenty years of his life looking for me, and I only lived with him for four months. Could he give me up so easily after he fought so hard to find me? I felt a little selfish as I thought about that. I probably wasn't as great as he imagined. Sighing, I looked at my cell phone to check the time. It was 4.

Groaning, I tried to think of something to do for the next three hours. I decided to go to Sephora to get some more makeup. I was running low on all my cosmetics. I don't know why, but walking into that store always calmed me down. The bright colors and hues of makeup always caught my attention.

I've always wanted to try out the outrageous colors, but I had no idea how or when I would wear them.

"Hello, my name is Amy. Is there anything in particular you are looking for?" a girl my age asked me. She was wearing a black t-shirt with a black smock on top. After seeing her genuine smile, I instantly took a liking towards her.

"Well, I need some more makeup," I began.

"Hence why you're in Sephora," she giggled. I mentally

slapped myself for being so stupid. "I'm just joking. I'll show you some of my favorite things!"

I looked at her face and saw the subtle yet beautiful makeup that she was wearing. I would die to learn how to do that with my face, "Thank you so much! I would actually really enjoy that."

"Great!" she led me to the foundations. "I always use this brand. It feels so light like you're not wearing anything, but the coverage is simply amazing. It also claims to be a foundation, moisturizer, powder, and concealer all in one. I don't know if it's true, but it does work." She took a bottle and held it up to my face. Shaking her head, she put it down and grabbed a lighter shade. "Perfect!"

She took me to a mirror and sat me down at her station. It was cluttered with brushes, sponges, and other tools that I had never even seen before, "I'm just going to apply a thin layer to your whole face with this sponge. If you decide to buy this, you can just use your hands to apply it." After she covered my entire face, I looked at myself. My skin certainly did seem like it was glowing more, and it did hide the imperfections on my face.

Amy ran around the store, collecting a sample of all the different things she used. She held about twenty different small containers in her hands. It was like she was a painter and my face was her canvas.

"Close your eyes. I need to put some of this eye shadow on," she said sternly. I looked into her hands and noticed that she was holding a dark gunmetal color. Giving her a skeptical look, I slowly closed my eyes. I could never pull off that color because it would just look like I had a black eye.

Knowing I was hesitant, she tried to reassure me, "It's okay. This is a tricky color, but if you know what to do, it looks absolutely amazing. Also, if you don't like it, there's always make-up remover." Laughing, I trusted her to do a good job.

Finally, after a few minutes, she was done. "Open your eyes honey." Slowly, I looked up at myself in the mirror. The color really gave depth to my eyes, and she hadn't put so much on so that it looked like I came out of a fight.

"You look absolutely stunning. Your boyfriend will love it," she smiled at me. When I didn't respond, she quickly blushed and amended herself, "I mean. If you have a boyfriend and all…"

Grinning at her, I tried to erase the awkwardness, "Don't worry, I do. Thanks so much. I think you could be a professional makeup artist or something. I would definitely pay for you to do this."

Amy beamed at me. Quickly, she dug around for her business card, "You seem like a really cool person. If you ever need any help, feel free to call me!" I stared at the card. I never met such a nice person in my life.

"Thanks again," I smiled warmly at her. Feeling like I should buy something, I picked up the foundation she put on my face.

Before I left, she called out, "Hold on! Let me get a bag so you can take home all these samples!"

I stared at the desk in front of me. There had to be at least ten samples of extremely expensive makeup. Could Amy or this store be any better?

After paying and quickly leaving the store, I made my way to Times Square. Although I was somewhat early, I still had to get changed into my dress and everything. There wasn't enough time to go home and come back to the red steps.

I made my way into the giant Forever 21. Prying myself away from the stacks of clothing, I randomly picked up a shirt to bring to the changing room.

"Hello, how many do you have?" the sales attendant eyed my hands, "Just one?" She answered the question by herself. I nodded as she led me to an empty room.

When I closed the door, I stripped of my clothes. Slipping on the red dress I bought earlier in the day, I completely ignored the shirt I picked up. I silently cursed myself when I realized that I wasn't wearing a strapless bra. A hot pink strap was left uncovered when I put the one shouldered dress on. Not knowing what else to do, I quickly stuffed the strap inside my dress. This was going to have to suffice.

Quickly, I made my way out of the dressing room and handed the waiting room attendant the shirt I didn't even bother trying on. She quirked an eyebrow at my new outfit, but didn't say anything. Laughing quietly to myself, I made my way out of the store.

Under normal circumstances, I would feel beyond self-conscious if I walked out onto the streets when I was wearing a formal dress. But since it was New York City, I felt like I blended in. There were so many different people here that it didn't even matter what you wore. That's why I loved New York so much. It just felt very homey.

I meandered around the city, taking in the different sites and sounds. I could never get tired of the city. If I could, I would definitely move into Manhattan, but the housing was so expensive. I looked down at my watch and couldn't help my heart from speeding up. It was almost time for me to meet Pierce at Times Square. Slowly, I walked back to the heart of the city and decided to wait for him on the steps.

As I was admiring the flashing lights of the billboards, two strong arms wrapped themselves around my waist. I relaxed into them once I took in a deep breath and recognized the familiar scent of Pierce's cologne. Spinning around to face him, I brought both my arms around his neck.

"Hello, I missed you," I breathed, noticing how close our faces were.

"I missed you too," he brought our lips closer for a little peck. I frowned when he pulled away again. His eyes were playful as he took a step back and looked at my new dress, "You look absolutely stunning"

"I better. You have no idea what I went through to get this," I muttered quietly under my breath. When Pierce gave me a strange look, I quickly smiled and told him it was nothing.

"Oh, really?" He didn't want to change the subject. He knew there was something wrong because of my fake smile.

"It's no big deal," I didn't want to ruin the night. "I'll tell you later."

He nodded suspiciously at my response, but thankfully dropped the subject. Instead, he chose to talk about the big surprise for the date, "So do you have any guesses at what we're doing tonight?"

"Um," I thought about why he told me to dress up. "A

fancy dinner?" He shook his head. "A party?" He shook his head again. I honestly had no idea.

When Pierce realized I didn't have any more guesses, he finally decided to fill me in, "We're going to see a play."

"Really?" shrieking, I saw Pierce cringe slightly from my loud voice.

"Yup," he popped the 'p' as he answered me. "It's called Next to Normal."

Raising my eyebrows, I looked at him skeptically, "I've never heard of that one." Not trying to be a brat or anything, my excitement level dropped significantly. I was expecting it to be something like West Side Story or another famous play.

"Don't give me that look," Pierce groaned. "I've only heard good reviews about it."

I wiped the disappointed look off my face. Instantly feeling guilty, I tried to raise my excitement level again, "Really? I can't wait to see it!"

Pierce laughed at my horrible acting skills, "Fine, but I think it's going to be a great show."

I playfully slapped his arm as we walked towards the theater, "We'll see about that."

About three later, I walked out with my head downcast. Pierce on the other hand, was happily skipping beside me whilst yelling out, "I told you so!"

Needless to say, the show was hands down amazing. The first half hour was extremely boring and confusing, but when I kept on watching, I was hooked. The music was incredibly catchy, and the storyline was beyond moving. I even started to tear up at the end. Not knowing that I would be crying because of that show, I didn't bring any tissues. I just hid my face from Pierce and kept on walking.

"When will you stop being such a baby and admit that you liked it?" Pierce poked me in the ribs as we walked back to the steps Times Square.

Blushing, I finally looked up to him, "Fine, I admit it. Aaron Tveit is a beast."

Pierce looked shocked for a moment and raised his eyebrows at me, "I told you to admit that the show was good, not that the guy in it was hot."

Smirking slightly, I continued talking about my new idol, "Oh whatever. I was watching him the whole time anyways. He is so freaking gorgeous and has such a sexy voice. When he first came out with no shirt on, I almost fainted." I nearly moaned when I thought about the stud, but I bit my lip and held it back. I'm sure Pierce would have appreciated it if I was lusting after another guy...not.

Pierce just let out a small humph, and didn't respond to what I said. I laughed internally when I realized I just crushed his ego. After my mini inner laughing fit died down, I felt a tiny bit guilty. I walked up to Pierce and pulled him into a hug.

He stiffened, and I realized I had to try harder to restore his ego, "Don't worry, Pierce. He has nothing on you, though. I prefer doctors over actors because doctors are so smart and skilled. Plus, I think you may be more ripped than Aaron was." I giggled to myself as I slowly brought one hand down to trace his abs.

"You're such a tease," he looked angry for a second before the sides of his lips were pulled slightly upwards.

"You know you love me anyways," I grinned happily as I stood on my tiptoes to give him a peck on the cheeks.

"Yeah, can't deny that one," he said as he pulled me into a hug and kissed the top of my head.

"Anyways, have anything else planned right now?" I mumbled into his chest.

Pulling away a little, he still held my waist with both his hands, "Nope, not really. Do you have something in mind?"

I smiled as my stomach growled angrily at me, "Well, since I didn't really have dinner yet, I guess we can have a midnight snack?"

Pierce let out a small laugh as I looked at him in confusion, "You're such a little pig."

My mouth dropped at his comment. Raising one eyebrow, I challenged him, "You do know that normal boyfriends are NEVER supposed to say that to their girlfriends?"

"So what? You're different than those girls who care too much about their weight. I don't like holding a girl who's like a stick and can break at any time. I like healthy, beautiful girls like you," he responded nonchalantly. "Plus, I'm not a normal boyfriend." He stressed the word 'normal.'

I rolled my eyes at the last part, but my heart melted at what he said earlier. How did I find such a perfect guy?

Not knowing how to respond to his comment, I blushed and pulled on his arm instead, "Come on. I know the perfect place."

After nearly an hour of walking around in circles, we were back at the steps in Times Square again.

"Where is the place you're always rambling about? Is

it even real?" Pierce raised his eyebrows at me, obviously thinking I was delusional.

I sighed and closed my eyes. I knew this place was real...I just didn't know exactly where it was.

Shivering, I shifted from one foot to another. Even though it was the summer, the cold air was slowly seeping its way through my thin dress.

Pierce sighed as he took out his cell phone to check the time. As he pressed a button, the screen glowed and lit up his face. It was well past midnight now, but no one could tell because there was still a throng of people on the streets. The lights from billboards emitted so much light that it looked like it was daytime.

"It's so late already...maybe we should just give up," he suggested gently.

"NO!" I yelled too loudly. A group of tourists looked over, but quickly lost interest. "I swear it's on the right side of this street. Then, all we have to do is walk north for a little bit."

He looked uncertainly towards the dark street. There weren't as many flashing signs, and there certainly weren't many people.

"Come on," I pulled on his arm again, dragging him towards where I thought the food cart was. "I promise it will be worth it."

I imagined the delicious food in my mouth. I was introduced to the food cart last year, but I couldn't remember exactly where it was. I just remembered that the food and white sauce was delicious. In fact, I think that this place was quite famous for its white sauce. Regular customers deemed it as "crack sauce" since it was so addicting.

"Fine. This is the last time we're looking for it though. If we can't find it, we'll come back tomorrow. It's getting really late," Pierce warned me as I nodded quickly. I knew this was the way. It had to be.

After ten minutes of walking, I almost lost all hope. But when I saw the familiar steam coming from the cart, I recognized the intersection we were at. "THERE IT IS!!" I screamed at I pulled him even harder.

There was a long line that stretched down the street, even thought it was already one in the morning. We stood at the end of the line, patiently waiting for the crack sauce and food.

"Two combo platters please," I barely looked at the guy who was taking our orders. Not able to look away from the amazing food in front of my, my mouth started to water. Right as my stomach growled, two steaming plates of heaven were thrown in my direction. Pierce quickly paid for them as I ran to the side of the cart and picked up a bottle with white sauce in it.

I literally drowned my plate so you couldn't see any of the food left. Then, I took Pierce's and did the same to his.

"Hey!" He screamed in protest as he realized what I was doing, "What if I don't like this white thing?" Looking at disgust towards his plate, he crinkled his face.

"Don't worry. I'm doing you a favor here," I reassured him while laughing.

"Mm hmm," he mumbled as he hesitantly took a bite. I saw his expression change from skepticism to shock to enjoyment. I smiled proudly as we walked towards a train. I took a bite and moaned at the deliciousness.

"I'm alive, I'm alive, and I'm so alive!" I sang happily at

the top of my lungs, trying to sing a song from the musical we just watched.

"You will never be as good as a singer as Aaron Tve-it," Pierce smirked at me, as I hit him upside the head. Not even his taunting could ruin the happiness that ran through my veins right then.

Chapter 23

It'd been a few blissful months since I had left the mansion. Life had been pretty good since both Pierce and I left for New York, but it was a whole different story for Blake. It'd been increasingly hard for him, and the pressure put on him by the newspapers and critics really got to him. At times when he was really stressed out, he would call Pierce and me.

I sighed as I flipped through the pages of Us Weekly. I was alone in the house right now because Mom was at the bakery and Pierce was at school. Lying on my stomach on top of my bed, my heart froze when my eyes landed on one page.

There he was with his head tilted back and mouth wide open, as if he was in the middle of a big laugh. His hands were holding onto Siri's. I could tell it was her because of her short, blond curly hair.

Blake was in some deep shit.

I growled as I quickly reached for my phone. Before I could find his name in my contact book, the devil himself called me.

"What the hell??" I screamed at him, skipping all the greetings.

"I can explain. It's not what it looks like," he began slowly.

"Save it, Blake. I don't really want to hear it," I snapped angrily.

"But you need to hear my side of the story," he tried to convince me to listen.

I huffed, "Fine. It better be a damn good excuse."

"Well," he began, pausing a little. "She set me up."

Looking at the picture again, I knew it was a candid shot. There was no way Siri could set him up so it looked like he was laughing like that. Threateningly, I warned him, "Don't lie to me."

The other side of the line fell silent for another moment. I sighed heavily as I realized Blake was lying to me.

"Okay, so I went to the beach once with her," Blake confessed. I sucked in a breath not believing my ears.

"Blake! What's wrong with you?" I screamed at him accusingly.

"I'm sorry, Melanie. But I was so stressed and lonely. She's always in the mansion with me, so she makes me feel less alone. I'm not going to lie when I say that I felt less stressed out after going on that date with her." I shook my head in disbelief. He was the one who said that he didn't like Siri. I thought we all agreed she was a gold digger.

"I can't believe what you are saying right now. If you felt lonely, you could've called me or Pierce! And remember, she and her dad are manipulative people!" I tried to knock some sense into Blake.

"Melanie! Whenever I try calling you or Pierce, you two are always together. I feel like you guys don't understand me at all sometimes. You guys always have each other, and it's not like you are completely by my side supporting me," Blake snapped back defensively.

"Siri is not supporting you at all. She's using you," I fired back at him.

"At least she's doing a better job at making me feel better than you are."

I stared angrily at the phone. He did NOT just say that. That was a low blow, and he knew it. After a minute of silence, Blake spoke up again in a softer voice, "I'm sorry, Melanie. I didn't mean that."

"Whatever," I knew he was sorry, but I couldn't let go of what he said earlier.

"Please come back. I need you," he pleaded me.

I opened my eyes in shock. I didn't expect him to say that at all, "Um…Blake? I'm with Pierce right now." I mumbled awkwardly.

"You're a stupid butt," Blake almost laughed into the phone. Wow, he had mood swings like a girl during PMS. "I meant you and Pierce. I need my friends to help me through this tough time. The stress is just getting worse and worse."

My heart almost broke at his soft and tight voice. It was like he was trying not to cry, "Blake, I don't know if we can come back!" I sighed desperately.

"Why not? It can just be for a short time or something. You don't have to move back in!"

I sucked in a breath. No matter how much I wanted to comfort Blake, I knew I couldn't go back to the mansion, "I can't, Blake. I made a deal with Evander. I can't go anywhere near the mansion anymore."

"Don't worry! I can take care of that!" Blake promised in earnest. However, it felt like he didn't know how serious Evander was when he said he "hoped to never see me again." I sighed, not knowing what else to say to Blake.

"You know what would be simpler? You and Pierce come back and take the company from me. I don't want to run it anymore," he sounded depressed.

"We can't do that, Blake. Deep down, you know you want to keep the company. You just have to fight through all the pressure," I tried to reassure him.

"But how can I fight it? Everyone hates me now! RM Productions has been on a downwards trend since I took over!" Once again, he rendered me speechless. I had no idea how to run a company, so my advice was basically useless to him.

I heard the front door open. Looking at the time, I realized it had to be Pierce. My heart soared as I realized Pierce could give him better advice than I could, "Hold on for a moment." I did a mad dash down the stairs and threw the phone into Pierce's surprised face.

"It's Blake," I muttered quietly, so Blake couldn't hear me from the other side of the line.

Pierce put his backpack down on the kitchen chair and took the phone from me. I walked back upstairs to give them more privacy. I didn't understand business jargon anyways. Looking down onto my bed, the picture of Blake was still open on my bed. Sighing, I flipped to the next page.

There he was again, and I gasped at the sight of him. I took in the dark bags under his eyes, the hollow look of his face, and the way his shoulders were hunched over. This was not the confident Blake I knew. He looked tired and weak in the picture. The caption claimed that he was not fit to be the CEO of RM Productions, and that he was being distracted by his fling with a blonde headed girl (Siri, of course).

I rubbed my face with both my hands. I desperately wanted to help him, but I had no idea how. I don't know how long I sat on my bed, but after a while I felt hands rubbing circles on my back.

I looked up at Pierce's worry filled eyes, "Are you okay?"

"I'm just worried about Blake! Look at him!" I tossed the magazine at him. The picture of the weak Blake was open, and I heard Pierce suck in a breath just like I had when I first saw the picture.

"I know, baby. Me too." He continued to soothe my worry. "I talked to him on the phone and gave him some advice. I think he might be better soon."

"You sure?" I asked, as I looked into his eyes, searching for the truth.

"Yeah, I'm sure. Blake is a tough guy, and can make it through this." He reassured me.

"Why isn't Chief helping at all? It's like he's just watching his company fall to pieces!" I muttered angrily. It was already a miracle I hadn't heard from him since leaving the mansion. I had thought that running away to New York would be a futile idea, but Chief had never stopped me yet, and it'd been a few months! I had an uneasy feeling at the pit of my stomach that something wasn't quite right.

"Maybe he's taking a step back and letting us run the scene for a while?" Pierce mused.

"And why would he do that?" I asked him in confusion.

"Maybe he's waiting for us to mess up and come crawling back to him?" he muttered, unable to come up with a better explanation.

"Mm hmm, sure," I muttered unbelievingly. However, I couldn't come up with a better idea. It's not like I would call him voluntarily. Not because I didn't like him or anything, but because I was scared that he would force me to go back. Or that Evander would find out and kill me somehow. Okay. I was overreacting…but still. Evander did seem capable of doing something like that…

A few weeks after Blake's worrisome phone call, it seemed like he was doing a lot better. There were fewer articles about his incompetency, and more articles praising him about how well he was doing. Needless to say, Pierce and I let out a big sigh of relief.

As we sat in the kitchen eating lunch on a lazy Saturday afternoon, a flurry of red hair burst through the kitchen door. The figure hunched over with her hands on her knees struggling to catch her breath.

"Jessica, nice you see you here…" Pierce commented without seeming too surprised. He had seen a lot of Jessica since I arrived back in New York and was used to her constant appearance. Jessica, however, was still not used to him being around and openly gawked at his gorgeous face.

"Earth to Jessica!!" I screamed out loud in her ear. Quickly, she shook her head to get her mind out of the daze. She opened her mouth to say something but closed it again after nothing came out. After repeating his several times like a fish, I snapped a few times in front of her face.

"What's up? Why did you come running over here?" I watched as she tried to gather her thoughts. A thin layer of sweat glistened over her forehead as she pulled out a chair to sit down across from me and Pierce. Her chest rose and fell while she caught her breath. Obviously, she sprinted over here for a reason. She's not the kind of person who would just run for fun.

"Did..." she panted between her breaths, "you...see... the news?"

"No..." I eyed her suspiciously, "What's the big deal? You could have just called me to turn on the TV or something instead of running over here."

She shot me a death glare, "Oh, I see. You don't want me here."

"NO!!" I held my palms out in front of me and shook them, "Of course not! It's just weird to see you running over here just to tell me to watch the news."

She sighed loudly, obviously not wanting to talk about it anymore. In a defeated tone, she muttered, "Just turn on the freaking TV."

I gave Pierce a look as he walked to get the remote. We could see into the family room from the kitchen, so it was pretty easy to watch TV while we were eating. With a flick of the wrist, he picked up the remote and turned on the TV. An ad for the Slap Chop filled up the screen.

"So..." I smiled at Jessica, "You came running here to tell me to buy a Slap Chop?"

"Hi, it's Vince with the Slap Chop. You're going to

be in a great mood all day because you'll be slapping your troubles away with the Slap Chop!" the man from the infomercial sang out cheerfully.

"Shut up," Jessica humphed, "You know what I mean… Just watch the news after this stupid commercial!!"

Smiling and shaking my head, I turned my attention back to the TV. During our moment of silence, Vince from the commercial blurted out, "Watch this! You're going to love my nuts."

"You have got to be kidding me," Pierce mumbled under his breath. He was obviously not finding this funny.

Jessica and I, on the other hand, were having a field day. We had watched the Slap Chop Remix on YouTube a million times about a year ago, and it brought back the memory of the video. Laughing to the verge of tears, we just clutched out stomachs while Pierce stared at us like we were idiots.

"Don't judge," I managed to gasp in between my laughs. My abs were burning like I had just worked out and my cheeks were cramping from the smile on my face.

"Sure," Pierce responded uncertainly. Finally, the long infomercial was over.

"Are you sure there's news on right now?" I asked skeptically as the TV channel began to broadcast a golf game.

Pierce raised his eyebrow at Jessica, "So…this is the breaking news? Although it is surprising how Rory McIlroy is in the lead. Isn't he our age and the youngest player there?" All his attention was directed to the tournament now. No offense, but I didn't, and still don't, understand what was so special about golf. It's basically people swinging metal rods, hitting mini white balls, and walking around on a green field.

"No! Wait! I know. Hold on," Jessica ran out of the kitchen and upstairs like she owned this house. A second later, I heard her heavy footsteps pounding back down the stairs. "I'm back!" She gasped out of breath once again. In one hand, she was carrying my laptop. With the other, she was clutching her side.

"You need to exercise more, missy!" I joked as I snatched my laptop out of her hands. Quickly opening it, I waited for the screen to light up so I could type in my password. When I got in, Jessica stole the laptop back.

"Okay. So...I was flipping through the channels and saw an ad or news brief or whatever for Access Hollywood," she spoke quickly as she opened up Firefox. Going to the URL bar, she typed in the address of the gossipy news show. "And guess who the topic of one of the stories was?"

I gasped at her, "Please don't tell me this has to do with Blake." I had told Jessie all about Blake, the other guys, Siri, and Evander. She knew everything about what happened in the mansion and my fear of Evander.

"Ding! Ding! Ding!" Jessica tried to sound like a bell ringing, signaling I had won an award. "Bingo! And they talked about someone else in the story too."

"Let me guess...the spawn of Satan?" I asked sarcastically. Jessica knew who I was talking about.

"How are you so smart?" she asked jokingly as she clicked on something. It seemed like she was waiting for something to load. Suddenly, she flipped the computer around so that the screen was facing me. "Take a look for yourself!"

I gasped at the screen. There was the picture of Blake and Siri at the beach. I had seen that before in another magazine. But there was a new one next to it that I haven't seen before. The two of them were sitting at the dinner table at the mansion eating a meal. It looked almost romantic, the way they were leaning in towards each other. The most shocking thing, however, was the headline.

Confirmed: Blake Miller and Siri Montgomery a Happy Couple

As I frantically scrolled down to the bottom of the page, I realized that there was a video. Hesitantly, I clicked on the little triangle to play it, not knowing what to expect.

"So tell me," the face of an interviewer filled up the screen. "Is it true or not that you are going out with one of the most eligible bachelors?"

A sound worse than nails on a chalkboard came out of the speakers. We could hear Siri before the camera switched over to her face.

"Oh! You mean Blake?" Giggle. "Let's just say he's not on the market anymore. The two of us are pretty close."

The interview was cut short as it went back to the host of the show, "And there you have it, America! This is Access Hollywood. Watch us weeknights at seven." The screen went black as the video finished.

I sat there in my seat trembling with anger. I could kill Siri right now! "That little…"

"Don't finish that sentence," Pierce quickly cut in. He never enjoyed hearing me swear, even though he had quite the sailor mouth himself. What a hypocrite.

"Fine. But at least you know what I was going to say," I

harrumphed in my seat. Crossing my arms over my chest, I stared at him with a hard glare.

"What?" Pierce looked at me innocently. "I'm not the one going out with Siri…"

I screamed out in frustration, "How can you even joke about that?!?"

"Come on, Mel!" Pierce sighed and calmly took my hand into his. "Have a little faith in Blake! Do you not trust him at all? Do you trust that gossip show and Siri more than Blake?"

I stared at Piece with wide eyes. Who knew he could be so sensible? Now I knew why Chief always thought he would be a great CEO of a company. "Pierce, you're right. Thanks for talking some sense into me."

"You guys should call Blake to see if he's alright. Also, you can ask him if it is true," Jessica's voice piped up from behind me. I had forgotten she was there.

"Right," I muttered as I pulled my hands from Pierce's and reached in my pocket to grab my cell phone. After finding Blake's number, I pressed call and put it on speakerphone. I had a sense of déjà vu. How many times have I done this before? Too many -- that's for sure.

I furrowed my eyebrows in worry when it went to voicemail after five rings. "Let me try again," I mumbled as I pressed the green button again. Still, no one picked up. That's strange. He always picked up on the first time I called him.

"He's probably off doing something important. After all, he is the CEO of RM Productions…" Jessica thought, trying to reassure me. But for some odd reason, I had a very bad feeling in the pit of my stomach.

"Yeah, Jessica has a point," Pierce looked at Jessie. Surprisingly, I saw her mouth hang open. I guess it was because Pierce and my best friend rarely agreed on anything. I tried to hide my smile.

"Okay, fine," I couldn't help but smirk a bit. Changing the subject I asked, "Anyways, what are you two doing today?"

Jessica looked everywhere but my eyes. When I glanced at her neck, I saw the slightest shade of pink. Aww, she was blushing! Guiltily, she muttered, "I'm sorry. I know I promised I would hang out with you today, but I'm actually meeting someone."

I stared at her with wide eyes as she looked at the floor, "Jessica van Hudson. Are you going out...on a date?" She never went out with any guys. It wasn't because no one liked her. In fact, it was actually quite the opposite. All guys drooled over her, but she was afraid of commitment because of her parent's relationship or something. That was why she only did one night stands...not that I really approved of her ways.

"Yeah," she muttered and ran out the door before I could say anything more. "That's unusual," Pierce looked at the door she just ran out of. "She is usually so talkative, it's annoying! This guy is making her quiet. I think I like him already."

I laughed along with him. Turning to me, he pulled me into a hug. "Sorry, my dear. I must go now. I have a meeting with my professor, but I should be back in about two hours." He pecked me on the lips.

"Okay, I'll see you soon!" I gave him a final squeeze before he left. Once again, I was in this house alone. With

Pierce and Jessica gone, my worries about Blake came rushing back.

The interview was only of Siri. Why wasn't Blake with her? Maybe it's really not true, and Siri was saying that to make it look like they were an actual couple. She wanted the company, after all. I think. She and her father were definitely up to something.

Sighing, I took my phone out to call Blake again. Still no answer. The uneasiness took over my body as my stomach began to churn. With shaky hands, I decided to call Chief. Although he may drag me back to the mansion, I needed to do this to find Blake. I laughed at myself for overreacting, but before I could chicken out, I dialed in Chief's number and held my breath as I heard the rings. I waited.

And waited.

"Hello, this is Ralph McKinley. I am not here ri…" I hung up my phone. Now Chief isn't picking up his phone? I laid my phone on the table and anxiously began to pace the room.

I was overreacting. Nothing was wrong. You're thinking too much. I chanted to myself over and over again. I don't know how long I did that.

The shrill ring of my cell phone echoed throughout the silent house and I jumped up a foot in surprise. Running towards it, I looked at the caller ID. Karter?

"Hello?" I asked unsurely, "Karter?"

"Thank god you picked up, Melanie! And who else would it be?" I laughed. I guess I wasn't the only one freaking out about people not answering their phones. My heart beat slowed when I heard Karter's voice again. It had been way too long.

"Karter! I've missed you."

"Yeah, yeah," he muttered dismissively. Then, he seemed to remember why he called. "Mel, have you talked to Blake in the past few days?"

My heart sped up again as I asked suspiciously, "No, why?"

"Oh, shit. This is not good," I could imagine him running his hands through his hair in worry.

"WHY?!?" I screamed, dying to know what's wrong.

"Mel," Karter paused for a moment. "Blake has gone missing."

Chapter 24

My heart stopped. What did they do to Blake? When I finally found my voice again, I screamed, "WHAT?!!?!"

"Blake. Is. Gone." Karter emphasized each word.

Holy shit. I repeated in my head a million times. My heart restarted itself and was now racing a mile a minute. This was not happening.

"Melanie! Are you still here?" Karter asked in a worried tone. I guess he was talking to me, but nothing was registering in my mind.

"Yeah, sorry. It's just…" I paused. "Wait. How do you know?" I asked skeptically. If this was a prank, Karter would not live to see tomorrow.

"I'm actually at the mansion right now for a visit. But when I came back, everyone was gone. I'm standing in my room right now, and I'm a little freaked out."

"Hold up. EVERYONE is gone…even Chief?" I asked, confused.

"Yeah. I know Chief is in the Caribbean right now to celebrate his retirement…at least that's what Evander told me. It makes sense, though, because he hasn't been picking up his phone or anything," Karter explained. "But Blake, Siri, and Evander are all not here."

I heard a door slam on his side of the phone. "That's really weird," I panicked. "Do you think Evander took Blake and killed him?!?"

Karter let out a hearty laugh. "Breathe a little, Mel. Don't worry. Even though the Montgomery family seems a little shady, I doubt they will kill anyone!" I couldn't help but smile at his answer. So we all thought that the duo was creepy.

"Okay, let's say that Blake wasn't kidnapped. Where would he run to? And why would he leave the mansion without a trace?" I wondered out loud.

I heard Karter opening another door. "No need to worry about the kidnapping theory. I doubt a kidnapper would let their hostage pack half of their closet!"

"So Blake wasn't kidnapped," I breathed a sigh of relief. "But that barely helps anything! Where is Blake right now?"

"Hmm…" Karter thought for a moment. "I have no idea."

Suddenly, my doorbell rang.

"Was that the doorbell?" Karter asked.

"Yeah," I stood up from my chair with the phone. "Hold on a second. Pierce probably forgot to take the key when he left the house. I'll open the door for him." I quickly put the phone down on the table and ran to the door. I had to tell Pierce the news about Blake.

Panting, I opened the door and began to speak in a rushed voice, "Pierce! Awful news!! Blake is…" I looked up and felt my eyes widen.

Oh. My. God.

"BLAKE!!" I screamed as I launched myself at him and caused him to drop his luggage. The worry that I felt a minute ago completely melted away as he gave me a friendly hug back. I pulled back a little as anger filled me.

"You stupid man!!" I hit his chest with my fist as I said each word. "Why didn't you call? You had me worried sick!!"

"I'm sorry, Mel!" Blake defended himself from my blows. "I saw your missed calls, and right when I was going to call you, my phone died."

Of course. How convenient. As I stood there, I realized that Karter was still waiting for me on the phone!! "Oh! Right!" I ran into the house, leaving behind a confused Blake.

I snatched up the phone from the table and squealed into the phone, "Karter! You will never guess what just happened!!" The excitement bubbling up inside me was about to burst.

"Let me guess," Karter said smoothly. "Blake just magically appeared on your front doorstep looking like a lost puppy." How did he already know what happened? The excitement in me evaporated, as I sat staring at the phone dejectedly. I wanted to surprise him with the good news!

Scowling, I grumbled, "How did you know?"

"Oh, I don't know…" Karter mused sarcastically. "Maybe because I heard you scream 'Blake' at the top of your lungs a minute ago." He did a poor imitation of my voice. "I just assumed he was at your door. It wasn't that hard to figure out."

"Oh," I sighed in defeat. "Was I really that loud?" I saw Blake drag his two suitcases into the kitchen.

"Yeah, you almost made me deaf," Blake joked as he overheard the conversation. I rolled my eyes at him and put Karter on speakerphone.

"Karter," Blake yelled from where he was standing so Karter could hear him. "Sorry for worrying you!"

"Mm hmm," Karter drew out, "That sounded so sincere."

"Whatever," there was a silence. Finally, Karter spoke up again. "So going to live with Mel now?"

"Uh," Blake looked at me uncertainly with an embarrassed look. He was probably ashamed that he suddenly had to crash at my house without any advance warning. I gave him a reassuring smile and a small nod. Of course I would let him stay here if he needed to. My mother loved company, so she should be fine with it too.

"Yeah, I think I am." Blake answered Karter's question.

"I'm jealous!" Karter huffed. "I don't think it's fair how you guys get to hang out without me. But I guess that's okay because you guys won't be able to have that much fun when I'm not there. I'm the one that brings the party."

"Well, nothing is stopping you from coming over, too." I mumbled sarcastically. Although I do love Karter, his large ego sometimes made me really annoyed.

"Thanks for the invite! I guess I'll have to go over to your house now," he laughed. I rolled my eyes at his silliness. "I'm not kidding."

"Yeah, sure. Whatever you say."

"Fine," Karter grumbled. "You don't have to believe me. But don't blame me when I show up at your door and you die from a heart attack because you're so surprised."

I paused, not knowing what to say. "Wait. So you're serious?" I never knew when to treat him seriously or not.

"Yeah, I promise. I had so many different gigs over here that I have saved enough money to buy a plane ticket!" Karter seemed very proud of himself. I smiled at his success as a musician and couldn't help but feel proud of him, too.

"I'm going to the airport now and seeing if I can get on a plane today on standby. I'll see you guys in a few hours!" Without waiting for a response, he hung up the phone. Of course he would do that. He was probably the most spontaneous person I knew. When he wanted something, he'd do anything to get it.

I stared at the phone in shock. He never failed to surprise me. Apparently, Blake was caught off guard by Karter's reaction, too.

"Well, that's a surprise," he mumbled.

"Not as much of a surprise as you showing up here!" I put my arms on my hips and leaned on one leg. "Why are you here? Why did you leave the mansion?"

"I quit."

"What?" I asked, completely lost and confused.

"I quit," Blake reiterated.

I let out a sigh of annoyance. I was too impatient to play his games. "Quit what?"

"My job."

I gawked at him, "You mean…"

"I'm not the CEO of RM Productions anymore," he stated calmly and slowly, as if he was talking to a little kid.

"What?" I was still dumbfounded.

He rolled his eyes and threw up his hands in frustration, "How many times do I have to say it?!?! I QUIT!"

"But...but...but..."

"BUT WHAT?!" Blake roared. I took a step back, scared of his reaction.

"What's going to happen to the company?" I asked when I finally wrapped my head around what he was trying to say. I couldn't believe he just quit!

Blake looked down in shame, "The only person I told my decision to was Evander and Chief. But Chief never picked up his phone, so I just left him a voicemail. Evander said it was okay and that he would handle everything."

"HOLD UP!" I screamed in disbelief. "You left EVANDER, the conniving father, in charge of the company??"

"Uh...yeah?" Blake said uncertainly. Now it was my turn to throw my hands up in the air.

"You stupid idiot! Didn't we all agree that the Montgomery duo were bad people?"

Something finally clicked in Blake's tiny brain, "Oh no."

"That's all you have to say?"

"Don't worry. I'll fix this, I promise. I didn't actually tell anyone else about this, so it won't be too hard to fix. The press won't know a thing about what is going on. And I will make sure Evander won't be in charge of anything."

Blake dug through his suitcase. After trashing the family room and kitchen with the contents of his suitcase, he finally found his cell phone charger. He ran towards an outlet, and his phone was revived in a matter of moments.

A few seconds passed before he was on the phone with someone.

"Hello, this is Blake Miller…" Pause. "I'm fine. What about you?" He waited for the person to respond. "That's good. Um, listen. I'm leaving for a while, so I need you to step up to the plate and be the CEO for a while."

I raised my eyebrow at Blake. Who was he calling?

"I'm not sure. I'm going to be gone indefinitely. Until I get back, you're running the business. Got it? Oh, and don't let a man named Evander push you around or make any big decisions for the company."

I laughed out loud when Blake said the last sentence. I gave up eavesdropping and plopped myself down on the couch in the family room. Reaching for the remote, I turned on the television and flipped through the channels.

About half an hour later, Blake finally finished his phone call and sat down next to me. "Got it all sorted out?" I asked, facing him.

"Yup!" Blake popped the 'p' very loudly. Obviously, he was in a very good mood now that he took care of all his business.

"Who was that?"

"The vice president of the company. He was one of the few people that actually supported me when the newspapers tore down my confidence. I completely trust him, and I can't think of a better person to take over the business. And I don't think he found it too disappointed that he had to become the CEO." Blake flashed a toothy grin at me. If he was this happy about quitting his job, he must have really hated being the successor. I had no idea he would be this relieved to get rid of his job.

"Well, congrats…I guess?" I smiled at him.

"Yes. Thank you!" He pulled me into a hug again. Right as we separated, I heard the front door open.

Blake looked at me as we shared an evil smirk, "You thinking what I'm thinking?"

"Yup," I nodded as we agreed to scare Pierce. This was going to be quite amusing.

I rubbed my hands in anticipation. I couldn't wait to see the shocked look on Pierce's face when Blake and I scared the wits out of him.

Happily, I skipped towards where Pierce was as I greeted him, "Pierce! You're back!!" I got up on my tiptoes and gave him a peck on the cheek.

"You seem like you're in a good mood," Pierce smiled as he took my hand and pulled me into the kitchen with him.

"I'm just glad to see you again!"

"Wait," he stopped walking suddenly, and I plowed into his back.

Slowly, he bent down and picked something up off the floor. Using the distraction to its full advantage, I turned to Blake and shot him a questioning look. We hadn't come up with and exact plan to scare Pierce, so we were improvising on the spot. Frantically, he waved his arms around like he was a zombie and mouthed the word boo. I nodded. He wanted me to stall a little and then bring Pierce to the family room where Blake would jump out and scare him.

As I turned quickly to face Pierce again before he stood up, I froze. Between his two fingers, he held a piece of fabric with anchors on it. "Would you care to explain why the hell there is a pair of boxers in your kitchen?? They're not even mine!"

I blushed and turned a deep shade of red. Stupid Blake! He probably accidentally threw them in here when he tore his suitcase apart to find his cell phone charger.

I looked up at Pierce to see him glaring accusingly at me. Uh oh. This was not good. Scared stiff at Pierce's expression, I decided to ruin Blake's plan of scaring Pierce.

"YOU ARE SO DEAD!!" I screamed over Pierce's shoulder at Blake. Pierce shot me a strange look as if he should be the one saying that to me. Whoops. I guess he thought I was talking to him because he had no idea Blake was here.

Before he could ask or say anything, Blake spoke out from behind Pierce.

"Pierce. Is someone jealous?" Blake cooed. "That's right. Mel and I just had mind blowing sex on the kitchen table."

I immediately blushed at his comment and was at loss for words. This was definitely not the way Blake would normally act. Pierce spun around so fast that one moment, he was glaring angrily at me and the next he had Blake in a headlock.

"Blake!! You're an idiot. I can't believe you're here." Pierce greeted him and squeezed Blake's neck even harder. "And you totally deserve this for nearly giving me a heart attack."

Pierce proceeded in giving him a noogie. Blake squirmed around, trying to get out of Pierce's death grip.

"I guess that's one way to scare him," Blake said

He winked at me, but I was still slightly pink from his earlier comment. Shaking my head, I gave him a small smile.

"So, Blake..." Pierce broke the silence. "What are you doing here in New York?"

"I quit!" Blake answered excitedly. He gave Pierce the same response as he gave me when I had first asked him.

"WHAT?!?!?" I had a sense of deja vu and shook my head in amusement.

"You know what? I'm not going to do this again," we looked at Blake in confusion.

"Do what?" Pierce asked the question on both our minds.

"Explaining why I or how I quit. I'm not going to do it three times!"

"Three times?" I asked. "The first time was to me. This would only be your second time..."

Blake scoffed at me as if I was missing an obvious fact. "Remember? Karter?"

"Oh, right!!" I slapped my forehead.

"What?" Pierce was still lost and confused in our conversation.

Suddenly, the three of our phones beeped simultaneously. I looked down at my and saw that I had an unread text. It was from Karter.

Just boarded the plane, suckers!! I'm expecting a limo at LaGuardia in about six hours.

Blake and I looked up as we finished reading and shared a smile. Pierce, on the other hand, reread the same two sentences over and over.

Finally he smiled widely and asked, "Karter is coming?"

"Yup!!" I laughed at his excited expression. "It'll be a reunion! I haven't seen the three of you guys together in months!! I am so excited!"

The two guys nodded their heads in agreement as we anxiously waited for Karter's plane to land.

Seven hours later, I sat impatiently in the driver's seat of my mother's minivan. What could be taking the three guys so long? I stared at the entrance to the airport.

Finally, I saw three unruly boys fight each other through the door. The three of them couldn't all fit through at a time, but they still tried to anyways. I laughed as I saw them clambered on top of each other.

"Boys! Calm yourselves!" I shrieked happily through the open window. We were all running on a high because we were together again. I had forgotten how much I had missed everyone.

"BUT I CALLED SHOTGUN!!" Blake yelled.

"BUT SHE'S MY GIRLFRIEND!! I obviously should sit next to her," Pierce argued as he pulled Blake back from the door. Blake landed with a thud on the ground as people began to stare.

"Shut up you guys!" Karter's voice boomed, rendering the other two silent. "I wanted a limo. But you came here in a crappy minivan. I think I deserve shotgun as compensation."

Karter quickly climbed into the backseat of the car and did an ungraceful somersault over the front seat so he landed in the passenger seat. In all my years of living, I had NEVER seen anyone do that. Pierce and Blake stared at him with daggers in their eyes. Reluctantly, they climbed into the back seat.

"Haha!" Karter's laugh resonated through the car. "Losers!"

Laughing, I threw the car into drive and sped away to

my little house. The hour drive was unbearable. Although Karter sat in the front seat, he managed to start almost all the arguments in the car. There were countless times where we almost crashed because they were such a distraction. It was like driving a bunch of two year olds around. Let me tell you...it was NOT fun.

Finally, the torture was over when I pulled up to the house. I sighed in relief and immediately got out of the stifling car. I thought that the mansion was way too big for five people, but now I realized that you could not keep the guys near each other for more than an hour. The house would be demolished if it was any smaller. I gulped as I thought about the fate of my own house.

"Nice home," Karter smirked at me. "It has been a while since I was last here."

I furrowed my eyebrows in confusion. He was here before? I mentally slapped myself as I remembered. Of course! He was here with Evander when I found out I was Ralph McKinley's granddaughter. It felt like so long ago, and so many thing had changed since then.

"I remember!" I smiled widely. "That was a while back."

"I know!" he shook his head in disbelief. "It has been half a year already!"

I led the way into the house. As we walked in, Mom was hunched over the oven door, taking fresh cookies out.

"Mom," I got her attention as she looked up. Pushing Blake forward, I introduced him. "This is Blake Miller."

My mother placed the cookies on the counter and took a step toward Blake. "It's so nice to finally see you in person! I have always heard Mel talking about you. And of course I've seen you in the news lately..."

"Mom!" I scolded as Blake looked down and blushed. I guess he really didn't like talking about the embarrassing articles. I changed the topic by grabbing Karter's arm and pulling him towards my mother. "I'm sure you know who this little thief is!"

My mom nodded while Karter tried to swallow the cookie he stole by pushing the whole thing in his mouth. Stupid move. His eyes watered as the fresh cookie burned his mouth. I laughed at his expression.

"Of course," my mom chuckled, too. "Karter right?"

"Yes, ma'am."

Shaking her head slightly, my mom spoke, "Okay guys. I'll leave you be. Oh, right! I can set up a bed in the basement, since Pierce is occupying the only guest room we have. Someone else is going to have to sleep on the pull out couch in the family room. Are you guys okay with that?" Everyone nodded in appreciation.

"I'm sorry for the intrusion," Blake began to apologize.

My mother waved her hands dismissively, "Honestly, it's not a problem!! And Mel, will you show the guys where everything is?"

I nodded. She smiled and went up the stairs to her own room.

"Okay," Blake clapped and rubbed his hands together in anticipation. "Let's bring these cookies into the family room so we can sit, talk, and eat."

"Great idea," Pierce swooped down to pick up the cookies and led us to the other room. I plopped down on the couch in between Pierce and Karter. Blake sat down in the armchair across from us and leaned forward to talk.

"I think we need to talk about several things," Blake

looked at each one of us. We all nodded in agreement. I wanted to know exactly why he quit his job.

"So, as Pierce and Mel knows, I quit being the CEO," Blake directed towards Karter.

Karter definitely didn't have the same reaction as Pierce and I had. Instead, he leaned back into the couch and placed both his hands behind his head. "Good for you, Blake."

We stared at Karter with wide eyes. I guess he takes shocking news like it is nothing. Based on his reaction (or more like non-reaction) when he found out that Pierce and I were dating, I shouldn't be too surprised.

Pierce looked pensive and shocked at the same time. Running his hands in his hair, deep in thought, he asked Blake, "Why?"

"Well, it was a mix of things, really." Blake looked off into the distance. I could see sadness in his eyes. My heart dropped when I realized he must have gone through a lot to have that kind of expression on his face.

Taking a deep breath and facing us again, he began to tell us, "Everyone hated me in the company. The newspaper articles really hurt my credibility as a CEO. Many of the employees began to distrust and disrespect me as a person. Some went as far as posting the articles on the public bulletin board. My confidence shattered when I realized that I was alone and that no one supported me."

"I'm sorry, Blake!" I whispered softly and placed my hand reassuringly on his shoulder. "I'm sorry I wasn't there for you."

He gave me a genuine smile, "That's okay. I'm fine now. So yeah, the stress and loneliness drove me to the point of snapping. But do you know what the weird thing was? Siri was there for me and helped me through some really hard times. Her conniving attitude was replaced with one of care, and she actually became a decent person."

Karter let out a sarcastic laugh, "Yeah, right. Is that girl even capable of being decent?"

"Laugh all you want," Blake glared at Karter. "She was really nice."

I gaped at Blake, " You're not defending her are you?!?"

"I'm just saying that I'm not lying. I really want you guys to trust and believe in me!" Blake sighed in frustration. We all gave him apologetic looks. Satisfied, Blake continued. "I couldn't help but feel suspicious with her sudden change in attitude."

"There is definitely something suspicious about her sudden acts of kindness. What could she possibly be up to?" I asked to the group.

Chapter 25

The four of us stared at each other in confusion. Not one of us could come up with a plausible reason why Siri would suddenly become nice to Blake.

Finally, Blake spoke up and continued his story. "Anyways, Siri was there for me through the hard times. So I wasn't surprised when an article popped up about the two of us being a couple. I just shrugged it off and continued going on. But after a few weeks, articles surfaced more and more frequently."

I remembered when I saw the first article about Blake and Siri. It would be an understatement if I said I was furious.

"I thought it was weird, especially because I, of all people, made it on to the cover of a popular gossip magazine am no famous actor or singer or whatever. They NEVER feature anyone like me...a business person. Hell, I don't think they ever put Bill Gates on the front page!!"

He's right...I thought in surprise. I never thought of that before. Come to think of it, CEOs never get THAT much attention in the gossip world.

"You do have a point there..." Pierce admitted slowly. "But what does that mean? Maybe it's because you're rich now!"

"I don't think so," Blake shook his head. "Have you guys seen the most recent Access Hollywood news?"

"Yeah!!" I gave him a harsh look as I remembered what Siri said in the video interview. "I was going to talk to you about that..."

"I am not going out with her," Blake answered my question before could even ask it. "But that's not the point."

"Then what is your point?" Karter asked somewhat impatiently.

"Did you guys pay attention to the pictures?" Blake asked each one of us. Karter and Pierce shook their heads.

I spoke up as I remembered the photos. They were imprinted in my mind and I knew them like I knew the back of my hand. "Well, there was a picture of you two at the beach. The other one was of you two eating dinner at the mansion."

"Exactly!!" Blake exclaimed loudly while pointing his finger at me. We shot him confused looks as he continued to freak out. "There was a picture of us IN THE MANSION." Even though he stressed the last three words, I was still lost by what he was trying to say.

"Do I still have to explain more??" Blake shook his head in disappointment because we didn't catch on to what he was saying. After a pause, he asked slowly, "How could paparazzi get inside the house, let alone get a picture from that angle?"

I gasped as it finally clicked in my head. It was impossible to get that shot...unless you were in the room with them.

"But how can you not notice someone taking a picture of you?" Pierce asked.

Blake's shoulders slumped. "I have no idea. But no matter what, I know there's something wrong with this picture...no pun intended."

I smiled at the last part, but my happiness was quickly wiped away when I came to a conclusion. "Someone in the mansion is trying to ruin your reputation. They know how much criticism you get from magazines when they talk about you and Siri."

"Yeah," Blake sighed. "They always think I'm losing concentration and only focusing on girls."

"If Siri was so nice to you," Karter began to talk in a suspicious tone. "Then why would she confirm that she is your girlfriend even though she knows it will ruin your image?"

Blake's eyes widened as they turned as large as plates. I guess he didn't think about this before. He stammered, "I don't know. I always thought she was a naive, selfish girl who was trying to boost her fame. I didn't even consider that she has an ulterior motive..."

"Then are you saying that Siri is trying to hurt Blake?" Pierce asked Karter.

"That's my only guess."

"If that is what Siri is doing," I wondered out loud. "Doesn't it mean that Evander is working on this, too?"

"Probably," Karter agreed.

"He might be the one who took the picture and sent it to the press," Pierce said, his voice full of disgust.

Blake nodded vigorously. "I wouldn't be surprised if he tipped the paparazzi on when and where Siri and I were going out. No wonder why they always magically appear out of nowhere."

"But there is still one problem," I pointed out. "We still don't know WHY Evander is doing this. It doesn't seem to have any benefits for him..."

Karter sighed in frustration, "You're right."

Blake, on the other hand, stared at me with hard and determined eyes. "I don't care what happens, but I will dig up the truth."

Pierce, Karter, and I nodded in agreement. The four of us would work together to find out what was going on... and end Evander and Siri once and for all.

I woke up with rays of sunlight penetrating my eyelids. Squinting against the sun, I looked up and saw that it was already in the middle of the sky which meant it was probably around noon already. Groaning, I turned over in my pillow so that I wasn't being blinded by the light.

I took a deep breath to calm myself down only to inhale a familiar scent. My eyes sprang open as I looked around. I felt my cheeks and ears heat up when I realize that Pierce's lap was my comfortable pillow.

While the four of us were planning our attack on Evander, I guess we all fell asleep in the family room.

I was awkwardly sprawled across Pierce and Karter while Blake slept in the armchair by himself. I was the only one that was laying down.

Feeling guilty about crushing Karter and Pierce, I tried to get up slowly without waking them up. I utterly failed by elbowing Pierce in the ribs and kicking Karter in the chin.

"Oww," Karter moaned as he opened his eyes in shock. "What the hell was that for?!?"

"Yeah! Why are you trying to kill us?" Pierce mumbled while clutching his stomach. He had not opened his ryes yet, so I could tell he was still tired.

"I'm so sorry, guys!!" I gushed as I sprang off of them, not wanting to impale them anymore.

"Will you guys keep it down?" Blake grumbled from behind me.

After a small silence, I heard the three of them start to breathe evenly. They were such lazy pigs. I looked up at the clock and grimaced at the time. It was already 12:37pm.

I loved to sleep, but sleeping in too late made me feel a little guilty. With the time I was sleeping, I could have done something more productive. Before my whole life turned upside down, I would have already run, helped out in the bakery, and gone to work.

Sighing, I decided to make brunch so that I was actually doing something. Although by now, it would just be considered breakfast for lunch...not brunch.

I walked over to the fridge and pulled the heavy door open. Looking around, I decided to grab the pack of bacon on the shelf. I poured some oil into a frying pan and waited for it to heat up before throwing the bacon in. The sizzling and cracking sound of bacon filled the air, joined moments later with the smell of the delicious meat.

"What smells so amazing??"

I whipped around, completely caught off guard and dropped my spatula in the process. I pulled my hand over my heart to calm the frantic beating.

"Jessica!! Never scare me like that again!!" I glared at the intruder. "How did you even get in here? I'm pretty sure the door was locked."

Laughing, she walked towards me while spinning a lanyard around her finger. I jerked my head out of the way as she almost hit my face with that thing.

"Whoops! Sorry, my bad!" She giggled. Not a trace of sorry was on her face at all. "I found this spare key under your doormat."

I rolled my eyes as she continued to tease me. "Can you be more creative with your hiding spot? It's like you're just inviting a burglar in!! You're way too predictable."

Shaking my head at her silliness, I quickly reached out to snatch the key out of her hand. I didn't want her to start swinging it around like a dangerous weapon again.

"Hmmm," she sniffed the air thoughtfully. "Your bacon isn't doing so well. If I were you, I would go and save them now."

My eyes widened as I caught a whiff of something burning. Running to the stove, I tried to salvage the meal. I quickly turned them over and saw that they were only slightly burned. The guys can deal with that.

Turning around, I was about to talk to Jessica when I realized that she wasn't there anymore.

Jessica's voice reached me a second later as she screamed "TIMBER!!" from the family room. It sounded like she was a woodchopper screaming out before a tree fell.

After a split moment of silence, I heard two loud

grunts. Chucking, I knew that Jessica probably fell on top of Karter and Pierce to wake them up.

Thundering footsteps made their way into the kitchen as I saw Jessica running away from Karter. Squealing, she ran and hid behind me.

"Jessica! You are so dead!" Karter's eyes blazed with amusement. "Since when were you this hyper?!?"

"Since forever!" Jessica smiled as she used my body as a shield. I picked up the hot pan of bacon just as Karter took a threatening step towards Jessica.

"Wait! Don't burn me!" Karter shrieked like a little girl and stopped walking towards us. "Why are you taking her side?"

I laughed as an annoyed Pierce walked into the room. I said, "I'm not taking sides! I'm just moving the food onto the table!"

Pierce sat down and looked up at me gratefully when I put the meat in front of him. Winding an arm around my waist, he pulled me toward, making me bend over so that our faces were level.

"Thank you, baby." he closed the distance between us as he hungrily sucked my lower lip.

"Get a room, you guys!! I don't want that to be the first thing I see every morning!" Blake rubbed his eyes as he walked groggily in. Suddenly, he froze in place. His hand remained hovering over his right eye, but not scratching it. It was as if time stopped for him as he stared ahead of him, not blinking.

Worriedly, I placed a hand on his arm. He immediately snapped out of it and blushed a deep shade is red. I looked up confusedly and saw what he was looking at. A huge grin crossed my face as I saw Jessica's confused expression. Blake totally liked her!

Karter and Pierce seemed oblivious to the whole scene in front of them, but I was on cloud nine. It was just too cute! I couldn't believe that he blushed.

Silently, with his head down, he walked towards the kitchen table and stuffed a slice of bacon in his mouth. He's so shy!! I cooed to myself in my head.

Happily, I skipped to the fridge and grabbed six eggs to scramble. As I cracked them into the bowl, I glanced up and saw that Jessica had sat down next to Blake and was talking up a storm to Karter and Pierce. Poor Blake, I laughed to myself as I saw him sit there awkwardly. He was as stiff as a board and rigid all over. Bless him, he was nervous!

"So," Jessica finally acknowledged him. "You're Blake, right? I came over here today because Mel was so worried about you yesterday! I'm glad you showed up!" She smiled at him, oblivious to his unease.

Blake gave a curt nod and turned away, never actually saying anything. Jessica shrugged her shoulders and turned away from him again.

I chuckled silently as a plan popped into my head. This was a wonderful distraction to the whole fiasco going on at the mansion.

After the large brunch, the five of us went out to explore Central Park, especially since Karter and Blake had never been there before…let alone New York City in general.

It was nearly summer and it was such a nice day we decided to have a picnic down there for dinner. Karter snatched up his guitar as we walked out of the house while

Pierce grabbed the picnic basket that we had prepared for the outing.

Grunting, Pierce struggled slightly with the weight of the food at first. Whoops…I guess we packed a little too much. I had insisted that we bring all kinds of sandwiches and fruits and snacks.

The sun was hovering high above our heads as we exited the subway nearest Central Park. A giant metal globe towered over our heads as we neared the entrance of the park. I squinted against a glare created by the sun's reflection off of the top of the gate. There were tiny gold sculptures situated at the tips of the gate.

"This is so amazing!! I love New York already," Blake mumbled under his breath. I nodded in agreement. Living in New York for as long as I could remember, I realized that I had become immune to the special qualities of the city. I had never noticed how grand New York really was and always took it for granted.

After a few more minutes, we chose a large patch of lush, green grass to sit on. Jessica produced a traditional red and white checkered blanket from her bed and placed it on the ground with Blake's help. I was originally going to help her, but Blake beat me to it. His eagerness was evident as he grabbed the two corners of the blanket opposite to Jessica.

First to sit on the blanket, I leaned back on my arms and let the rays of sun wash over my face. I felt the warmth on my skin and basked in it for a few minutes. Suddenly, a presence blocked out the sun and cast a shadow over me. I opened my eyes, ready to tell at the person who took the warmth away from me.

The harsh words I planned to use were never spoken

when I realized it was Pierce. My heart nearly stopped as I saw the pure emotion of love in his eyes--and it was all directed towards me. Blushing, I quickly sat upright and picked at the grass next to me.

I felt him sit behind me as he put his legs on either side of my body. Not knowing what to do, I brought my legs up again my chest. I had never really enjoyed PDA, especially in front of the other guys and Jessica. I would never hear the end of it. Looking around nervously, I realized that they weren't even paying attention to me and Pierce.

Blake had finally gathered enough courage to start a normal conversation with Jessica. On the other side of the blanket, Karter was unzipping his guitar case and getting ready to play. Sighing, I decided it was safe to relax a little.

Pierce's arms wrapped around my waist and gently tugged me back towards him. I happily obliged as I leaned against his strong chest. After a few minutes, my breathing fell into sync with his. I could feel the steady rise and fall of his chest against my back, which was really quite soothing.

"You looked so mesmerizing when you sat with your face in the sun," his breath tickled my ear as I tried to suppress the shiver that traveled down my spine. "I swear you looked just like an angel."

My mouth fell open at his sweet comment. Twisting my back so that I could see his face, I could see his eyes were full of sincerity and seriousness. I still don't know how he seems to see me in a perfect light, even though I am obviously far from being flawless.

At loss for words, I remembered that actions could speak louder than words. I hooked my hand around his neck and pulled him closer to me. My stomach fluttered in anticipation when our lips brushed against each other. Teasingly, I pulled back a centimeter when he tried to deepen the kiss.

Growling, Pierce brought his hand around to the back of my neck and held me there so I couldn't move away. Within seconds, our lips finally met with a great force. Roughly, he moved his mouth over mine, taking complete dominance. I gasped when he nibbled on my bottom lip. Taking my gasp as an invitation, his tongue flicked into my mouth and found my tongue.

I moaned and raked my fingers through his hair when he managed to deepen our kiss even more. He tasted of fresh spearmint, and I craved for a better taste. I ran my tongue along his, and I felt him shudder against me.

Someone cleared their throat behind me, clearly not amused. Quickly, I pulled back from Pierce and felt my face heat up like an oven. Pierce, on the other hand, groaned in frustration this time.

"Will you two please, PLEASE try to control yourselves in front of us? I'm begging you!" Jessica got down on her knees and clasped her two hands together.

"You're just jealous," Pierce quipped.

"Eww!" Jessica scrunched her nose. "Definitely not."

"Sure," Pierce flashed his signature grin. "Whatever you say."

Jessica rolled her eyes in annoyance and ignored Pierce. She turned back to Blake and they resumed talking. As I watched them, it reminded me to come up with a plan to get the two together. They were just too cute!

"Pierce," I got his attention in a hushed whisper. "Do you see what I see?"

He raised one eyebrow in confusion, "A carousel?"

I rolled my eyes at his stupidity. Even though we were sitting close to a carousel, it was definitely not what I was talking about. "No, you idiot!! Blake and Jessica!"

A knowing smile crossed his face, "I knew what you were trying to hint at. I just wanted to mess with you."

Slapping his shoulder gently, I scolded him. "This is not a joking matter. Can't you see they are made for each other?"

Pierce looked over at the two of them, "I guess. But they obviously cannot see that for themselves…except maybe Blake. He's turning into a tomato over there."

I could see that Pierce was right. With every moment that passed by when he was talking to Jessica, he would turn a shade redder. First, it was a slight flush in his neck. Then it crawled up to his cheeks and eventually made it to his ears. Silently, I laughed. This was better than watching a movie.

The sound of a guitar drew my attention as I turned from Blake to Karter. With a guitar slung over his shoulder, I don't think I've seen Karter in a more natural environment. It was like he was born to be a musician. Even though I don't think he realized it, he had a look of passion and dedication when he lightly stroked the strings and tuned the instrument. Being cooped up in an office as a CEO would have definitely wasted his talent.

Blake and Jessica's chatter stopped when we hear Karter start to play the chords to a familiar song.

"Hey, there Delilah. What's it like in New York City? I'm a thousand miles away but girl, tonight you look so pretty, yes you do. Times Square can't shine as bright as you. I swear it's true..."

Karter's golden tenor rang out and broke through the silent, peaceful air. I have never actually heard him play the guitar or sing before, but I was not expecting anything like this. We all sat stunned into an awed silence as he finished the song. I hung onto each word, only wanting him to sing more.

When he finished the song, no one dared to say a thing. However, our trance was broken when a few bystanders began to clap for Karter. I quickly joined in on the applause, and cheered him on.

"That was amazing, Karter!! I can't even describe it..." I looked at him in a completely new light. He was no longer always the playful, lighthearted fool. I knew he had a passion for music that was stronger than any passion I had for anything.

Karter shrugged at the compliment I gave him and put the guitar down. "Thanks, Mel. But really...it was nothing."

We all fell into an easy conversation after that, and time passed by quickly. In the middle of it, Pierce excused himself to meet with his professor at NYU. After giving me a peck on the lips, he promised to be back within two hours.

"Love you," I whispered in his ear as I hugged him before he left.

"I love you, too." With that, he left.

* * *

An hour later Karter started getting a little restless. Obviously, he wasn't used to sitting in one spot for too long.

"Come on, guys!! I promise it will be fun!!" Karter pleaded us after he suggested we go on the carousel.

"That's for little kids!!" Jessica argued back, not wanting to move from where she was.

"Not necessarily," Karter answered without elaborating. "I'll pay for all your tickets!"

I was convinced. Needing to do something, I hopped up and grabbed Karter's hand. Dragging him towards the carousel, I called over my shoulder, "Feel free to join us, but we're not going to wait around all day for you!"

Blake looked torn. He wasn't sure if he wanted to stay with Jessica more or go with Karter and me. When Jessica finally stood up to join us, Blake looked relieved. I guess he didn't have to make a decision now.

"I guess this could be fun," Jessica reasoned. "I haven't been on one of these in years!"

"That's the spirit!" Blake grinned at her. Surprisingly, she smiled back and grabbed his hand and dragged him along, much like what I was doing to Karter.

Moments later, we were all sitting on our own plastic horses. Mine looked like it was beginning to jump over something and was frozen in time. The carousel began to spin at a very slow pace at first, but then the ride began to pick up speed.

Happily surprised, I realized that it spun a lot faster than I expected it to. Although it was still rotating at a slow pace, it wasn't an agonizingly slow process. The green trees around us started to blur together as we passed them. I began to see whirling colors of red, orange, and blue. Laughing along with the others, I was exhilarated by the feeling of being a child again.

A flash of brown passed my vision, and my heart started to beat faster as I realized that it was the exact same color as Pierce's hair. He was probably back from his meeting with his professor!! Waiting until I passed where he was standing again, I realized that he was indeed watching us on the ride.

"Pierce! You're back!" I waved and managed to yell out before passing by him again. After another rotation, I saw the look on his face

His mouth was pressed into a hard line, and his eyes were distant. It was like he was thinking of something important. His good mood from earlier today was gone, and I frowned. What could have caused this sudden change in mood?

No longer amused by the ride, I patiently waited for the carousel to slow down and eventually stop. When it finally did, I jumped off the horse and made my way to the gate. Pierce was there, waiting for me. I did a double take as I saw a smile on his face. Maybe I was just imagining the scowl he had on a few moments earlier.

Shaking the thoughts out of my head, I threw my arms around his neck and pulled him in for a hug. "I missed you!"

"Missed you, too." Pierce said back, almost like a robotic response. Pulling back, I saw him smiling at me still. However, the smile didn't completely reach his eyes.

"What's wrong?" I asked gently, not wanting to force him to talk.

"Nothing!" Pierce tilted his head and regarded strangely. "Why?"

"I don't know," I responded unsurely. "It's just that... forget it."

The normal Pierce would have bugged me about it until I told him why I thought he was acting strangely. The normal him would have not just dropped the subject.

Sighing, he slung an arm around my shoulder, but I could feel the stiffness in it that wasn't always there. He was obviously preoccupied with something, or else he wouldn't be acting this way.

But what in the world could have caused him to give me the cold shoulder? And why was it after he met with his teacher?

Suspicion and doubt swirled around my head, as I pretended to listen to what Karter was saying. A feeling of unease came crawling into my body, and I couldn't shake it away no matter how hard I tried.

And just as I thought things were going uphill for once...it all had to come crashing down again.

Chapter 26

Pierce's unusual actions did not let up as the days passed by. Days turned into weeks, and if anything, Pierce's mood worsened. At times, he didn't even bother covering up his frustration at the world.

I sighed in defeat. What could I possibly to do cheer him up? It's like walking on a tightrope and one wrong step would send me plummeting down. With every attempt, he managed to shoot me down and pull me into a dark mood. But at least he wasn't just snappy at me. His anger lashed out at anyone who got in his way or disturbed him.

The tension between us was like a time bomb, just ticking away and ready to explode at any moment.

"I can't do this anymore," Pierce's tired voice was muffled by his two hands that were covering his face. He rubbed his face in desperation, trying to clear his mind.

I looked around the room, trying to figure out how we managed to get to this point. We'd had several small confrontations, but nothing seemed as foreboding as this meeting. I had just stumbled into the study room in my house while he was in there. Knowing he wouldn't be in a good mood, I tried to quietly make my way out without disturbing him. Unfortunately, things didn't go as I had hoped. He stopped me in my tracks with his vague words.

"This?" I questioned, unable to say anything more. My body was paralyzed and my mind braced for what he was going to say next.

"Yes. This," He stressed the last word and gestured his hands back and forth between the two of us. "I don't think it's a good idea to be together anymore."

My mind couldn't process his words. It was like it just shut down and turned numb.

"Why not?" I demanded when I could finally make my mouth form words, needing to know what was going through his mind. I didn't want to sound like a desperate girl, but it was hard to hide my breaking heart.

"Because," Pierce didn't even show any remorse on his face as his eyes met mine. "I can't concentrate with your constant presence. Having you around is hindering me from reaching my dreams of becoming a doctor."

I paled. What is this about? What is going on?

"That doesn't even make sense! You have to tell me exactly what I did wrong! I can't live with that pathetic explanation. I might even understand what you are saying if you just elaborated a little. Maybe I could even agree with you…seeing that we could barely tolerate each other for the past few weeks!" Even though my heart wrenched at the thought of being around Pierce and pretending nothing happened between the two of us, my mind told me this is what I had to do.

Sighing in defeat, Pierce finally admitted what had been bothering him for the past month. "I've been failing my classes, Mel. I can't possibly afford to waste spending time with you."

It was as if he plunged a knife deep into my heart. If words could wound someone, I would be dead by now. But a nagging question formed in the back of my head. How could Pierce possibly be failing a class? That was just unusual. But then again, he had been acting quite differently lately. I wouldn't hold it past him to suddenly fail. Scowling, my depressed mood quickly turned sour.

"Okay," I laughed bitterly. "Now I see what you're saying. You feel that being with me is a waste of time. I get it."

Pierce's face twisted a little in guilt, "That's not what I meant..."

"No, save it." I held up my hand to stop him from saying his explanation. I was ready to walk out of the room.

"Mel, wait. Hold on!" He grabbed the hand that I held up and clasped his fingers over mine.

"What?" I muttered, staring down at our connected hands...not amused by his hot and cold feelings.

"Look, I'm sorry. But I think we need to take a break or something so I can refocus on what's important," Pierce let go of my and looked down at his hands. Quietly he mumbled, "What other options do I have?"

When I shrugged my shoulders in response, he sighed. After moments of silence between us, he finally broke the silence again, "I could always go back to the mansion."

Shooting him my coldest glare, I responded icily, "Do

you really think that going back will magically solve your problems? If you return to the mansion, you are not half the man I thought you were. I always believed you were strong and could face any challenge. Please don't prove me wrong."

"I don't live my life for you, Melanie. I can make my own decisions, and I couldn't care less if you judged me," Pierce glared back at me.

"So are you just going to forget about all your dreams and what you promised your family?" I knew my hit was a little under the belt, but he deserved it.

"You have no right to bring my family into this. They are MY family and you didn't even know them. Plus, you should take care of your own family problems first." Okay. He just went over the line.

I cringed as I realized he did have a point. Chief never responded to any of our calls, so we had assumed he was incredibly mad and didn't want to talk to me. But nevertheless, I couldn't help but stand up for my grandfather.

"Don't forget who took you in after you became an orphan. You can't talk about Chief that way!" I shot back at him, tears threatening to leak over the bottom rim of my eyes.

"Whatever. I'm just saying that I am going to live my life the way I want to and you are not going to change that no matter what you do." Pierce almost spat the last part at me.

A single tear betrayed me as I tried not to show how hurt I was by his words. With a determined voice, I looked Pierce straight in the eye.

"Then I guess you don't need me in your life anymore."

With that, I quickly turned and ran out of the room, not even waiting for his reaction.

The ticking time bomb of our relationship had finally exploded. Pieces of my heart were shattered everywhere.

When I was no longer in the same room as Pierce anymore, I allowed the tears to flow freely. My legs gave out from underneath me as I crashed into a wall for support. Slowly, I slid down the length of the wall and crumpled into a ball on the floor. What had I done to deserve this? We were fine a few weeks ago! Everything was working out for the best when we all reunited in New York.

What changed everything?

A large crashing sound brought my mind back to the room that I was still sitting outside of. Terrified, I trembled at the sound of glass showering over the wooden floor. I heard Pierce scramble furiously around in the room, picking up the shattered pieces that had once been a cup.

This was not the Pierce I knew and fell in love with. This was more of an uncontrollable man who had let rage consume him.

Suddenly, the door was ripped open. When he saw me crouched defensively against the wall, I caught a glimpse of the soft, once caring Pierce. I looked into his eyes as pain, regret, and sorrow flashed through them. As I was about to approach him, he quickly put up his guarded face again. His eyes were filled with a look of emptiness. Devoid of all emotions, he pushed past me, not turning to look back at all.

My heart wrenched at the finality of that gesture. I wanted to follow him so badly and see what was wrong and possibly heal his hurt...but I couldn't.

This was it, and there's no going back.

Deep down in my heart, I knew he was a stubborn fool. He wouldn't accept me, and my heart could not take another rejection. We had hurt each other badly with our words and actions, and there was only one remedy to our wounds…time.

Letting it go, I slowly pushed myself up onto my legs and walked to my room. Falling onto my bed, I finally let another round of body wracking tears rip through me.

Tired from all the emotional exertion, blackness found me as I fell into a dreamless sleep that night.

I was aware of the sunlight hitting my face as my eyelids fluttered to meet the new day. Groaning, I pushed myself up into a sitting position. I tried to clear my dry throat.

It did nothing to help except remind me of what caused my sore throat. Pierce had changed. Struggling to breathe right, I felt like I was suffocating. I managed to regain my sanity after a few seconds.

Scoffing at myself, I realized how truly pathetic I had become. Since when did I need a guy to survive? I was an independent girl and had fended for myself before Chief and the guys entered my life.

And I could still find that girl within me. A rush of strength surged through my body as I stood up and got dressed like any other normal day.

"Be strong, Melanie. Life has strange ways of making everything okay."

My mother's voice drifted into my thoughts. I could still feel the embrace that she pulled me into years ago when I found out I was adopted. I've already been through so many life changing experiences, and this is just another one to add to the list.

Arranging a smile on my face, I bounded down the stairs and into the kitchen. Everyone was already down there, happily eating their breakfast.

When my eyes landed on chestnut hair and a pair of gray eyes, my smile wavered. However, I managed to pull myself together and cast an even wider smile in his direction. He looked away with no reaction.

Sighing, I sat down next to Karter and began to eat. He gave me a strange look when he saw me stabbing my eggs, but didn't comment. An awkward, tense mood swept throughout the room as Blake and Karter noticed something was wrong. The only thing you could hear was the sound of chewing and utensils scraping.

A shrill ring pierced the silence making me jump a foot into the air. Realizing it was the telephone, I ran to go answer it. Thank God for an excuse to get away from the table. The atmosphere was slowly suffocating me, and I needed to get away from there.

"Hello?" I gave myself a mental slap as I greeted my savior a little too excitedly.

"Hello, Melanie," the voice brought shivers down my spine…and not the good kind. Suddenly, I'm not so grateful for this interruption anymore. "It has been a long time since I have last talked to you."

"It has been quite a while, Evander." I greeted him coldly. "How are you?"

"Regrettably, this is not a casual call, so I'll just skip the pleasantries and get to the point." Evander said slowly with a dry sense of humor. "I have some unfortunate news for you."

I sucked a breath in through my teeth. I was not expecting that. "What's wrong?"

"It's Mr. McKinley."

My heartbeat quickened, and I mentally prepared myself for the worst. "I thought you said you were getting straight to the point. Just tell me what is wrong! Is he okay?"

"No," Evander answered casually. He paused and I waited for him to continue. If I could, I would be strangling him right now for making me wait in suspense. "His health is quickly diminishing and he is currently bedridden. However, all the doctors have no idea what is wrong with him."

"When did this happen?" I seethed.

"About two weeks ago."

"And why didn't you call sooner?" I spat at the phone in disbelief. What was going on here, first Pierce and now Chief?

"We both didn't want to drag you into this. We thought he was going to get better."

"Anything that has to do with Chief is my business, goddammit."

Evander ignored my comment. "Mr. McKinley is asking for all you guys to come back. I'm afraid he thinks there isn't much time left."

Numbly, I nodded. After a moment, I realized he couldn't see me through the phone. "Of course." I hung up the phone without hearing his response. Slowly, I walked to the kitchen.

The three of the m looked up at me, worry crossed their

expressions as they saw my pale face. Looking at each one of them dead in the eye, I began to talk.

"It's time to pack up. We're going back to the mansion."

"Wait…WHAT?!" Blake's voice broke through the stunned silence in the rom.

Karter spoke up right after Blake. "What are you talking about, Melanie? Why would we go back?"

I opened my mouth to answer, but Pierce cut in. "I thought you said you never wanted to go back there." He looked at me accusingly. I gulped as I realized he was right.

Isn't it ironic how I just yelled at him yesterday for wanting to go back to the mansion? Now I'm the one bringing it up. But nevertheless, this was a special circumstance, and the guys had to realize that.

I ignored Pierce's swipe at me and got to the point, "Chief is really sick right now. Evander told me he's not doing so well."

"Sick!?!" Karter asked in disbelief. "With what?"

It seemed like three of them leaned closer to me while they waited for me to answer. The anticipation was killing the guys. However, I had no definite answer for them.

Anticlimactically, I sighed and admitted, "I don't know."

The guys let out a sigh of disappointment as Pierce scoffed and rolled his eyes, "How do you not know?"

"I'm not the doctor here, am I?" I stared pointedly at him. "Then again, I guess that no one in this room is really qualified to be a doctor." I laughed bitterly as Pierce glared at me.

Karter and Blake shared a confused look. I should

probably have updated them on our relationship status, but that would have to wait.

Blake cleared his throat uneasily and tried to lessen the tension by bringing up an important point, "Should we believe what Evander is telling us? What if it is a trap or something?"

"Blake's right. Evander already manipulated Blake enough. We all don't need to run straight into another one of his games," Karter reasoned.

I thought about their ridiculous claims. Even though Evander may be really deceptive, I highly doubted he would physically harm us. "Come on. It's not like he is a serial killer or something. He can't really do anything to us."

"Uhhh, Melanie. I beg to differ," Pierce spoke up once again. However, he wasn't using his arrogant tone. I was surprised when I heard his voice illed with concern and thought. "Remember the night of New Years? At the ball?"

I paled as the scene came back to me. I remembered earlier that day I was sitting in the passenger seat of Evander's car and was about to be squished into a pancake by another car. Later that evening, there was a really sketchy conversation that basically implied that Evander arranged for it to happen.

"Oh. Yeah. I almost forgot about that," I muttered.

Karter and Blake shot me a confused stare. I had never told them about what happened that night. As I began to retell the story, their eyes grew wider and wider.

"Nope! No way! I'm never going anywhere near that man ever again!" Karter exclaimed right when I finished telling the story.

"I second that!" Blake nodded aggressively. "I don't trust that man for one second!"

"But guys," I pleaded. "What is Chief is really sick? What happens if we're not there and he…"

My voice cracked, and I couldn't finish the sentence. Suddenly, my vision began to blur as tears filled up my eyes. Chief was my grandfather, and even though he was forcing me into a loveless marriage, I still loved him. He's family, after all.

"I think Melanie is right," a soft voice spoke up. Surprised, I looked up and met Pierce's eyes. They looked as soft as his voice sounded. "Even if it is a trap, we cannot risk Chief's life. We can always just take precautions around Evander. If the whole thing is fake, we can just come back here."

I looked gratefully at Pierce. He was talking in a more reasonable voice than I could pull off at the moment. So quickly that I thought I imagined it, I saw a ghost of a smile on Pierce's face when our eyes met. After blinking once, it was gone and Pierce was now looking at Karter.

"Fine. Once the voice of reason talks, we cannot go against him." Karter teased Pierce.

"But no matter what, I'm not planning on staying there!" Blake warned us. No one said anything in response.

Silently, after a few minutes, we split ways and started to pack our bags. Why was it that it was nearly impossible to escape the glamorous life? It's like a black hole…full of mystery and impossible to escape from.

I stood there, facing Los Angeles with a suitcase in one hand and my cell phone in the other. Anxiously, I dialed in Evander's number and pressed the green call button. He picked up on the third ring.

"Hello, Melanie. I'm assuming you're at the airport right now?" his voice greeted me.

I didn't even bother asking how he knew. He always knew everything.

"Yes. I am," I answered. Then I corrected myself. "We all are."

"Excellent," Evander let out a small laugh. "Mr. McKinley will be very happy to see you all."

He paused when I didn't say anything. After a minute, he continued, "I've sent out a limo half an hour ago, so it should be arriving shortly. I'll see you later." A dial tone signified the end of that conversation.

I turned around to look at the guys. "Evander sent us a limo. It should be here soon."

I sighed when no one spoke up. It was like this the whole plane ride, and I was not sure how long I could survive the silence. A few minutes later a black limo finally pulled up to meet us. I recognized the driver from the first day I arrived, and he took our suitcases and put them in the trunk. Wordlessly, we all climbed into the back.

Butterflies flew around in a jumble in my stomach. It was almost to the point that I felt sick. I wrapped my arms around my waist and stared out the window. Everything reminded me of when I first arrived here. The scenery was the same – trees flew by as the houses became increasingly larger. But the atmosphere was completely different this time around. When I first arrived here, I was nervous, but in an excited way. This time, I am nervous, but in a dread-ing way. I could sense something big happening soon, but it could easily just be my mind telling my crazy things.

During half the ride, I was expecting something to go horribly wrong. At every intersection, I sucked in my breath and kept a lookout for runaway cars that headed in our direction. Thankfully, no one crashed into us the whole way to the mansion.

The limo pulled up to the all too familiar gates, and the driver rolled down his window to talk to the gatekeeper. After a few moments, the gates slowly pulled back to allow us through. Apprehension filled me as the mansion came closer and closer. Soon enough, it loomed overhead as if it was taunting us. The weather did not help, the sun hid behind clouds, making the world seem a little grey.

"We're finally back," I muttered under my breath to no one in particular. I stepped out of the limo first and faced the mansion again. The front door swung open, and as it hit the wall with a loud bang, I jumped.

"Welcome home, Melanie."

Evander's voice floated through the air, but I couldn't see where he was. I took a step closer and saw that he was behind the door, holding it open for us. Under my breath, I scoffed. This was not home anymore. I don't know what changed everything, but I no longer felt attached to this large, empty and echoing house anymore.

Slowly, I walked up the marble steps leading to the front door. With each step, I felt more uneasy. I told my brain to stop thinking too much as I paused at the threshold. Taking a deep breath, I squared my shoulders and stepped through the door.

"Thank you, Evander." I muttered as I passed by him.

While standing in the large, open foyer, I turned around and waited for the guys.

Karter was the first to enter. He was followed by a glum looking Blake. Finally, Pierce walked back into the mansion that he had run away from about seven months earlier. Evander let go of the door and allowed it to slowly close again.

It let out a loud groan before it clicked shut with a sense of finality.

"It is nice to see you all here again. I'm sure that Mr. McKinley will be very pleased," Evander stepped so that he was in front of us. I took in his appearance. For an older guy, he looked quite cleaned up. The suit he wore was pristine, and there was no trace of lint anywhere. His face bore a small smirk, almost like a leer.

"Where is he?" Pierce spoke up for what seemed like the first time in five hours.

"Follow me," Evander turned on his heels and walked through a hallway on the opposite side of the foyer. He turned by the library where I first met Chief and took the stairs up. After two turns, we arrived outside a large set of oak doors.

"You guys have never been here before, but this is Chief's room. He doesn't usually enjoy having people encroach on his private place. However, this is a special circumstance, and he told me he wants to see all of you." Evander paused and added. "I'll be waiting out here."

He placed one hand on the door handle and the other knocked the door. After a moment of silence, a raspy voice called out. "Come in."

Evander smiled at us and pulled open the door to reveal

a large room with a king sized bed facing the right wall. I could make out a body lying in between the sheets. My breath caught in my throat when I took the sight in.

Hesitantly, I stepped into the room. I could make out Chief's head turning towards me. His eyes widened a little as he weakly reached out a hand towards me.

"Melanie."

That single word pushed me over the edge as I ran towards the bed with tears forming in my eyes. It was scary to see my grandfather look so weak and helpless. Grabbing the hand that he held towards me, I sat down on the edge of the bed. I barely heard the guys' footsteps as they walked into the room behind me.

"Chief, are you okay?" I asked with my voice full of concern.

"Of course I am. I'm still alive, aren't I? I admit that I have seen better days, but I'm doing well now that you're here." Chief lightly squeezed my hand. I looked at his face and saw tubes coming out of his nose. Looking at the other side of the bed, I noticed that the tube led to an IV pole.

I smiled at my grandfather's lightheartedness. Even though he was so sick, he could still joke around with me, "What happened?"

"I don't really know. I was fine until I collapsed one day. Evander found me passed out in the kitchen and brought me to this bed. Ever since then, I've been stuck here all day. It's like I'm being quarantined!" Chief smiled at me. "But I should've seen my health deteriorating. I'd noticed that I had been getting more and more health problems before I fainted. I guess my age is finally catching up to me."

"Aww," I cooed. "Don't say that! You're still pretty young!"

"You flatter me too much…just like your mother. You two always say things just to make an old man feel better."

I just smiled down at him, not knowing what to say in response. He barely ever talked about my mother or father, except for the day that I arrived in the mansion. It was as if he didn't want to remember the painful memories that came with the thought of my parents.

"I see you brought along the whole gang, too." Chief nodded his head towards the three guys.

"Hi, Chief." Karter saluted as a joke.

"Long time no see," Blake greeted him. Although he didn't want to be back at the mansion, I could tell he actually sincerely missed Chief.

"Hey," Pierce said with his head down. I guess he remembered the last time he saw Chief was when he was turning down the position as a successor. The last thing Chief did was kick him out of the mansion. I guess they need to discuss some things before we left for New York again.

"It's so nice to see you all again," Chief's eyes wrinkled in happiness as he looked at each and every one of us. I could see the glisten of a single tear sliding down the right side of his face. Whether it is from happiness or sadness, I don't know.

All I knew was that at the moment, I was glad to be here. Back in the same house as my grandfather and the boys like the old days.

Chapter 27

After ten minutes of talking to us, Chief slowly dozed off to sleep. I looked down worriedly at his sleeping figure. His once strong face was now vulnerable and hollow. A shadow fell over his features and I saw that he was really frail and skinny. How much was he eating?

Turning around, I saw the same sad expressions on the guys' faces. They all knew that something was terribly wrong, and we all wanted to do something to fix it. But we just didn't know how. How could we possibly help him if doctors couldn't?

I turned around and quietly made my way out of Chief's bedroom. Blake quickly followed behind. Like me, I guessed he couldn't handle seeing Chief like that.

I leaned against the wall outside Chief's door waiting for Karter and Pierce to come out. I pressed my face into my hands and tried to block out the world. Why was everything going so badly, first Blake, then Pierce, and now

Chief? All our lives were turned upside down in the past month.

Silent tears began to leak out of my eyes. I was surprised I had more tears left in my body. After crying for Pierce, I was sure that my tear ducts were all dried out. A small gasp accompanied my effort to get some air through my tears.

I felt arms wrap around my shoulders. Looking up, I saw a worried Blake. Gently, he pulled me in and made my head rest against his chest.

"Shhh," he said. "Everything will be alright."

"H-How do you know?" I managed to get out between my gasps.

He started to stroke my hair. After a moment of silence he sighed. "I don't."

The words struck a chord in my heart. Even though he had no idea what was going to happen, he had hope. And that's something that I needed the most right then. Crying would not solve the problem. Slowly, my tears dried and I was able to stand up on my own. Before leaving Blake's embrace, I gave him a quick hug back.

"C'mon. Karter and Pierce already left." Blake gently steered me towards the lounge.

"They did?"

"Yeah, you probably didn't notice. They slipped past us when you were still crying."

"Oh," I muttered, slightly embarrassed.

We turned the corner when we reached the top of the stairs and walked into the lounge. Karter and Pierce were sitting silently on the long couch across the TV. Blake sat on the loveseat while I made my way over to the oversized bean bag.

No one knew what to say, now that we had just seen Chief. I think that we all had expected this to be a trap and that everything was okay. But knowing that Chief was actually sick, it was hard for the information to sink in.

"Does anyone else find this situation really…strange?" Pierce spoke up, causing me to jump. It was so silent before, and his sudden comment surprised me. "I mean, he was perfectly fine a few months ago!"

"Of all people, you should know that it is possible to develop a sudden illness," I muttered.

Pierce ignored me and continued to talk, "It's not only that, though. Have you realized he's never spoken to us directly after we left the mansion?"

"Yeah, I always thought that was a little weird," Karter agreed.

"I always thought it was because he went off on a vacation…or business meeting or whatever," Blake commented. "He left for about two weeks after Mel disappeared. But before he left, he just told me to take care of the company. He was going to figure something out with the shareholders on his trip. And we all know Chief. Even though he is filthy rich, he hates spending money and paying for international calls. He probably just kept his phone off since he was in Mexico. He also came back for a little bit, but had to go back there because there was some unfinished business. That's when I left the mansion."

"I guess that makes sense," I thought about it. "That explains why he wasn't picking up his phone for a while. But why didn't he call us back when he saw all the missed calls?"

"It doesn't make sense because no matter how mad he

was at us, I know he has the decency to call people back," Karter mumbled.

"Plus, he didn't even seem mad when he first left for Mexico…" Blake commented.

"Wait," I held up a finger at Blake. "He wasn't mad when I ran away?"

"Of course not…if anything, he was really sad." Blake rubbed his chin in thought. "Why? Did you think he was mad at you?"

"Uh-huh. Yeah. I honestly did…for a lot of reasons. One: I ran away to New York when he didn't want me to go back. Two: I went back to Pierce even though I'm supposed to marry you. Three: he cancelled my credit card, which was basically a sign of disinheriting me. Four: he has been ignoring me." I held up a finger for each reason I listed off. I'm sure there were lots more reasons, but my mind was drawing up a blank at the moment.

"What?" Blake shook his head in disagreement. "What are you talking about?"

"What do you mean?" I raised my eyebrow at him. Pierce did the same while Karter just leaned back to listen to the conversation.

"One: who told you Chief didn't want you to go back to New York? Two: he understood your situation and knew you wanted to work things out with Pierce first. Three: What? He did not. Four: he's been ignoring all of us." Blake copied my motions and countered each reason I had.

"Okay. First of all, Evander told me that Chief didn't want me to go back to New York because Pierce was there. He said that Chief would fly all my friends and family from New York to California. Secondly, I'm positive that he cancelled my credit card. I tried using it one day, but it was denied." I furrowed my eyebrows in confusion. This doesn't make sense.

"Chief made a deal with you and said that he would let you go back to New York after four months. He is a man of his words, and would never break a promise," Blake said calmly. "And why would he cancel your card? He loves you more than you think, Mel. He wouldn't do anything like that…no matter what you did to him."

I was at loss for words. Why wasn't anything adding up??

"This is so…" Karter finally spoke up. "Bizarre."

I snorted at his word choice. Of course he would say something like that.

"Okay. Let's just think about this whole thing some more," Pierce reasoned. "Who's behind most of the questionable events going on?"

It was a no brainer.

"Evander," I automatically said like it was a knee jerk reaction.

"Exactly," Pierce smiled at me. "I feel like he's smarter than we give him credit for. There's something bigger that he's hiding."

"What about his little evil daughter?" Blake shivered at the thought of her.

"I don't know. It seems like she is fairly innocent in this whole thing. I mean, the only thing she did was go after Blake and I. But that's not surprising because we all know girls can sometimes be gold-diggers." Pierce ran his hand through his hair then shot a quick glance at me. "No offense, Melanie."

"None taken," I muttered. Although his statement was quite offensive, there was some truth in it.

"Until we can pin something on her, I think she's innocent in this whole thing. Maybe she has no idea what her father is up to," Pierce said.

"But…" I argued. I knew Siri was evil. However, Pierce just waved me off and continued to talk about Evander. How could he be on Siri's side after everything she did to him? She blackmailed him for heaven's sake!

We continued to talk in hushed whispers until we heard footsteps on the stairs. Shutting our mouths immediately, we tried to look like we were resting on the couches together. It wasn't the best way to look inconspicuous though, as I looked around to see Karter and Pierce both pretend to snore. If we weren't in the mansion and in this situation, I probably would have laughed out loud.

"Eh my gawd!! You guys are back!!" I rolled my eyes and internally groaned. Speak of the devil…it was Siri. I opened my eyes and saw her standing right in front of me.

"Siri," I spoke with sharp sarcasm and too much fake enthusiasm. "Long time no see!"

"MEL!! I missed you too, darling!" She ran up to me and gave me a quick hug. Who said I missed her in the first place? And did she forget how she had treated me before I left? She had basically thrown daggers at me with her eyes when she was about to tell Pierce's secret to Chief.

I exhaled a deep breath as she moved on to her next victim.

"Pierce! How are you? I haven't seen you in seven long months! I heard you went to New York," Siri babbled on about random things. Surprisingly, Pierce was civil towards her. After answering all of her questions, he even gave her a small smile.

My heart panged at the sight. Pierce used to give me those smiles, but not anymore. Just thinking about him smiling at Siri like that made me feel disgusted. How could he treat her like that? I thought angrily.

"Oh, yeah! Chief is awake again and wants to talk to you! That's the main reason I came up here," Siri told Pierce after there a small break in their conversation.

"Me?" he asked with his eyebrow raised.

"Yup," Siri popped the 'p' loudly. "Oh, and he wants to talk to you alone."

I was taken aback by what she said. Why would Chief want to talk to Pierce alone? What was he going to do?

"Okay…" Pierce answered hesitantly and slowly left the lounge.

After he was gone, Siri turned back to the three of us, "Nice seeing you guys again. I must go now." She walked away, with an extra swing to her step. I nearly gagged at the sight and saw that Blake did too.

"Well…" Karter let out a breath. "That was interesting."

"What's her problem?" Blake spat.

"Aww, is little Blakey jealous that Pierce got more attention from the devil than you did?" Karter cooed at Blake's face and stuck his finger in between Blake's eyes.

"Shut up!" Blake swatted Karter's finger away. "You know that's ridiculous."

"Then again, why was she so interested in Pierce again? It's weird." I asked bitterly.

"Ooh…now I see!! Blake isn't the jealous one here… you are!!" Karter teased me. I remained silent, not knowing how to respond to that. Deep down, I knew that I was... but how could I forgive the guy who broke my heart?

The silence was stifling as Karter shifted awkwardly in his seat. I guess he regretted what he said. Suddenly, a loud growl filled the silence. My head snapped to Blake as he turned a little pink.

"What was that?!? Are you secretly a monster?" I stared incredulously at him.

"Nah," Blake muttered. "That was my stomach."

Karter and I shared a look before bursting out into laughter. Later, Blake joined in.

"C'mon," I smiled as I stood up and glanced at the clock in the corner of the room. "Let's go eat something. We haven't eaten anything since we left New York!! Anyways, it's already dinnertime."

"Ahh, maybe that's why I'm so hungry."

Karter rolled his eyes as he walked out of the lounge with me. Blake quickly ran to catch up with us. I gasped a little as I took in the dining room again. If possible, it was even grander than I remembered it. The high ceiling arched and reflected the glow cast by the lights. I didn't think I would ever get used to how amazing this place is.

The room was empty as the three of us sat at one end of the long table. A few minutes later, waiters brought out our food on large silver platters.

"Thank you," I muttered before tucking into my food. I didn't realize how hungry I actually was until now. The three of us sat there in silence, our attention all on the food.

The sound of a chair being scraped along the floor interrupted my thoughts. I looked to my right and saw Pierce pulling a chair back. I looked at him questioningly, wanting to know what Chief wanted. However, he looked away before I could ask anything. The look on his face was grim and solemn, so I decided to ask about it later. Turning back to my food, I realized I had lost my appetite.

Not a minute later, someone brought out Pierce's food. Instead of leaving after placing the food down, he stood beside Pierce.

Odd. I thought as I looked up.

My eyes met Evander's as he smiled at me before patting Pierce on the shoulder. What was going on? Pierce ducked his head down and shifted slightly away from the butler.

"Congratulations Pierce. You deserve it," Evander smiled. His grin was too gleeful to be normal.

"Congratulations for what?" I asked, unable to contain my curiosity. I knew I bit the bait when Evander turned his creepy smile towards me.

"For taking over the company!" His voice drawled out sweetly. "You're looking at the new CEO!"

My mind blanked. Karter choked on his food and Blake whacked his back. When Karter was done hacking up the food, we all turned to Pierce with questioning eyes. I could feel that mine were filled with surprise, betrayal, and confusion.

The so called "new CEO" looked down and didn't meet our gazes. Why would he do this?

My mind still drew a blank. Did Pierce really accept the job as the CEO? Muttering an excuse, I pushed myself back from the table and escaped from the room. He knew that I would seriously disapprove of this decision, but he still chose to take over the company. I guess he was serious when he said that he didn't need me or my opinions in his life.

I quickly ran up to my room and sat on the windowsill, wanting to be alone with my thoughts. At first, sadness had filled me when I heard the news. But I was done crying over Pierce and his stupid decisions. I couldn't let him hurt me anymore.

Anger surged into my body the more I thought about Pierce. A thousand thoughts went flying through my mind, but only one question stuck out.

What bullshit was he trying to pull now?

Too restless to sit still, I got up and snuck into the hallway. I wasn't ready to face anyone else yet. For once in my life, I wanted to be alone. Walking around the house aimlessly, I let myself wander.

After a few minutes, I rounded a corner and faced an unfamiliar hallway. That's weird…I thought I knew the mansion like the back of my hand by now. I looked around at my surroundings, trying to figure out where I was. The stairs that led to my parents' bedroom loomed above my head. I never knew there was a hallway underneath the stairs. The entrance was usually blocked off by a door, so I always thought it was a coat closet or something.

Hesitantly, I took a step into the hallway. Shivers ran down my spine when the single light bulb flickered above me. The short hallway was lined with two doors on either side, all of them closed. Moving towards the door closest on my right, I was able to discern a voice.

My curiosity got the best of me as I carefully laid one ear on the door.

"It was almost too easy," a deep voice said. "I thought

they would be inseparable, but it looks like they're not as 'in love' as we thought."

"Excellent." I gasped as I recognized that voice. Evander. "It looks like everything is falling perfectly into place as I planned."

"And the delivery came in today," the first guy said something again. His voice seemed like he was proud.

"That's good. We were running low on the milk," Evander said coolly as usual.

What the hell!?? Milk? Is that a freaking code word or something?

After a pause, Evander spoke up again. "It won't be long before it's all over."

Before what's over? I racked my brain for ideas, but I just drew a blank. The new information might as well be as good as junk since I had no idea what it was supposed to mean. I toyed around for different meanings the word 'milk' could have, but none of the puzzle pieces fit together.

Suddenly, I was aware of the heavy footsteps that came from the other side of the door. They were approaching in my direction…fast. As quickly and as silently as I could, I ran out of the hallway and up the stairs to my parents' room. Turning around and looking down the side of the stairs, I saw the two men disappearing towards the main part of the house.

A weight felt like it was lifted off my shoulders as I was finally able to breathe again. I placed a hand over my heart to try and calm it down. I smiled a little as I made my way to my parents' room. It felt like I haven't been here in forever. A light coat of dust covered the door handle, so I gently brushed it away before opening the door.

Even though I never really knew who my parents were, I felt a sense of calmness flooding through me as I took in the room again. I really missed this place. Walking to the far side of the room, I picked up the picture frame holding my mother and father's smiling faces.

"Hi mom and dad," I stared at the picture, feeling slightly silly. "So many things have happened since I left for New York. Obviously, I'm back now."

Walking over to the bed and sitting down on it, I poured my heart out to the photo of my parents. They listened without interrupting or judging. Of course they couldn't talk back…they were dead. My eyes watered at the realization. Once again, I found myself alone in this large, empty mansion. Silence filled the air around me as I just stared off into space, not really thinking about anything.

A soft knock on the door broke the silence. My heartbeat quickened as I tried to figure out who it was. "Who is it?"

Without answering, the person opened the door and popped his head in. Pierce.

"Can I please talk to you?" his eyes begged me to let him in.

I didn't say anything and turned my attention back to the picture in my hands. After a moment, he took my silence as a 'yes.' Slowly walking into the room, he whispered, "I know you probably hate me right now, but I want to explain to you why I chose to take over the company."

I snorted. "I thought you said you didn't need me in your life and you didn't care about what I thought of you."

He flinched as his harsh words were repeated back to him. "I didn't mean to make it sound so harsh."

My heart sunk. He didn't want it to sound that harsh? Does that mean he still meant what he said? I looked over at Pierce, which confirmed my suspicion. He did mean what he said the other day. His eyes were now cold and distant.

What bothered me the most was that we were in my parents' room…the place where Pierce poured his heart out to me and told me that he wanted to become a doctor. There were so many memories of us in this room, but this one would certainly overshadow the happy ones.

"Whatever," I muttered.

Pierce looked over at me and let out a sigh. "When Siri told me that Chief wanted to talk to me, I wasn't even thinking about the company…let alone taking over it. I just walked into Chief's room, not knowing what to expect. He looked so pale and weak."

I couldn't help but remember the image of Chief laying in his bed, completely drained of energy.

"So when he asked me to come to his bed, I had to comply. I remember the sound of his weak and raspy voice when he asked me the question. I was so caught off guard; I had no idea what to do." Pierce avoided my gaze and ran a hand through his hair.

"What did he say?" I needed to know.

Pierce paused and took a breath before repeating what he heard. "Will you grant my last wish and take over the company? I can't have it in the hands of someone I don't trust."

I sucked in a breath. All my anger towards Pierce subsided, and I finally understood why he agreed to take up the title as the new CEO.

"How could I possibly say no to him?" Pierce's voice

cracked as his head dropped into his hands. He looked so torn that my heart reached out for him. Hesitantly, I moved to place my hand on his shoulder. Before I could, he looked up with more resolve and determination that I had ever seen in his eyes.

Looking straight at me, he said with strong conviction, "So don't you dare judge me, Melanie Cartwright. Don't you dare."

Turning around on his heels, he quickly walked out of the room. My hand flew to my mouth as my eyes filled with tears of guilt and helplessness. No matter what I did, it's like I couldn't do anything to make our lives better. If we continued the way we're headed, all of us were on a one way street to hell.

After a few minutes, I quietly walked out the door like Pierce did. The loneliness was back, and I needed to find someone to talk to. Closing the door behind me, I quickly ran down the stairs. I didn't know where I was going, but my subconscious did. I didn't stop running until I stood outside of Chief's door, not knowing whether to disturb him or not. I hoped he wasn't still sleeping.

Softly, I knocked on the door waiting for a response. I heard a cough and some words I couldn't make out. Assuming Chief was telling me to come in, I pushed open the door.

"Melanie," a smile lit up his face. "It's so nice to see you again!"

"You too Chief," I walked over to his bed for the second time that day.

"So what brings you here?"

"I just wanted to see my grandfather," I grinned as I pulled up a seat next to his bed.

"Well, don't I feel special?" he coughed a bit, and scratched his arm. "I missed you so much, sweetie."

"I'm back now, don't worry about anything. And I'm sorry for not coming sooner," I took one of his hands into mine. I nearly blanched at the sight. His hand was so much paler and had a tinge of yellowness to them. What made him so sick like this? "I love you, Chief."

"I love you too, Melanie." He forced a smile even though I could tell he was in pain.

Slowly, I saw his eyes grow heavy right before he fell asleep again. It's not normal for a person to be sleeping this much, even if they are sick, I thought worriedly to myself. Walking towards the door, I allowed one last glance of him before I left.

Chief coughed heavily in his sleep, rolling over to his side. In the following instant, I heard a gurgling sound as he vomited in his bed.

"Chief!" I screamed and ran towards him. I shook him so he was awake, but still not aware of his surroundings. His eyes were in a straight stare, looking at everything but not taking anything in. His stomach growled as he heaved again.

Frantically, I rolled him over onto his other side so he wouldn't choke on his own bile. With tears running down my eyes, I ran out of the room desperately to find some help.

"Pierce! Blake! Karter!" I screamed at the top of my lungs. "Chief needs help! Come here!!" I ran back into Chief's room hoping the three of them heard me. Sure enough, fast footsteps fell onto the floor above me as people came running.

Pierce was the first one to burst through the room.

"What's wrong?" he asked worriedly while looking around the room. He took one glance at Chief and paled.

"We need to get him to a hospital as soon as possible!" Pierce tossed me something as he ran towards Chief.

I caught whatever he threw, and realized it was a phone. Shaking, my fingers pressed the three buttons that I have been taught about since childhood. Holding the phone up to my ear, I waited for the person to answer.

"9-1-1. What's your emergency?"

Minutes, but what felt like hours, passed before I heard people rushing into the room beside me. I don't know when Karter or Blake arrived, but they were suddenly standing next to me. My mind was in a daze, and all their faces started to blur together. Moving on their own accord, my feet dragged the rest of my body outside where red and blue lights flashed rhythmically. Nothing made sense as I climbed into the ambulance behind Chief. I grabbed onto his hand as the ambulance sped off into the night. The sirens echoed through the empty streets.

Abruptly, my hand was jerked away from Chief's and I desperately cried out to him. I noticed that we already arrived at the hospital. Running after the stretcher that carried my grandfather, I was stopped by a lady dressed in white.

"I'm sorry, Ma'am." A nurse stood in front of me to restrain me. "We cannot let you pass at this moment. He needs to be brought to the ER immediately."

I tried to protest, but she gave me a sad look and shook

her head. With that, she disappeared behind those large metal doors, along with the other doctors who held Chief's life in their hands. My heart broke as I let out a strangled sob.

Defeated, I fell to my knees, feeling all alone in the white washed hallways of the hospital.

Chapter 28

I felt a pair of arms wrap around my shoulders and gently pick me up from the ground. Gratefully, I turned around and buried my face into their chest. The familiar scent calmed me as I looked up to Pierce's worried face.

Snapping back to my senses, I realized I shouldn't be this close to Pierce. I tried to wiggle out of his arms, but he managed to hold me firmly into place.

"Pierce…" I protested.

"Shh," one of his hands wrapped around to the back of my neck and pulled me in closer so that my face was buried in his chest again. "Just don't say anything right now."

I nodded into his chest as a fresh wave of tears crashed through me. Thoroughly wetting Pierce's shirt, I finally finished crying and took a step back. This time, he let me.

"Thank you," I muttered, not meeting his gaze.

"It's the least I can do after everything that happened."

I avoided meeting his gaze, scared that he'll snap out of

it and suddenly stop acting so nice to me. Trying to find an escape, I looked around and saw that Karter and Blake were sitting on the chairs in the waiting lounge. Slowly I disentangled myself from Pierce's arms and made my way over to the other guys. Taking a seat next to Karter, I stared blankly ahead at the wall on the other side of the room.

There was a crack running along the upper side of the wall. Two more met up with it near the corner of the room. It was like all the cracks in the wall led to that one point near the corner.

I let my head rest against Karter's shoulder as I stared at the point for a long time. It was the source of all the problems. The more I stared at it, the more I wondered what caused it. My eyelids drooped a little as I lost focus of the point on the wall. Right before I fell asleep, I heard Evander's voice in my mind.

Milk.

"Melanie!" I felt someone shake me. "Wake up! The doctor is coming!"

Groaning, I slowly opened my eyes only to be blinded by the bright, fluorescent lights. There were no windows in here, so it was impossible to discern what time it was or how long I was sleeping for.

"What time is it?" I asked Karter while rubbing my eyes.

"It's almost five in the morning," he answered after glancing at his watch.

"Oh," I muttered. It was around eleven when we brought Chief in. It took six hours for the doctors to finally come?

Anxiously I stood up to face the man wearing a white

lab coat. Unsurprisingly, he was carrying a file in one hand and had a stethoscope wrapped around his neck. Too impatient for him to walk all the way over here, I ran to meet him halfway.

"Well?" I asked impatiently.

"It seems like Mr. McKinley is in a stable condition right now," the doctor gave me the good news. I sighed a breath of relief and almost laughed with happiness. However, I glanced at the doctor's face and knew that wasn't the end of his diagnosis. Of course they would save the bad news for last. "But I'm sorry to say he has cirrhosis."

"What?" I snapped mad that he didn't care to explain what cirrhosis was. I can't understand the medical jargon that doctors spew. However, I heard a small gasp on my right and saw that it was from Pierce. I rolled my eyes because I forgot that he probably knew what it meant.

"It's basically a liver disease," the doctor began to explain slowly. "The cells in the liver become scar tissue."

I gave him a pointed look, still not understanding what that meant.

Pierce cut in when he saw my expression, "It's when the cells die."

My heart stopped. Even though I didn't have a lot of knowledge in biology, I knew that dead cells were not a good thing. "Is it deadly?"

This time, the real doctor answered. "This disease will eventually lead to liver failure, which is deadly. The good news is that we discovered the cirrhosis early enough so that a good chunk of his liver is still functioning."

"Okay," I let out another breath of relief. But before

I could celebrate, the doctor had to burst my bubble yet again.

"That means we have to operate on him as soon as possible. The only way to save his liver at this point is to cut out all the dead parts."

"What are the rates of survival?" Pierce asked.

"It's pretty high…around 65 to 80 percent," the doctor smiled. "On the other hand, since Mr. McKinley is older, the chances of complications increase a little."

My nerves gnawed at my stomach as I thought about Chief dying. I shook my head. That will NOT happen. Suddenly, a question popped into my head.

"What causes cirrhosis?" I asked curiously.

"There are a lot of different causes, so we don't know for sure. It could be a hereditary disease. It could also be caused by hepatitis A or B or a handful of other diseases." The doctor shrugged. "But we will save him, don't worry."

After a pause, it was clear to the doctor that we had no more questions. "Now, I'm going to talk to Mr. McKinley about his health status when he wakes up. If you please excuse me…"

The doctor went back through those metal doors.

I turned to Pierce, "When do you think we can see him?"

"Probably when he is out of the intensive care unit," Pierce guessed, not completely sure of his answer.

Karter, Blake, Pierce, and I walked back to the waiting lounge to sit again. There was a solemn silence that swept through the air, as none of us spoke up. Finally, Karter couldn't take it anymore.

"Hey," he said in a teasing tone. "At least we know Evander isn't behind any of this. Chief was actually sick!"

I scoffed. "Evander is still really, really sketchy though. I think we're going to have to do something with him even if he is innocent. He just gives me the creeps."

"You can say that again," Blake muttered. "He's a mysterious guy."

Nodding, I agreed completely with him. His comment struck a chord in my mind, making me remember what happened yesterday with Evander. "He is mysterious! Oh, and I forgot to tell you guys something. Yesterday, I heard him and this other guy in a room talking about milk."

The three of them gave me a baffled look. In unison, the questioned, "Milk?"

"Yeah. I have no idea what it means. The one guy just said, 'the delivery of milk came in today.' And Evander seemed happy about it. Maybe it's a code word for something?"

"I have no clue as to what it means," Karter scratched his head. "That man has some serious issues. Maybe it's for himself…like he needs milk to make soap or something."

I scoffed. "Yeah, right. I'm sure Evander needs milk to make soap." My tone dripped with sarcasm.

"Hey! It's just an idea. No need to shoot it down like that," Karter defended his idea.

"Whatever."

"What about something more…realistic?" Blake suggested. "It could be a code word for something. It could have to do with money."

"That's more believe-able," I muttered, but still not entirely convinced.

I looked at Pierce to see if he had any ideas. He seemed as stumped as the rest of us were. His eyebrows were furrowed, as if he was in deep thought.

"Do you guys think it has something to do with Chief's condition? Or something else entirely?" I mused, not sure of an answer myself.

"I feel like it has to do with something else," Karter input his opinion. "You heard the doctor. There are so many different causes to the disease Chief has, and it seems fairly common. It could be running in your family."

I rolled my eyes at him, "Thanks a lot. Are you saying I'm going to get it when I'm older too?"

Karter held up his hand in defense. "Hey, I didn't say that. You're the one who said it."

"Sure, sure."

"Who knows? Maybe you won't get it," he continued to tease me, trying to lighten up the atmosphere some more. "Just avoid drinking Evander's milk." Karter joked as he poked me in the side.

"Har, har. You're so funny," I flinched away from his finger and swatted his hand away from my body.

No one bothered to react, and I sighed. Taking my phone out of my pocket, I checked the time. It was nearly six. I snapped my phone shut and tapped on the screen, impatient to see Chief again. Every few minutes or so, I hit a button on my phone to see how much time had passed, but it seemed to drag on slowly. Everything was just so freaking quiet and sluggish.

"I figured it out!"

Pierce's outburst had me falling out of the chair in surprise. He jumped up, running his hands through his hair frantically as he paced around as if he was looking for something.

"Keys…keys…" he mumbled as he patted his pockets furiously. "Where the hell are the keys?! I need the keys!" Pierce turned to Blake and held out his hands expectantly.

Karter, Blake, and I stared at Pierce with concern. It seemed like he finally lost his mind. Hesitantly, Blake reached into his pocket and produced a set of car keys.

"What's going on? What did you figure out?" Blake asked before surrendering his keys to Pierce.

"I don't know for sure, but I need to check something to confirm my guess." Pierce talked quickly and curled his fingers in a come-hither motion. He wanted the keys badly.

"I think I should drive," Blake said cautiously as he looked into Pierce's crazed eyes. "Are you okay?"

Pierce let out a loud groan of frustration and swiped the keys from Blake's hand, "Of course I'm okay! And you don't have to come with me. You guys need to be here for when Chief wakes up. I'll be back soon."

Before anyone could protest, he was running out of the hospital like a mad man. I stared after him for a moment, not knowing what he was up to. Without thinking, I sprang to my feet and followed Pierce out of the building.

"Wait up!" I huffed as the morning rays of sunshine began to pierce through the sky. I shielded my eyes away from the glare and focused on the figure running in front of me.

As he fumbled with the keys a little when trying to unlock the car door, I managed to make it to the passenger door. I heard a little click and knew the door was unlocked a second later. Before Pierce could say no, I slid into the car and buckled my seatbelt.

"What's going on?" I asked him as he started the engine.

He backed out of the parking lot like a pro while look-ing back through the rear window. Shifting his eyes be-tween me and the road, he let out a sigh and filled me in on his theory.

"I think that the milk Evander was talking about is actually milk," I raised an eyebrow at him in confusion. Rolling his eyes, he began from the beginning. "Remem-ber when Karter was teasing you about how you shouldn't drink 'Evander's milk' if you didn't want cirrhosis?"

I nodded, not knowing where he was going with this.

"Well, if my theory is correct, he is right." Pierce shook his head at Karter's indirect way of solving the mystery.

"How can he be right? He was only joking!" My mind was still all over the place, trying to figure out what Pierce was telling me.

"In my pathology class, we learned about cirrhosis and liver cancer," Pierce explained. I didn't say anything, so he continued. "Apparently, it is really common all over the world, but for different reasons. The main reason here is because of alcoholism." He looked over his shoulder and switched lanes quickly. I'm pretty sure the way he was weaving through traffic was illegal.

"But the most common cause of cirrhosis in Asia and Africa is either hepatitis B or a mold called afflation." My brain finally registered what he was trying to say.

"So are you saying that Chief got his disease from drinking moldy milk?" I scrunched my face, trying not to think about how disgusting that was.

Pierce nodded in confirmation, "There's only one way to find out if I'm right."

My body lurched forward as Pierce slammed on the brake when we arrived in front of the mansion. We quickly sprang out of the car and up the front steps leading to the mansion. Pushing past the butlers and workers, Pierce and I ignored all of the questioning stares that were thrown at us.

When we made our way through a dark and narrow hallway, I whimpered slightly, not knowing where we were going. I felt something warm slide into my hands and my fear evaporated as I realized Pierce was holding onto my hand as support. Using our connection, he gently guided me towards the kitchen.

I took in my surroundings as I felt Pierce's hand slip away from mine. A row of fluorescent lights shone down on metal countertops, reminding me slightly of the hospital I was just in. It was cold and clean in here, the only sound you could hear was the hum of the appliances. The room gave off a slightly chilling atmosphere.

I heard a light clank and whipped my head toward the source. Pierce had opened the refrigerator, revealing large shelves of liquids and foods. Silently, I made my way so that I was standing next to him.

"There it is," I whispered, as I pointed to a quart sized glass container holding some white liquid.

"That's the one," Pierce smiled at me before gingerly reaching in and grabbing the bottle around its neck.

Chapter 29

"Is that even a question?!!" I yelled at Chief in disbelief.

"The doctor said I should think about the surgery very carefully," he responded to me calmly. "He warned me about all the complications. It just doesn't seem like it is worth it..."

I sighed in frustration. "If you don't get the surgery, it might develop into cancer! And then the complications would be even worse."

"It MIGHT develop into cancer. There is still a chance that it won't."

I threw my hands up into the air, annoyed by his attitude. Even though I desperately wanted to knock some sense into him, I feel like it would be unethical to hit an old man in a sick bed...especially since we were still in the hospital.

"Chief, I know you are a very smart guy," I started to take a different approach in convincing him. "But I think you lost a serious amount of brain cells because of that fever last week..."

It had been about nine days since we had rushed Chief to the ER and approximately eight days since Pierce and I reported our suspicions about Evander to the police. However, we never got a reply from them.

Chief chuckled a bit and then let out a sigh. After a moment, he asked me, "Do you really think I should do it?"

I smiled at him ruefully, "Yes. I need my grandfather in my life, and we've only been united for half a year. The doctor seems to know what he is doing, and I really trust him."

At that moment, the doctor walked into the room. With a large smile on his face, he turned to me, "Thank you for your trust." Then he said to Chief, "There is one thing I can guarantee - you'll be in good hands."

Chief looked between the doctor and I, seeming like he was deep in thought. "Fine. Why not? I'll do the surgery for Melanie."

The doctor smiled and looked at Chief's charts before leaving the room again. I let out a sigh of relief and ran over to Chief with a grin. Wrapping my arms around him, I put my mouth to his ear. "Thank you so much for doing this, Chief. I know it's really hard on you, but I feel like this will really help your health."

"I know, I know. I just wasn't 100% sure about everything, but now, I am." I pulled back from him so I could see him talking. "Anyways, don't you have a date with Pierce right now?" Chief's eyes darted to the clock on the opposite wall.

There was a small pang in my chest, but I quickly covered up my emotions in front of Chief. Forcing out a fake laugh, I crossed my arms and gave Chief a pointed look. "Chief! How many times do I need to tell you? I'm not dating Pierce!"

"You were when you angrily stormed out of the mansion right after him..." he rubbed his chin in thought as he remembered that day months ago.

I rubbed my hands over my face to hide the blush spreading across my cheeks. Groaning in frustration, I refused to either affirm or deny Chief's accusation.

"Think what you want to think," I rolled my eyes and gave Chief a quick peck on the head. "But you were partially right. I have a MEETING with Pierce...NOT a date." I emphasized those two words before briskly walking out the room. Chief's muffled laughter followed me after I closed the door to his room.

In record time, I drove back to the mansion and walked up the marble steps to my parents' old room. Dust no longer lined the railing or door handle because of my frequent visits.

"Pierce?" I whispered quietly as I opened the door.

"Shh," a hand pulled me in and shut the door behind me. "Did anyone see you come here?"

"Calm down!" I wrenched my arm away from his grip and angrily scolded him. "It doesn't really matter if anyone sees me coming here! Evander won't hunt us down or anything like that. But no. No one saw me."

Pierce ran his hand through his hair while walking away from me, clearly annoyed.

After an awkward silence, I spoke up again. "So what did you call this 'emergency' meeting for?"

Since no lights were on and the curtains were drawn shut, I could only see his silhouette bend down and pick up something off the bed.

"The lab results are in."

My heart pounded as I registered his words and walked over to where he stood. We had sent the sample of milk to the lab eight days ago! We pulled some strings at the local community college so they would run the liquid through microscopes and tests to determine if the mold was actually in the milk. "Finally! What were the results?"

"I don't know yet. I was waiting so we could see together." Pierce shrugged his shoulders nonchalantly. My heart sputtered at what he said. Was it bad that I found it extremely sweet of him to do that? I shook my head lightly as Pierce proceeded to stick his finger under the seal of the envelope.

The sound of ripping paper filled the room as we held our breaths. Opening the envelope, Pierce pulled out a small packet of paper stapled together. I looked over his shoulder, but was unable to understand any of the graphs and words on the paper. Pierce nodded his head while reading several things, and I pretended to process the information, not wanting to seem stupid in front of him.

"The test results are..." I paused for dramatic effect, hoping he would finish the sentence for me.

Thankfully, he did. "Positive."

"Positive," I repeated, all my emotions jumbling together. I was glad that we could prove Evander "poisoned" Chief, but it was sad that we were all deceived by someone we thought we knew so well.

"What are we going to do now? We already tried calling the police, but they won't do anything! They should be dealing with these kinds things...it's their job!" I huffed angrily.

"It's because they can't do anything without 'probable cause.' Our tips aren't good enough to start an investigation." Pierce sighed angrily, too.

My heart dropped at our predicament. The justice and law enforcement system was usually great, but in some situations, it was seriously flawed. It's awful to know that there was an obviously guilty criminal walking among us and we could do nothing about it...unless they actually killed someone and we caught them.

"We can hire a private investigator..." I suggested as I thought of Sherlock Holmes. Aren't there people like that who can help catch the bad guy without dealing with the police?

"Do you know how expensive they are?" Pierce asked incredulously.

"Do you know what Evander is going to do to the company if things go his way? We don't know if he'll somehow formulate a plan to take over the company and completely drive it to the ground!"

It seemed like I had finally made Pierce silent as he considered my words. "Fine. But we're going to have to pool our money together in order to do this."

"So I guess we have to tell Karter and Blake about this whole thing. I was hoping we didn't have to drag them into this mess." I sighed.

Pierce nodded and made his way to the door, signaling that our 'meeting' was over. Holding the door open for me, my heart pounded against my chest as I had to squeeze past him to get through the opening. My shoulder brushed against his chest, and butterflies exploded in my stomach.

Looking up at Pierce, I was met with his grey eyes. He held my gaze for a second, completely unblinking, before turning away. Feeling like an idiot for staring, I mentally slapped myself for not turning away first. No matter how much my brain said it hated him, my heart beats told a different story. And I hated it. I hated not being able to control my heart.

And so I led the two of us out of the room, with my heart still fluttering like a falling leaf in autumn. Slowly, we walked back to the lounge outside our rooms. As we approached the room, the sound of quiet gunshots came from the television. Karter and Blake sat in front of the screen with their eyes glued to the figures they were controlling. It looked like virtual Blake was successfully sneaking up to virtual Karter when Pierce and I interrupted the game.

Pierce cleared his throat, but was ignored by the two morons. Taking matters into my own hands, I walked up in front of the TV, blocking both of their views. They both grunted and moved to opposite sides of the room so they could see again. I sighed in frustration as I turned around and switched the game system off. Blake had a disappointed look on his face when his eyes met the black screen.

"What was that for?" Karter yelled, throwing the controller down onto the table in front of him.

"We have something to tell you." Pierce stated calmly.

"It better be good!" Blake muttered.

"Are you going to tell us that you two are finally together again?" Karter asked.

My mouth fell open as I gaped like a fish. Pierce, on the other hand, seemed like he was less affected by that comment.

"No." Pierce answered flatly with a grim look.

"What? But you..." Karter didn't finish his sentence as his eyes glanced over to me like he just remembered I was in the room. I saw him and Pierce share a look. Karter's was more pointed and Pierce shook his head lightly. I furrowed my eyebrows in confusion. What was that silent conversation all about?

Pierce cleared his throat and started his announcement over. "It's really important, so listen up."

I took over talking as everyone found a seat.

"Remember when Pierce acted like a madman at the hospital and kept on asking for the car keys?"

Karter and Blake's confused expressions turned into one of understanding when I mentioned the car keys bit.

"How could we forget that? And you guys never told us what it was all about! All you said was that his guess was wrong and it was all for nothing." Blake commented.

I looked down in shame for lying to the two of them. Pierce noticed my hesitation and picked up where I left off.

"Well, actually…" Pierce scratched the back of his head. "It turns out I was right."

Karter and Blake both raised their eyebrows in confusion, waiting for Pierce to elaborate. After minutes of explanation, they both looked murderous for being kept in the dark.

"So you decide to finally share the information with us when you realize that you need money?!" Blake asked accusingly.

Pierce and I shared a guilty look. "Sort of, but we also realized that you guys should know what's going on, too." I mumbled a lame excuse.

"That's complete bull," Karter rolled his eyes. However, the corners of his lips turned up into a grin. "But I do think this could be really interesting. I'll donate all the money I made from my gigs."

I smiled, relieved that he wasn't too mad at us. Karter proceeded to pull out his wallet from his back pocket and leafed through it. Throwing a five dollar bill onto the table, he smiled proudly.

"And that's about it." He snapped his wallet shut and stuffed it back into his pocket.

"You're too funny for your own good, you know that?" I laughed as I punched his shoulder.

"Sure. Whatever." Karter leaned back into the couch with his hands behind his head. "I say we hire Inspector Jacques Cousteau."

Pierce shot him a funny look. "Who?"

"Oh, come on! You don't know who he is?" Karter looked around at Blake, Pierce, and I. We all have him blank stares. "You know…ohm-berr-gare." He did a terrible impression of a French guy trying to say 'hamburger' in English.

"You mean the weird guy in *Pink Panther*?" I asked with one eyebrow cocked.

"Exactly! That's the one. Thank you!" Karter gestured towards me gratefully.

"For some reason, I feel like he wouldn't be much help in this situation. We need a real PI to crack this case." I muttered to no one in particular.

I hoped this plan wouldn't fail us.

Chapter 30

Ryan Carter. That was the man's name. I looked down at the business card he started to hand out to each of the four of us. On the left hand side of the card, there was a small picture of a magnifying glass with an eye in the middle of it. On the other side of the card, there was a small seal that ensured he was a licensed detective. Smack dab in the middle of the two things, his name was printed boldly in italics.

Looking up from the business card, my gaze was met with the detective's old, expressionless eyes. Wrinkles creased the skin around his eyes, and his silver hair showed us he had years of experience. "Thanks for coming." I told him sincerely. He was our last hope to solve this whole fiasco with Evander.

"It's really no problem," he answered mechanically, without emotion. To him, everything was a job. Through years of working with the CIA and as a detective, he was conditioned to never reveal anything personal about himself. The only reason why he was helping us was because we paid him a fat sum of money we had managed to collect.

"So…" Karter eyed the man warily. "What's next? What are you going to do?"

"I'm going to start with the basics," Ryan began to explain his strategy to us. "Contrary to popular belief, I am not allowed to do anything more than a mere citizen like you guys."

His gaze met each of ours, and I couldn't help but let out a small sigh of disappointment. I expected him to be able to sleuth through confidential files and make dramatic arrests. Needless to say, I already doubted our decision to hire a private investigator.

"But I do have more knowledge than an average person on how to use my resources. There are ways of obtaining information legally, but it is really tricky sometimes so we'll just have to find ways around that." Blake nodded at what Ryan was saying, hanging on to every word. He was clearly impressed by the older man. "I usually start out with phone records. Although it is nearly impossible to see someone's records without permission, it is okay if we use connections and contacts. From there, it depends on what I find before I decide what to do next."

I voiced my approval of his methods. It was simple, concise, and we had nothing to lose. "Okay. So when will you start looking into things?"

"Probably right after we finish this little talk," he answered professionally. "It's best if we start quickly and finish quickly."

I smiled at his efficiency. Although I did appreciate his

work ethic, I felt a little sorry for him. Did he ever let loose a little? Did he have a wife? I shook these thoughts from my head as Ryan began to close his briefcase next to him.

"Do you have any more questions or concerns?" He turned his head towards the three of us again. When he was met with silence, he started to leave the room. "Then I hope you have a nice day. I'll keep in contact when I find new information."

With that, he opened the door and showed himself out of the mansion. He's probably going off into his headquarters or something and doing what detectives do.

"Well that was…interesting," Karter huffed as he ran his hand through his chocolate hair so it would stay out of his eyes.

"Yeah," Pierce agreed.

"Well, let's see if he does find something helpful for us," I fiddled with my hands, nervous that Evander would get away with what he did.

"I know that guy will find something to tack onto Evander. He seems like a really talented guy," Blake stood up for Ryan, even though they had met only a few minutes earlier. "I believe in him." He put his hand over his heart dramatically, making me shove him lightly and laugh.

"I hope you're right, Blake." Pierce shook his head. Under his breath, he muttered it again as if reinforcing it would help our cause. "I really hope you're right."

* * *

"Are you ready for this?" I looked at Chief hesitantly.

"Of course I am!" He shook his head with a small

smile. "Weren't you the one pushing me to do the surgery? Are you regretting your decision?"

"No!!" I quickly shot back. I still wanted Chief to go through with the surgery--I was just a little nervous for him, even though the doctor had reassured me a thousand times that Chief would be okay.

I twiddled my thumbs a little as we checked in to the hospital. In a few moments, Chief would be whisked away so they could operate on his liver. I shook the thought from my head. Blood always made me uneasy.

Chief seemed to notice my unease and placed a hand on my arm. Gently, he urged, "Melanie. Don't worry. I'll be okay. You have to calm down for me, okay?"

Taking a shaky breath, I nodded. I was such a loser. I should have been comforting him. He's the one getting the surgery. I looked up and smiled at Chief right as the doctor came out and called his name.

"Ralph McKinley, we're ready for you now." The doctor looked up from the clipboard.

Chief patted my hand one last time and slowly stood up. I quickly stood up too and pulled him into a hug. "I love you, Chief."

"Love you, too," I could hear Chief struggling to stay unemotional. I think that was the second time I had ever said 'I love you' to him. "I'll see you in a few hours."

I nodded as he patted my back and pulled away from the hug. I stood in my spot until he disappeared from my view. Sighing, I took my car keys out and made my way to the car. As I was driving home, I heard my phone ring.

Looking down, I saw 'Ryan Carter' flash across the screen. Knowing I was breaking the law, I quickly picked up the phone. It must be important if he was calling my cell phone. Usually, he would call Pierce and leave a voice-mail if Pierce didn't pick up.

"What's up? Any new news?" I kept my eyes on the road, hoping no police would see me while I was on the phone. It had been a little over a week since the guys and I hired Ryan. We had made little progress since then.

"Actually, yes. I found something really interesting," his scratchy voice answered mine.

My heart sped up a little, and a little adrenaline rushed through my body. I needed this good news. "What is it?"

"It would be best if I can meet you in person. Can we set up a date for all of us to meet?" Ryan's disappointing answer came through the line.

I frowned. How important is this news if it can wait for a group meeting? I sighed as I pulled through the gates of the mansion.

"Sure. When do you want to do it?" I asked impatiently as I drove up the long drive. The sun glared against the windshield and I squinted my eyes to see better. In the distance, I could make out a figure walking towards the house. Strange, everyone was supposed to be busy and out of the house today.

"I'm sorry, but I can't do it today. I have some other important business to take care of," he apologized gruffly.

"Then how about tomorrow?" I said absentmindedly, still concentrating on the person who was walking into the front door now. Quickly, I parked the car and quietly followed him. I didn't recognize him, but he may just be one of the workers.

"Yeah, sure."

"What time?" I asked, somewhat groaning because I lost sight of the person. I walked through the house and sat at the base of the stairs leading to my parents' room.

"I think five o'clock would be best."

"Good," I twirled my hair absentmindedly in my hand. I caught a movement in the corner of my eye, and whipped my head towards the source. The door underneath the stairs had opened, as someone made their way into the hidden hallway. I remember hearing Evander talking about "milk" when I first went in there.

Scrunching my eyes in suspicion, I waited until the door closed. "Hey, Ryan. I have to go. I think Evander is up to something." I whispered into the phone.

"What are you talking about, Melanie?" I could hear the confusion in his voice.

"I think I am on the verge of catching Evander red handed," I told him, ready to hang up the phone and solve the mystery myself. I was tired of waiting for Ryan to make progress in the case. At this rate, we would never get Evander in jail.

"Melanie!" I heard alarm in his voice, "Don't follow him! He's dangerous! You don't know what you're…"

I rolled my eyes and snapped my phone shut. Ryan was just being too defensive. If he ever wanted evidence, he had to go out and find it…like what I'm was going to do. I knew I was being a little reckless, but the thought of Chief going through surgery made me angry. He wouldn't have to go through all of this if it weren't for Evander!

Slowly, I crept up to the door and twisted the handle. Opening the door fully, I made my way into the hallway.

The place was still eerie and it gave me the creeps. Right as I shut the door behind me, a door to my right opened.

I yelled in surprise as my heart dropped and beat furiously. Standing in front of me was Evander himself, his eyes full of coldness.

"Hello, Melanie." He greeted me, almost too calmly. "I've noticed that you've been following me. What is that?"

I shivered at his voice. Nothing was more disturbing than the way he sounded. Taking a deep breath, I gathered all the courage I had and pushed my fear aside. I returned his cold glare. "I think you know exactly why I'm following you."

"I actually don't. Please enlighten me," Evander tried to seem innocent. No way was I letting him off the hook.

"Stop lying, Evander. You hurt someone who is really important to me, and I can't forgive you for that." I got straight to the point. Suddenly having an epiphany, I subtly turned on my phone and went to the voice recording function. Thank God for all those spy movies I had watched. This could be the evidence we needed to get him locked up.

Evander's eyes suddenly changed from an innocent look to one of rage, but he still didn't say anything. Egging him on, I hoped to catch a confession escape from his mouth.

"I know you're the one who poisoned Chief with the moldy milk. But what I don't know is why you did it. What's in it for you?" I pushed on, ignoring that his whole body was shaking.

In the instant before his arm lashed out to hit me, I finally felt fear rush through my body. Panic made me freeze in my spot, unable to defend myself against his attack. I hit the floor with a crash before I felt the pain in the side of my head. Evander's punch rendered me blind for a moment, and I could see nothing but dark spots blocking my vision. I vaguely heard the clatter of my phone as it slid across the room.

"You have nothing to prove it was me," Evander laughed hysterically as he paced the room, obviously distraught. From his actions, it was painfully obvious that he was guilty and panicking.

"Not yet," I grimaced as I tasted the salty irony blood in my mouth. "But I will. I know I will."

I was still lying on the ground when Evander made his way over to me. The last thing I saw was one of his giant, black leather shoes swinging towards my face. I closed my eyes and turned my head, preparing for the impact. As quickly as the pain coursed through my body, it receded as I slipped out of consciousness.

Chapter 31

The first thing I felt was a dull thudding on the left side of my head. It felt like a hangover, but probably a thousand times worse. Groaning, I tried to sit up, but was pushed back down by a firm hand.

Cracking one eyelid open, I immediately shut it again. Those damn, bright florescent lights seriously needed to die. I sighed, trying to remember where I was. I didn't recall going to a party the night before, so I didn't think this was some kind of mega hangover.

Forcing myself to open my eyes and take in my surroundings, I fought against the bright lights and looked around. I was wearing an extremely unflattering white paper gown. Looking up, I found the owner of the hand that restricted me from getting up.

Pierce. His grey eyes were piercing into me so worriedly that I immediately felt self-conscious.

Suddenly, everything came back to me. I had stupidly

confronted Evander, and he had kicked my head. No wonder why I was feeling awful right now.

"How…" my throat croaked from the dryness, and Pierce snapped out of his worried expression and quickly handed me a glass of water. After taking a gulp, I cleared my throat and tried again. "How did I get here? I thought Evander…"

I didn't finish the sentence. Did he try to kill me? Was he really that evil?

"I actually don't know what exactly happened. I just got here with Karter and Blake." Pierce confessed and finally sat down on the chair next to my bed. Taking one of my hands into his, he began to rub circles with his thumb. I can't deny that it felt somewhat comforting and good.

Dumbly, I looked around the room and realized that Blake and Karter were standing on the other side of my bed. My eyebrows shot up in surprise when I saw Ryan Carter sitting at the foot of my bed.

"If you want to know what happened, ask Ryan. He's the one who brought you here." Karter told me when I met his eyes. Nodding, I turned my head back to Ryan. He stood up, knowing that I wanted to talk to him.

"I told you not to go in after Evander."

I cringed at the first thing he said to me. I looked down ashamed, knowing that I should have listened to him.

"And when you hung up on me, I knew you just ignored what I had told you to do. I had a feeling you would be in trouble, and I knew I couldn't stand by idly and wonder if you got hurt." Ryan sighed.

I saw sadness flash though his eyes. However, I knew this had nothing to do with me. Something probably happened to him while he was on a mission when he was younger, and it had hurt him badly. But I knew I wouldn't get his story. It wasn't something he was willing to tell. Maybe that's why he was so dedicated to his work and completely devoid of emotion.

He continued telling me what happened. "I figured you were back at your mansion, so I followed my instincts and drove straight to your house. And sure enough, your car was parked outside. I didn't have to walk far into the house before I heard a loud crash. I followed the sound and ran into a room in a strange hallway. You were on the ground, and I could tell you were unconscious. But Evander was pacing the room like a madman. He didn't know what to do."

I nodded. Even though Evander was evil, I knew he couldn't murder someone directly. I guess that's why he hired men to do the dirty work for him--and probably why he chose to use poison on Chief.

"When Evander saw me, he panicked and bolted out of the room, but I couldn't chase after him because you were still unconscious." Ryan didn't look too upset about that, though. "It isn't a big deal because police are already out looking for him. We have enough evidence to lock him up, especially now that we can charge him with assault... thanks to you."

I grimaced, not entirely sure whether to be proud or not. On one hand, I had almost gotten myself killed. On the other, I am the reason why Evander was going to go to jail.

"I'm just glad you're okay," Blake gently leaned down

and pushed my hair out of my face for me. I smiled up at him.

"You gave us a heart attack when Ryan called us and told us about what you did. Can't you be more careful?" Karter shook his head at me.

"At least I'm still alive…" I tried to joke, but obviously no one found it funny.

"Never do anything like that again," Pierce squeezed my hand a little harder to get my attention. "We all care about you, and I don't think we can imagine our lives without you anymore."

I blushed and my eyes watered a little at his comment. I didn't know I was so important to the guys. I looked up at Ryan and noticed that he was off in his own world. What was he thinking of?

Suddenly, the doctor walked in. I grinned when I realized it was the same doctor who had treated Chief when we brought him to the ER that night.

"Fancy seeing you again, Melanie….although it's quite unfortunate that you are the one that is in need of medical attention."

I shot him a wry smile as he flipped through my charts and checked up on the machines that were hooked to me.

"Everything looks quite normal. We already checked your head for any brain injuries, but we didn't find anything severe. Not even a concussion."

"Well…I guess we should be thankful that Melanie has quite a thick skull." Karter decided let out his humorous side. Scowling at his double meaning, I shot him a death glare.

The doctor chuckled in response. "Yes, I do agree."

My mouth dropped at his comment. "Did you just agree with that idiot?" I asked the doctor, referring to Karter.

Waving off my question, he began to ask me questions. "How do you feel? Any pain?"

"I feel like I have a massive hang over right now. But other than that, I'm fine." I answered truthfully.

The doctor placed a hand on the left side of my head and began to gently press down. I winced when he hit the spot that Evander kicked. "Okay. It seems like you'll have a bruise over there, but otherwise, you should be good to go. I'll go get you some painkillers that may help you out."

I smiled at him. "Thank you so much."

"No problem," he said warmly before he walked out of the room.

A calm silence settled over us before Ryan cleared his throat. "I have something to tell you, and since we're all here, we don't need to make a team meeting."

I nodded as I remembered what he said in his call before I ran off to face Evander. I didn't think it was going to be anything important.

"Evander uses a cell phone that Mr. McKinley pays for," Ryan began to tell us. I raised my eyebrow in confusion. What does that have to do with anything? "I guess he forgot about that fact when he started to make some suspicious calls. I can track them because I got consent to see the phone records through Mr. McKinley."

Everyone nodded at his ingenuity. "And trust me; he has made some really weird phone calls."

"Like what?" I asked, eager to hear the answers to all the questions that had been bugging us.

"First, he called a number based in Wisconsin about eight times. That's about one too many times for it to be suspicious. Hence, last week, I flew over there and met with the owner of the number personally. Turns out, he was a farmer."

We all could see where this was going. Ryan confirmed our guesses. "Evander has been paying the man quite a large sum for some of the spoiled milk he had. Apparently, the cows ate some infected wheat, which made their milk unhealthy."

I smiled sadly at what he said. I was glad the whole fiasco was over, but it's still sad to see how far some people will go to hurt someone else.

"Thank you so much, Ryan. You've done so much to help us. And you managed to find some evidence to pin on Evander." I beckoned him to come over to my bed.

Adamantly, he stayed where he was. "I'm not done telling you what I found."

Pierce's eyes scrunched together. "There's more?"

"Evander had all his bases covered. His plan was more elaborate than just spoiled milk," Ryan shook his head pitifully.

"What else did that man do?" Blake's usually friendly voice suddenly carried an edge of anger in it. He must be furious at the thought of Evander doing more to cause harm.

"I went back several months in his call records. It took a while, but I found some interesting information. I'm not sure what they mean, but they were significant enough to take note of them." Ryan took out a worn yellow notepad from his breast pocket and flicked through several pages.

"A few months ago, he made calls to a news broadcasting company on a weekly basis. I found that he sent the same company a few letters. Do you know why he may have contacted them?" Ryan looked up, waiting to see if we had any epiphanies. I raked my brain for some ideas, but came up with none. Karter on the other hand, had a grim expression on his face.

"I think I may know what it means," Karter muttered under his breath. "A few months ago, I remember we all left the mansion, except for Blake. I was around California playing some gigs, and Mel and Pierce were in New York."

We all wanted to hear what Karter was thinking. "Don't you remember your time at the mansion, Blake? You were miserable."

Blake frowned at the memory. After a few moments, something clicked in this brain. "It was all because of those stupid news articles coming out about me!"

"Exactly!" Karter pointed at him in affirmation. "Maybe Evander gave gossip to the news companies about you. Maybe he knew you would crack under pressure and quit the job."

"And I was about to leave the company in his hands for a while…" Blake shook his head in disbelief. "Thank God Mel told me to leave the real vice president in charge."

I grinned at that memory. Blake had flipped out and turned his suitcase inside out to look for his phone. I remembered how he had left a pair of boxers in the kitchen, and Pierce had found it.

"You're welcome," I joked. Everything was starting to make sense now.

During the whole conversation, Ryan looked between

us in silence. When he realized we were done talking, he went on. "I also found that he made some calls to credit card companies and cancelled a credit card. If I wrote this down correctly, the card number ended with the digits: 1601."

"Wait. Pierce." I looked over at him. "Isn't that my card?"

"Yeah," he rubbed his chin. "I remember you telling me that you couldn't buy something in New York because Chief cancelled your card. You were furious."

I nodded in agreement. But I also felt a twinge of guilt-iness in my heart. I was mad at Chief for nothing? It was all Evander's fault? I guess Evander did that so I would get mad a Chief and never come back to the mansion. Oh, that man was despicable and too smart for his own good.

"Please don't tell me he did more things to make us hate him," I looked to Ryan. He had an expression on his face that told me that it wasn't the end of his story. "I guess I can't hate that man more than I already do."

"There is one last thing that he did." Ryan admitted. "And this one is technically a misdemeanor."

"What is it?" I sucked in my breath to prepare myself.

"He bribed a teacher at New York University." Ryan turned to look at Pierce. "Specifically, it was one of your teachers."

All of our gazes gravitated towards Pierce. I could see that he was literally frozen in his spot. Taking this as a sign to go on, Ryan kept on talking. "He gave the teacher $100,000 to fail you."

Pierce was still standing there…expressionless. This re-action was as scary as the time when we broke up. I knew something deep inside him was bottled up and ready to explode at any second.

"Pierce," I begged in a small voice, not wanting to push him over the edge like last time. "Please calm down. What's done is done. And I'm sure the teacher and Evander will be punished for this."

Slowly, I could see him take deeper breaths and his eyes regaining some sad and angry emotion. "I can't believe that they would do that to me," he whispered finally.

"I know," I shook my head. "I can't believe he did all of that to us." I referred to everything we just learned about. "He probably made you think you were incapable of being a doctor so you would come back and lead the company. That way, he could find a way to manipulate things his way again."

Pierce sighed. In a small, determined voice, he stated, "But we won't be his victims anymore. We won, and now he's paying the consequences."

Ryan Carter had left after he told us everything he knew. Everything took a while to sink in, so we walked around in a haze. But at the moment, we all stood at the foot of Chief's bed, waiting for him to wake up after his surgery. According to the doctor, everything went smoothly.

I walked over to the seat on his right side and took his hand in mine. Softly, I gave it a small squeeze. There was no response. Patiently, I waited for him to open his eyes.

A knock on the door snapped me out of thoughts running through my head. I looked up at the least expected person walking into the room – Siri.

Shooting her a glare, I snapped, "What do you want? Do you still want our money? Our lives?"

I was met with silence. To my greatest surprise, I saw her eyes water up slightly. "I'm sorry." Her voice broke in the middle. "I had no idea what my father was capable of doing."

Everyone was shocked by her apology. Not knowing what to say, we didn't say anything.

Her tiny voice spoke up after a minute. "I just knew that he encouraged me to try and get with Pierce. He just said that he was the perfect guy for me, especially since you and Pierce had broken up. I had no problem with it because I didn't think there was an underlying motive to his actions."

Deep down in my heart, I knew she was telling the truth. In a whisper, I acknowledged her apology. "I know."

"And the more I think about it, the more I'm ashamed. My father probably broke you two up on purpose, just so I would be free to go after Pierce." She sniffled a little and wiped the corner of her eyes. "When I got the call that my father got arrested, I knew I had to find you guys first. I'm sorry."

Before any of us could respond or accept her apology, she quickly ran out of the room. My heart broke for her, and to some extent I could tell what she was going through. The only parent she knew had just broken her heart. Evander was no longer a role model and perfect dad for her. I didn't know what I would do if my mother was arrested for anything that Evander was charged with.

Suddenly, I felt a small tug on my hand. I looked down and realized that my hand was still wrapped around Chief's.

"Guys! Chief's waking up!" I quickly yelled, almost forgetting about Siri. Although I forgave her for what she did, I didn't think we would be friends anytime soon--if I ever see her again.

Karter, Blake, and Pierce all rushed up to the bed, trying to get closer to the man who had taken them in and trained them for the past few years.

"Chief!" Karter yelled, trying to speed up Chief's waking process. I grinned and slapped Karter on the arm.

"Be nice! He's just waking up!'"

"Exactly my point!"

"Kids," I heard my grandfather's voice call out. He coughed to clear his voice, but winced in pain. I quickly hit the call nurse button so they could do something to help his discomfort. "Stop your bickering."

"Chief," I muttered, "I missed you."

"I wasn't gone for long," his eyes finally fluttered and opened the smallest fraction of a centimeter, "I hope I didn't miss anything too exciting." He joked as he forced his eyes to open fully. I could tell he was blinded by those fluorescent lights too.

Blake let out a hearty laugh. "Oh, you have no idea."

Chief raised an eyebrow. "Oh, really?"

I smiled a wistful smile, "Yeah, really."

Starting from the very beginning, I began to tell him the story. "One day, there was this girl known as the heiress bride. She had an evil butler that only wanted her family's money, and would do anything to get it…"

The four of us sat there, and the guys filled in the story at parts where I skipped over some details. By the middle of my recollection, Chief realized it was about us. Worry filled his expression and then some anger. At some point, a nurse came in to give him a pain killer, but it made him sleepy.

Chief's eyes were drooping by the time we had finished, but I could tell they were filled with regret. "Melanie, I'm sorry for putting you through this whole thing. If I had known any of this would happen, I would have never contacted you."

My heart clenched at what he said. Even though I had to live through the events, I would still choose to move into the mansion if I had the choice to redo everything.

"Don't think like that, Chief." I reassured him. "I wouldn't change anything for the world."

He smiled sadly. Slowly, he turned to Pierce. "Pierce, you would be an amazing doctor. If it weren't for you, I probably would have died of liver cancer." Pierce shook his head in disagreement. "Don't be modest."

"I hope you know, Mel." Chief started to say drowsily. "You are no longer in an arranged marriage. You and Pierce can move back home to New York."

"Chief," I muttered quickly before he fell asleep, so he knew how I felt. "I'm not going anywhere. I am at home, right here with you."

Chapter 32

"Shh!! Move over!!"

"Stop shoving me!"

"You deserved it! Look, you're taking up all the space!"

My butt was numb from my awkward position. A few moments earlier I had pushed Karter over so that I had a little extra room to make myself more comfortable...not that it had helped. It was impossible to move around without bringing too much attention to us.

I turned around to look at our surroundings. A few yards away, a mother gave us a weird look and quickly ushered her child away from us. I sighed. They probably thought Karter and I were insane--not that I blamed them. It was not every day that you see two people wearing green outfits, hiding sketchily in the bushes with leaves in their hair. According to Karter, it would help us "blend in." I guessed not...

"Are you freaking kidding me?" Karter glowered. Using

his hands, he gestured at the ground behind me. "You have so much room behind you!"

"Shut up! They're going to hear us!!" I shot a death glare back at him. If they found out we were there, everything would be ruined.

Karter didn't bother to say anything and rolled his eyes in response. Directing my attention back to the couple sitting outside at the restaurant a few yards away, I squinted to get a better look at them. It was almost impossible to see their faces clearly at that distance. The leaves of the bushes didn't really help the view either.

At least Karter and I had been able to keep tabs on them all day. Thanks to the red hair, it was almost impossible to lose them in the crowd. Suddenly, something very interesting caught my eye.

"OH MY GOD!!" I shoved Karter to get his attention. Unfortunately, I put a little too much strength into my push which sent Karter sprawling on the ground. The bush shook around us, causing more leaves to rustle and fall into my hair.

"What the hell was that for?" Karter hissed at me while pushing himself upright again.

I didn't bother to apologize as I forcefully turned Karter's head so that it was facing the couple we were stalking. "Look!"

My eyes were glued to the scene unfurling in front of me. It was almost as good as a TV show. Blake's golden hair blew gently against the wind while his eyes were focused on my best friend. Ever so slowly, he brought his head closer to hers.

My fists clenched together in excitement as I began to

bounce up and down in my spot. I was dying from anticipation. Even though I wasn't the one about to be kissed, it
sent butterflies fluttering around in my stomach.

"C'mon, Blake!! You can do it!" I quietly urged him on.

"Shut up!" It was Karter's turn to shove me.

Even though I should have seen it coming, I didn't
have time to brace myself. I tumbled ungracefully into the
ground face first. Realizing I fell out of the bushes, I quickly crawled back so I was partially hidden again. I heard the
leaves rustling as Karter hurriedly pulled me up.

When I was back in my spot, I quickly glanced over at
Blake and Jessica to make sure they hadn't noticed us.

The two of them separated as Blake's head turned to my
direction. Our eyes met for a brief moment before I broke
the eye contact and grabbed Karter's hand.

"We have to get out of here," I screamed at him, not
bothering to be quiet anymore. "NOW!"

"Melanie Cartwright, you are so dead!" I heard Blake's
voice call behind me, but I didn't bother to respond. "You
too, Karter!"

Quick as a ninja, Karter did his infamous backward
somersault and jumped out of the bushes...all while sticking his middle finger up at Blake. I, on the other hand, just
sprang up and sprinted out of there. We didn't turn back
and look over our shoulders. We just ran and ran until we
were several blocks away, both gasping for breath.

"Nice going, Karter. You totally ruined our mission." I
grumbled angrily in between my gasps.

We had been so successful at staying hidden the whole
day! We had followed them from Jessica's new apartment

in California all the way back to the restaurant near the mansion.

The company Jessica worked for in New York had a job opening at their branch in California a few months ago. She thought it was the perfect opportunity for her because not only was it a promotion, but also because it was near where I lived. Although she wouldn't admit it, she probably came here to be closer to Blake, too.

In New York, Blake and Jessica had an interesting relationship. He had a huge crush on Jessica, and the whole world knew…even her. It was actually adorable. However, nothing came of it because we had rushed back to California when Chief fell ill. But now that she lived only two hours away from us, she and Blake had a chance to be together. Every weekend, she came to the mansion and hung out with us.

Recently, I could tell that Blake and Jessica had been getting closer. They weren't officially dating and wouldn't admit to anything, so Karter and I had decided to take matters into our own hands. We wanted to see if they were hiding something from us.

And from the kiss they almost shared a few minutes ago, I could tell that they were definitely hiding something. But thanks to Karter, it was only an almost-kiss…not an actual full-on kiss.

"It was not my fault. You started it by shoving me first!" Karter retorted.

"Stop being such a child and grow up for once in your life! Learn to take responsibility for your actions!" I stomped my foot. Karter raised his eyebrows at me. Ironically, I was acting more like a kid than he was at the moment.

"Fine. Whatever. At least we know that they are certainly more than friends," I huffed.

"Yup," Karter nodded in agreement. "I would say that our mission is not a total failure."

I nodded, and we started to walk back to his sports car. There was no point in stalking Blake and Jessica any more with our cover blown. Pulling open the door handle, I plopped myself down on the passenger seat.

"Where are we going now?" Karter asked me as he turned the key to start the car. The engine slowly purred to life.

"Back home."

My mouth curled into a smile at the sound of the word 'home.' To me, the mansion was my home. A month before I wouldn't even call it a home. It had been a cold place full of secrets. But now, it was the homiest place I knew. All the people I loved were there, except for my mother; but I always knew that I eventually had to move out. Anyway, Jessica had her own room in the mansion that she used on the weekends when she came. Karter, Blake, Pierce and Chief also decided to stay at the mansion with me. It was the most convenient, since all of our jobs were in California.

"We're home," Karter said and snapped me out of my thoughts. He parked the car in front of the door and left keys in ignition so that someone could move it into the garage later. The two of us stepped out of the car and walked up to the mansion.

When we entered the house, we were immediately greeted by a stressed out Chief. He was frantically running around the house, trying to find us. I laughed at the sight in front of me. My old grandpa was scuttling around the place with his arms flailing everywhere.

You could barely tell that he was just had surgery a month and a half earlier. At such an old age, it was a miracle to see Chief up and running again after only a month of rest. I guess being the founder of your own company will make you stronger than usual.

"Where the hell is Blake?" Chief snapped at us without even saying hello.

Karter and I shared a knowing glance. I tried to keep the smile off my face as Chief shot me a glare.

"Why? Is something wrong?" Karter asked sweetly. I let out a small laugh.

"That boy is in big trouble," Chief used his warning tone. Unfortunately, Karter and I weren't scared of it since it wasn't directed to us. I felt sorry for Blake when he got back. Chief was going to give him an earful for whatever he had done wrong.

"What did he do?" I asked the question we were both thinking.

"That little rascal has an interview in two hours! He needs to get ready and drive all the way to the studio!" Chief looked down at his watch to check the time for what probably was the billionth time.

I laughed out loud. Oh, Blake is so dead. "Last time I saw him, he was at the restaurant down the street." Chief looked like he was going to blow a gasket.

"What is the interview for?" Karter asked.

"I promised ABC that they would get an interview from the new CEO of my company!" Chief yelled impatiently. "But I don't know if there even will be an interview because Blake is MIA."

"Breathe a little, Chief." Karter placed his hand reassuringly on Chief's shoulder. "Just go outside and drive my car to the restaurant. You still have two hours! Just grab him and leave. The car is right outside the door."

Without a word of thanks, Chief stormed out of the house. I laughed at him. It was amazing how much energy he had.

A few moments later, I realized that Blake's date was going to be ruined! But I guess that was what had to happen, since that he was the CEO again. With Evander gone, there wouldn't be awful articles about him. He was actually a great CEO, but he had doubted himself because of all the negative publicity he had surrounding him. Now that the stress had significantly decreased for him, he had decided to take over the business once again.

"I love Chief," Karter ran his hand through his hair and laughed. I nodded in agreement. "Oh yeah! Speaking of the company, I have something to show you!" Karter grabbed my hand and led me up to his room.

"Ooh!! Is it another song you wrote?" I asked eagerly, hoping the answer was yes. Recently, he's been writing a ton of songs and I was the person he experimented on. I told him if I liked it or not and if the lyrics were good. Most of the time, I just applauded him for his musical genius…I guess my opinions were a little biased.

"You guessed it!" He smiled widely at me as we walked into him room. Picking up his guitar, he began to tune it and hum a little tune. "Here it goes."

Needless to say, the song was amazing and I lost myself

completely in the melody. Too soon, Karter strummed the last few chords of his song as my eyes filled up with tears. This time around, he had written a sad song about heartbreak and starting over. The instrumental was slow and sad, catching the mood of his lyrics.

RM Productions was lucky to have gained a wonderful artist. Yup, you heard me right. Karter has a record deal with Blake's company. How great was that? You could say that everyone's dream was finally coming true. We all had a clean slate to start from.

"That was beautiful," I whispered, afraid to break the peaceful silence that followed the song.

"Don't be afraid to hurt my feelings. You can be harsh…I think I can handle the criticism." Karter joked, but was seriously looking for some feedback. Too bad I had no negative comments to give him.

"The only bad thing is…," I paused for a dramatic effect. "You're going to break so many hearts when it plays on the radio. I almost cried at the end of it."

Karter let out a loud guffaw and threw an arm around my shoulder. "Thanks, Mel. You always know how to make my day."

"No problem, big bro!" I smiled up at him. He was really like an older brother to me. We had grown closer recently, but not in any romantic ways. He was such a caring person, and the girl who won his heart would be lucky to have him.

However, Karter was completely content to play his guitar. It seemed the instrument held his heart at the moment. You could see the passion he played with as he poured his soul into the music. Even the way he carried and touched his guitar was like he's caressing the most fragile thing ever. My thoughts were interrupted by a knock on the door.

"What's going on in here?" Karter's door opened to reveal a smiling Pierce. My heart banged against my chest as I saw his perfectly mussed up hair. "I heard some music coming from in here. Did you just write a new song?"

"I sure did! But you'll have to wait and see what it sounds like," Karter smiled smugly at Pierce. "Only Mel can hear my songs right now. The rest of you can buy my first album."

"You're such a brat…you know that right?" Pierce came in and playfully punched Karter in the shoulder.

"Sure, whatever floats your boat."

I smiled at the two of them, glad that things had returned to normal after Evander and Siri had gone.

"What were you up to, Pierce?" I asked him after a moment.

"What do you think?" He grinned at me. "Studying like crazy for my test tomorrow!"

I scoffed at him. "You're already at the top of your class! What do you need to study for? You'll do fine."

"Yeah, sure." He agreed sarcastically. "It's one of the most important tests! It determines if I will be a doctor or not…" Pierce wrung his hands nervously as thoughts of the test filled his mind.

"You say that for every test," I pointed out gently.

"But it's true!"

I laughed and my heart soared over our silly banter. It was like the ones we had before we had split up. Karter left his room at some point and gave us some privacy. He knew that Pierce and I needed to properly talk to one another because we had done so after our big blow up.

After a comfortable moment of silence, Pierce made his way over to the bed I was sitting on. I felt the bed sink down as it accommodated his weight. I looked down at my hands, suddenly nervous.

Gently, I felt Pierce's cool fingers as they curled under my chin and pushed my face up so I looked into his grey eyes. A hint of sadness flashed through his expression as he said the three words I had been waiting the longest time to hear. "I'm so sorry."

My breathing hitched as my heart violently pounded against my chest, trying to break free.

Those words held so many different meanings for the both of us. They marked the end of one chapter of our lives and the start of another. It showed that he was ready to move on from what Evander and Siri had done to us and our relationship. He was finally here with me, asking for my forgiveness.

My vision blurred as my eyes filled up with wetness. Blinking furiously, I tried to clear them and few tears slipped down my cheek. I felt a warm hand cupping my cheek and wiping the tears away. Looking into his eyes, I knew he was serious and that he still had some feelings for me.

I took one of his hands into mine and leaned into the hand that was still on my cheek. Closing my eyes, I gave him a shy smile. "I'm sorry, too."

In one fluid motion, Pierce pulled me up against his body. I stiffened for a minute, but quickly relaxed into his chest as he continued to hug me. My arms instinctively wrapped around his strong torso. With one hand stroking my hair and the other pulling me closer, he planted a kiss on the top of my head.

While in his arms, I closed my eyes and relaxed. I let my mind melt away its inhibitions and hesitation as I allowed myself to enjoy this small moment of peace with him.

That was when I realized that I was ready to just start my life over again. Everything just felt so right, like I had finally found a place in this world. Even though I had no idea what would happen in the future, I was ready for whatever life threw at me next.

About the Author

Brie Kraus always dreamed of being a writer, but put that ambition on hold, while pursuing working in the fast food industry and putting herself through college. After graduating and losing her employment, Ms. Kraus turned back to her forgotten dream: writing. *Don't' Ask* is her first novel. She has gone on to write a mystery series (*Closed Case*) and *I Hate You Rock Stars*.

More by Brie Kraus

Closed Case

Curious Confession
Over the Hills
Murder on the Eiffel Tower
Unfinished Business

Other

I Hate You Rock Stars

www.ingramcontent.com/pod-product-compliance
Lightning Source LLC
Chambersburg PA
CBHW020211260626
47156CB00002B/326